MUNCHEM ACADEMY

THE BOY WHO KNEW TOO MUCH

MUNCHEM ACADEMY

THE BOY WHO KNEW TOO MUCH

COMMANDER S. T. BOLIVAR III

DISNEP • HYPERION

LOS ANGELES   NEW YORK

Printed in the United States of America
First Edition, October 2016

1 3 5 7 9 10 8 6 4 2

FAC-020093-16246

Library of Congress Cataloging-in-Publication Data

Names: Bolivar, Commander S. T., III.
Title: The boy who knew too much / by Commander S. T. Bolivar III.
Description: First edition. | Los Angeles ; New York : Disney Hyperion,
    [2016] | Summary: When Mattie Larimore is sent to reform school he
    uncovers a creepy conspiracy, led by Headmaster Rooney, to fix all the
    problem children, including Mattie's brother—for good.
Identifiers: LCCN 2015042271 | ISBN 9781484753583 (hardcover)
Subjects: | CYAC: Reformatories—Fiction. | Schools—Fiction. |
    Conspiracies—Fiction. | Brothers—Fiction.
Classification: LCC PZ7.B4551354 Bo 2016 | DDC [Fic]—dc23
LC record available at http://lccn.loc.gov/2015042271

Visit www.DisneyBooks.com

SUSTAINABLE FORESTRY INITIATIVE   Certified Sourcing
www.sfiprogram.org
SFI-00993

THIS LABEL APPLIES TO TEXT STOCK

For the Commander's mother, who knew
Mattie was corrupt from the beginning.

Munchem Academy Rule

1

DO NOT STEAL

THE FOLLOWING STORY IS THE ONLY TRUE ACCOUNT OF HOW Mathias Littleton Larimore became the world's greatest thief. Other books may claim to know the truth behind the man who stole the Queen's jewels and then mailed them back to her. They may even claim to know the real story about the man who stole all the toilet paper from the White House bathrooms.

Those books lie.

They don't know anything about how a rather-small-for-his-age Good Boy began his life of crime. They don't know anything about how the youngest member of the Larimore family became the world's greatest thief.

They do know how everything started, though. Everyone does. You see, there was a subway train, and several bad decisions that resulted in Mattie Larimore being arrested for the first (and only) time.

Later, when he was asked why he would steal a subway train, Mattie said it was because of the following:

Reason #1: His parents were fighting. Again.

Reason #2: His brother kept calling him girls' names. Again.

Reason #3: The door to the control room was wide open.

His parents' lawyer said these were "extenuating circumstances," which seemed to mean "Why, everyone should go home and forget this ever happened." Only nobody did. They stayed to yell at Mattie.

Then Mattie's father arrived at the police station, and he yelled at everyone else.

"You are so dead, Matilda," Mattie's brother, Carter, said as they watched Mr. Larimore bellow at two police officers. Both boys were sitting against a butter yellow wall, on a bench worn smooth by hundreds—if not thousands—of butts before theirs. "You think they'll just bury your lifeless body in the back garden?"

Mattie gaped. He had no idea. He had never been in trouble before.

"What were you thinking, anyway?" Carter asked.

"I was trying to . . ." Mattie trailed off. He couldn't bring himself to say he was trying to impress Carter. He couldn't bring himself to say he regretted stealing the train the moment it passed the first stop. He definitely couldn't bring himself to say he was so worried his parents *were* going to bury him in the back garden that he had now sweated through his underwear.

"I just wanted you to stop calling me girls' names," Mattie said at last.

"Listen up, Melissa." Carter did not look at his brother. He was too busy using his cell phone to type out all the new swear words he was learning from Mr. Larimore. "That's a stupid reason to steal a train."

Sadly, Mattie had to admit this was true. He knew being called Madeline was not a good enough reason to steal a subway train that smelled like vomit and hair spray. It was not a good enough reason to take all of the passengers trying to go to the south side of the city to the north side of the city. But in the moment before he locked himself in the train's control room, all he could think about was:

Reason #4: If he stole the train, his big brother would stop treating him like a little kid.

Even if he was a kid—and, let's face it, little—Mattie was small for his age. His size didn't seem to matter except for when it came to dealing with brothers and going to gym class. And buying clothes that didn't have baby ducks on them. Sometimes that was a problem too. Mattie could never figure out why adults seemed to think that if you were a little kid you wanted baby animals on your T-shirts. It was like they thought he was stupid.

Mattie wasn't stupid. Although one of the police officers was currently asking his parents if he might be.

"Of course he's not stupid!" Mattie's mother cried, wobbling on her pink high heels. Mrs. Larimore always wore high heels. She wasn't very good at it, but she said it was part of her job as an actress. Mattie's mother was once the star of the telenovela series *Como Pasa El Tiempo (As Time Goes On)*. She played a beautiful farmer's daughter who was always looking for love.

Mattie knew this because he had just spent the entire summer watching and rewatching the series with her. Sometimes it was the only thing Mattie could do to make his mother smile.

She certainly wasn't smiling now. Mrs. Larimore jammed one finger in her son's direction. "My son is not stupid! He's eleven!"

The first police officer exchanged a look with the second. It was a silent look, but Mattie could tell what it meant. It said, *But eleven-year-olds* are *stupid.*

"And you, sir, smell like cough syrup," Mattie whispered.

"What's that, Beverly?" Carter asked. He had stopped typing swearwords into his phone because their mother was now crying and their father was trying to get her to stop. "Talk louder. I can't hear you when you whisper."

Mattie glanced at his parents and then at the police officers.

He wasn't sure if he was supposed to be talking to Carter about the officers. Actually, he wasn't sure if he was supposed to be talking, period.

"I said that police officer smells like cough syrup," Mattie said at last.

"So does Dad's accountant," Carter said.

"Ugh," both boys said. Mattie and Carter spent a lot of time with the accountant because Mr. Larimore wanted his sons to know all about the Larimore Corporation. Unfortunately, the accountant never taught Mattie anything he wanted to know, and if Mattie asked his dad questions he *did* want the answers to, the vein on Mr. Larimore's forehead would stand up . . . kind of like it was now.

"Why, if I ran my company the way you run this horrible excuse for a police station, I'd be out of business!" Mr. Larimore yelled. He took a white handkerchief from his suit pocket and dabbed his shiny, bald head. "I'm not even sure you can *prove* my son took that train! What proof do you have?"

The first police officer shook his fist. "He admitted it himself!"

"He's eleven!" Mrs. Larimore shrieked.

"Exactly," said Mr. Larimore. "And he's our good son. Now if you had been talking about my other son, Carter, that would be different."

Everyone looked at Carter. Carter waved. This was what Mr. Larimore meant when he said Mattie was "the good son."

Mattie made good grades (mostly). He was polite (almost always). He never stole stuff (until today). Meanwhile, Carter had terrible grades, was never polite, and once peed off their third-floor balcony. He had wanted to hit the pigeons below. He missed. Or scored, depending on whether you would give Carter points for missing the pigeons, but hitting old Mrs. Kirby-Clegg as she walked home from seniors' yoga.

Carter was the Bad Brother. He even went to a special school with other bad kids. It was called Munchem Academy, and it was way out in the countryside so that none of the students could escape.

"And so no one can hear us scream," Carter would always add.

Mattie hated when his brother said that. It always made his skin prickle. Bottom line: everyone knew Carter was a bad kid. Everyone said Carter was a bad kid. Carter was even sort of proud of being a bad kid. Or at least he seemed proud, especially now when all the police officers were glaring at him and Carter was waving and grinning.

"That's enough, Carter," Mr. Larimore said, eyes narrowing.

Carter stopped waving, the adults started talking, and Mattie slumped down on the bench. If his shoulders touched the bottom of the backrest, his sneakers could almost hit the dirty yellow floor. If his parents and the officers argued much longer, he would have to make a game out of seeing how far he had to slump before his feet completely reached the floor.

"We're going to let Mattie off with a warning," the first police officer said to Mr. Larimore. "But we better never see him doing anything like that ever again."

"Of course you won't see him doing anything like that again!" Mrs. Larimore was wobbling again and Mattie couldn't tell why. It was either her high heels or her crying. His mom kept making hiccuping noises like she was crying, but her makeup never smeared. It was a trick she had learned on the set of *Como Pasa El Tiempo*. "What kind of parents do you think we are?" Mrs. Larimore demanded.

The police officers exchanged another look. Mattie understood this one too. It said, *We don't like these people.* Mattie's parents got that look a lot, but they never seemed to notice. Only Mattie did. Sometimes noticing how other people looked at his parents made Mattie cringe. Mostly, it made him try to be even nicer.

"Let's go," Mr. Larimore said, grabbing both boys by their shirt collars. He steered them down the butter yellow hallway and past the chipped reception desk. But when Mr. Larimore pushed through the wooden double doors, the whole family was greeted with pops of light.

Cameras, Mattie thought as he shielded his eyes. No, worse, he realized. They were reporters with cameras. His father *hated* reporters with cameras.

His mother loved them. Mrs. Larimore stopped on the

police station steps and began to pose. She turned right and then left and then blew them a kiss.

Mr. Larimore shook his fist. "Out of my way!"

"Mr. Larimore!" one of them yelled. The man wore a red vest with pockets and shouldered past the others to shove a tape recorder in Mr. Larimore's face. "What can you tell us about your son's recent lawbreaking?"

Mr. Larimore's face went purple again. "No comment!" he roared and hauled both his boys toward the parking lot. The reporters followed, but there wasn't much to see. Mr. Larimore was stomping like he usually did. Mrs. Larimore was teetering like she usually did. And the boys were eyeing each other like they usually did.

But something felt very off to Mattie, like something really bad was about to happen to him, and in a way Mattie was right, because Mr. Larimore was coming up with a plan.

Munchem Academy Rule

PREPARE FOR THE WORST

MR. LARIMORE LIKED BIG THINGS: BIG MEALS, BIG HOUSES, bigger office buildings. But most of all, he liked the Larimore family's big SUV. It towered over the other cars on the road and made him feel like he was sitting on an enormous leather couch as they flew down the interstate.

It made Mattie feel like he might hurl as Mr. Larimore jerked the SUV around another reporter's van. Someone honked behind them and Mr. Larimore stepped on the gas. The SUV swerved into the next lane.

"You know what your problem is, Mattie?" his father asked.

Mattie thought about it. There were plenty of problems to choose from. Mattie had some problems in math, a few problems reaching top shelves, and a few more problems making friends. In short, Mattie didn't know which problem his father meant, but he was pretty sure his dad was going to tell him.

"Your problem is you're turning into Carter," Mr. Larimore said.

Next to Mattie, Carter blew out an enormous sigh and became very interested in his cell phone. Mattie's stomach gave a little twist. He thought about patting Carter's knee . . . or shoulder . . . or something, but Carter wasn't big on Mattie patting him. To be honest, Carter wasn't big on anything to do with Mattie.

"Both of you boys think that life is just this big game," Mr. Larimore said. He had craned his head around to look at his sons, causing the SUV to drift into the next lane. Mr. Larimore corrected it with a jerk. "And life isn't a game, is it, Maria?"

Mrs. Larimore agreed that life was indeed not a game.

"See?" Mr. Larimore pounded one fist on the leather steering wheel and changed lanes. "Even your mother knows I'm right."

The boys' father braked for a red light. Once the SUV stopped, he turned in his seat to better glare at his sons. "You're going to inherit the company one day, Mattie! You better shape up!"

Mattie nodded. "Sorry, Dad."

"Is that all you have to say?" Mr. Larimore demanded in a tone that sounded very much like that of a father who would bury his bad son in the back garden.

Mattie swallowed. If he were Carter, he would suck in his mouth and round his eyes until they were huge. The move always worked on their mother. It sometimes worked on their father. Mattie was pretty sure it wouldn't work for him because at the moment all Mattie could do was sweat.

"I won't ever, ever, *ever* do it again," he said at last.

"You're darn right you won't," Mr. Larimore said and smacked his lips. "I can't have this sort of behavior. It's going to put us in all the newspapers. Again!"

The light turned green and Mr. Larimore floored the gas pedal. The SUV lurched forward. Mattie slumped in his seat. Just when he thought disappointing his parents couldn't get any worse, the newspapers got involved.

"Both of you are turning into hoodlums," their father continued. "I have to do something or people will think I'm a terrible father and then they'll think I have a terrible company and then sales will go down!"

Everyone in the SUV gasped. Well, everyone except for Carter, who might have laughed.

But he did it very, very quietly.

"We have to do something, Michael!" Mrs. Larimore was back to wailing.

"Of course we will," Mr. Larimore reassured her. "I'll show those reporters how serious we are. We'll send Mattie to reform school. That'll shut them up."

Mattie sat up straight. "But *Dad*, that's for kids like Carter!"

Next to him, Carter made a little coughing noise and Mattie winced. He winced because it wasn't a nice thing to say, and he winced because he knew his brother would make him pay for it. A small voice in Mattie's head wondered if Carter would make him pay with a wedgie? A swirly? Mattie didn't know, and he'd finally found something that scared him even more than being half-drowned in Carter's toilet. He couldn't go to Munchem. Being buried in the back garden would be a better fate.

"I'm not like those kids!" Mattie's voice swung so high that, for a second, he really did sound like a Matilda. "I've never done anything like this before!"

"And you won't do it again," Mr. Larimore said. "I can't have this kind of behavior. I *won't* have this kind of behavior. You boys need discipline!"

"Dad," Mattie pleaded. He was thinking fast. He was thinking hard. It was important to use words like adults did. Mostly that was all they understood. "Please don't do this. It was a thoughtless mistake, and I've learned from it. I'm a better person now."

Carter started laughing, but Mattie ignored him. He concentrated on his father and tried to squish his smile into the same smile Mr. Larimore used when speaking to customers. It seemed to make customers happy, so it should make his father happy too.

Mr. Larimore shook his head. "You two need real-life school! School's important, right?"

"Right!" the boys said, because they knew that if they didn't, their father would yell some more. Mattie kind of agreed anyway. Or, at least he knew he was supposed to agree. School *was* important. But it was also boring.

And filled with kids who didn't like Mattie. As his father often said, Mattie was still trying to "grow into that market," which mostly meant "find someone to sit with at lunch." But however Mattie looked at it, he still ate alone.

"You're going to Munchem Academy with your brother from now on," Mr. Larimore continued. "It's done wonders for Carter. He hasn't peed on any people in ages."

Carter smiled.

Mrs. Larimore started crying again. "But Michael, you can't! What about Mattie's school here? What about his *friends*?"

"He doesn't have friends," Carter said.

"I do too!" Mattie snapped.

Carter shook his head. "Manfred and Mom don't count."

They did *too*. Their mom was their mom so of course she counted, and Manfred was the Larimores' butler. He had taught Mattie how to tie his shoes, how to fly a kite in the park, and how to polish silver. Honestly, Mattie had been a bit confused about the silver-polishing part, but Manfred had been quite adamant this was the sort of thing friends did. And Mattie believed him. Sort of. Mostly.

But all of that was too much to say. Mattie knew he needed a proper answer here, but he couldn't think of one, and it didn't matter anyway because the sound of Mrs. Larimore's crying had become piercing.

"He's so small!" she howled. "He's too young!"

"Dad," Mattie said and, because it was now or never, he put his hand on his father's shoulder just as he had seen his father do with his employees—usually when the employee was crying and holding a box of his stuff. Mattie thought it made his father look gentle, and the employee usually thought so too because he would always cry harder.

"It was one mistake," Mattie said.

Mr. Larimore snorted. "That's how it always starts. Pack your bags. I'm calling the headmaster *tonight*."

BE HONEST

MANY YEARS LATER, BIOGRAPHERS WOULD SAY, "IT WAS NO wonder Mattie Larimore grew up to be so horrible. His parents were terrible, terrible people."

And those biographers would be right.

Others would say, "In many ways, Munchem Academy was just the ticket for Mattie Larimore. It was the perfect place for a pint-sized criminal."

And they would be right too. Munchem Academy *was* the perfect place for a pint-sized criminal. The world's greatest reform school ended up being Mattie Larimore's great beginning.

Which, in this case, meant he learned how *not* to get caught.

But, at the moment, Mattie had no idea he was speeding

toward his destiny. Three weeks after "the train incident," he was trapped in the back of the long black car their father had reserved to take them to Munchem.

"Stop looking like you're going to pass out," Carter said to Mattie. Carter had one hand on his schoolbag, fingers drumming like he was singing along with a tune in his head. "This is your fault, Astro."

"Stop calling me dogs' names."

"They're not just any dogs' names," Carter said. "They're *famous* dogs' names. You should be proud."

Mattie wasn't proud. Mattie felt sick. His stomach was starting to squeeze, and his armpits were wet. He was nervous. He was scared. And in that moment, he kind of hated Carter, who didn't look like he was feeling either of those things.

The long black car sped up the gravel drive, and the boys watched the school's brick towers draw closer and closer. Once upon a time, Munchem Academy was called Munchem House, and it had been very, very grand.

Now, Munchem looked more like a place ghosts would vacation or where zombies would have family reunions. Vampires would definitely like it, Mattie thought with a shudder. Munchem Academy had three and a half towers, four stories, two huge gardens, and more chimneys than he could count.

Luckily, however, Mattie had spent most of the night before researching the school's Web site. So he didn't have to count the chimneys. He already knew how many there were.

"Munchem Academy has twenty-two fireplaces," Mattie told his brother. The long black car hit a pothole and both boys bounced. "And before it was a school, it belonged to the Munchem family. Then they lost all their money and they had to sell everything to the first headmaster."

Carter, who was still drumming his fingers, stared at his brother. He didn't say anything, but he didn't call Mattie a girl's name or a dog's name, so Mattie considered that a win. Mattie had read all about the school's success rates and activities and happy parents. It was all part of his Get Out of Munchem Plan. Mattie had wanted to know everything he could about the school. But right now, all he could think about was how Munchem didn't seem so big on the site. Looking at it now, he didn't know how he would find his way around.

All that ivy on the walls? On the Internet, it looked trim and tidy. Now that they were here, it kind of looked like a jungle was eating the buildings, and the stone statues were watching. And laughing.

In the pictures, the students were smiling and leaning toward each other as if sharing their favorite jokes. But none of the passing students was smiling. They didn't look like they wanted to share jokes. They looked like they wanted to shove someone to the ground.

If Mattie were being honest (which he mostly was), the whole place looked rather terrifying. Mattie sneaked a glance at his brother. Carter was staring at the school's tallest tower and punching the seat ahead of him. Mattie swallowed and looked straight ahead. He could do this. He *could*. He just had to do as he was told and get good grades and then the teachers would call his parents. He would get to go home.

Although, if he squinted hard enough, Munchem almost looked like home: it was just as big as Mattie's house, and had the same prickly, black iron fencing surrounding it. But no matter how hard he pretended, Mattie knew he would be staying here tonight, not in his own bed on his own floor at home, and no matter how hard he squinted, he couldn't make his mom or Manfred appear.

It wasn't the same, and the reminder was like a punch to Mattie's gut. Until now, he hadn't realized missing someone could be a terrible weight, so heavy that he felt pasted to his seat.

"So what'd you read about the cemetery?" Carter asked, his dark eyes bright.

"The cemetery?" Mattie squirmed as they passed the spiny wrought iron fence that surrounded a few dozen uneven headstones. "Um, you know, the usual. It's where they buried all the Munchem family."

"And the students who didn't work out. You should think about that, Snoopy."

The car pulled to a stop in front of a wide sweep of granite steps. Above the steps was a pair of heavy oak doors and above the doors was a shiny plaque, but Mattie couldn't read it because Carter shoved him out of the car. Mattie hit the gravel and skinned his hands.

"Hello, Carter," said a pleasant voice. Both boys turned in time to see a youngish woman not much taller than they were walking toward them. Two girls in red Munchem uniforms passed her, and she waved at them like they were old friends.

"Hello, Miss Maple," Carter said gruffly.

Mattie picked a bit of gravel from his palm as he watched his brother's ears go pink. "Why do you sound so stuffy?" Mattie asked.

"Are you getting sick, Carter?" the woman asked. She had bright yellow hair and brighter blue eyes.

"No, Miss Maple," Carter said. He bent to pick up his schoolbag, which had fallen from the car when he kicked Mattie out. "I have no idea what you're talking about, Mattie."

Carter's eyes were very wide, and he kept blinking them as he stared at Miss Maple.

"Do you have something in your eye?" Mattie asked even though he was pretty sure Carter didn't. Carter glared at him. Mattie smiled back. Carter looked like he wanted to kill him, but Mattie was pretty sure Miss Maple would intervene. There was something about her smile that made him think of having your hair brushed back from your sweaty forehead or being given a piece of candy after a bad day.

"And you must be Mattie," Miss Maple said. She shook

Mattie's hand, squeezing it like she was very glad to meet him. "I heard you were a very-last-minute enrollment."

"Yes, ma'am," Mattie said.

Crash!

Mattie jumped. To his right, a piece of slate had fallen from the roof and shattered on the ground, splintering into a million pieces. Mattie stared, openmouthed—*that could've been his head!*—but Miss Maple and Carter didn't seem to notice.

The driver of the long black car noticed. When he came around the car with Mattie's suitcase in one hand and Carter's in the other, he eyed the broken slate, looked up at the sloped roof, and took a big step back.

"You can leave those here," Miss Maple said to him, sounding very clipped and sharp for a woman who was so pillowy and round. "I'll have the cases sent up to the boys' rooms."

The driver nodded and dropped the suitcases on the ground. Maybe with a bit more force than necessary because they landed with a mighty *whump*, and Miss Maple's pale eyebrows drew together like caterpillars.

"Marcus? Jay?" she called and, for the first time, Mattie noticed two older students watching them. Marcus and Jay joined Miss Maple by the long black car. Miss Maple smiled like she was on television and had just won a washing machine. "Could you take these suitcases to Carter's and Mattie's rooms?"

"Yes, Miss Maple!" Marcus and Jay chimed in unison.

Miss Maple smiled even wider. She leaned close to the Larimore brothers and whispered, "See how good they are? One day you'll be that good too and your father will be so proud."

Mattie nodded and smiled back. He hoped it implied he was taking Miss Maple's words to heart. Carter made a honking noise deep in his chest.

Miss Maple straightened. "Are you sure you're not getting sick, Carter? Let me feel your forehead."

While Miss Maple checked Carter for a fever, Marcus and Jay picked up the Larimore brothers' suitcases . . . and that's when something rather funny happened. Perhaps it wasn't funny, perhaps it was just *weird*. Marcus bent down to take Carter's suitcase and jerked. His shoulders snapped back like they were pulled with invisible strings, and his floppy dark hair fell in his eyes. He stared into the distance as if something was there.

All Mattie could see was trees and grass and the teeny-tiniest glimpse of the cemetery.

"Yobbo," Marcus whispered.

Mattie swallowed. Was this a Munchem thing? A way to say hello to new students? "Uh, yobbo to you too?"

The bigger boy's eyes focused on Mattie and narrowed.

Jay shouldered in between them. "What did you say?" he asked in a tone that suggested Mattie better not have said anything.

"Nothing," Mattie assured him. "Nothing at all."

Jay nodded. "That's right," he said, and he and Marcus walked off with the suitcases. Mattie stared after them. What was "yobbo"?

"Thank you, Marcus. Thank you, Jay." Miss Maple smiled as the two boys passed her. Then she smiled at Carter and Mattie. Maybe she just kept smiling. Mattie was starting to think Miss Maple might take the same vitamins Mrs. Larimore got from the pharmacist.

"Follow me, boys," she said, and the boys did. They followed Miss Maple up the granite steps and through the heavy oak doors and under the plaque. It said THE BEST YOU IS A NEW YOU! but Mattie didn't get to think on it for long because Carter tripped him and he nearly fell on his face.

"Carter," Mattie whispered. "What's 'yobbo'?"

"Toe fungus," Carter muttered without looking at him.

Somehow Mattie doubted this, but he didn't get to doubt it for long because Miss Maple turned to him.

"Mattie," she said, her heels *click-click*ing on the shiny hardwood floors. "This is the main hall. Most of your classes will be on this side of the house and the boys' dorms are that way." She pointed down a long hallway to their right. Mattie's feet slowed . . . and slowed . . . until he stopped.

Mattie stared. He couldn't stop staring. The long hallway to their right was hazy with dust. Spiderwebs clung to the chandeliers. Wallpaper dangled in faded ribbons.

Mattie's home might be as old as Munchem, and it might

be just as big, but Manfred would *never* let their house look like this. Ever.

Crash!

Another piece of slate hurtled past the windows. Mattie cringed. Miss Maple and Carter continued walking.

"The administrative offices are this way," Miss Maple said as they turned a corner. Mattie dashed after them and they walked down another set of stairs to another long hallway. This one was cleaner. Much cleaner. The windows left squares of silvery sunlight on the floorboards, and the gold-framed portraits glinted as if they'd been polished recently. Everyone in the portraits was old or bald or, in the case of someone named Olga Higgins, old and bald.

"If you ever need me," Miss Maple said, "you can find me here." She waved one hand toward a simple wooden desk, stacked with folders and files. She smiled at the boys before pulling an orange folder from one of the piles, flipping through a few pages before passing each of them a printed schedule. "These are your classes for the semester."

Mattie quickly read through the list and felt his nerves settle. He had history, math, natural science—all stuff he'd taken at his last school, Wicket Prep. If Mattie tried hard enough, he would do well. Maybe Munchem wouldn't be so bad after all.

Mattie looked at his brother and realized Carter didn't seem nearly as excited about his classes. Carter scowled at the paper and then scowled at Mattie and then stuffed his schedule into his pants pocket.

"Any questions?" Miss Maple asked, her smile as shiny as her hair.

"Uh, yes," Mattie said, and Carter sighed. "I'm sorry to be rude, but why was everything back there so dirty?"

Miss Maple blinked. "It's dirty so you can clean it."

Now Mattie blinked. "What?"

"Cleaning is good for you," she said. "Doing something over and over and over again prepares you for life."

"It does?"

Miss Maple nodded so hard her curls bounced. "Any more questions?"

The boys shook their heads.

"Okay, then, Carter, can I trust you to show your brother to his room?"

Carter grunted.

Miss Maple smiled wider.

"Does that mean we can go?" Carter asked, hoisting his schoolbag onto his shoulder.

"Oh, no. I'm afraid not." Miss Maple frowned and tilted her head so her pale blond hair spilled across her shoulder. "You'll have to see Headmaster Rooney first."

Mattie's eyes went huge. Miss Maple looked at him and made a clucking noise. "It's nothing to worry about," she told Mattie. "Right, Carter?"

"Wellll," Carter said, drawing out the word like he really had to think about whether Mattie should worry.

"Stop it," Miss Maple said. She sounded mad, but she was still smiling. "I'll be right here."

And, as if to prove her point, Miss Maple sat down at her desk and collected a big blue purse from underneath it. It looked heavy and huge. In Mattie's experience, women's purses were always heavy and huge because they were always filled with makeup and gym clothes and—Mattie leaned a little closer—office supplies?

Miss Maple's purse was stuffed with boxes of pens and paper clips. Mattie looked at Miss Maple. Miss Maple looked at Mattie.

Miss Maple closed her purse. "You can wait in the headmaster's office," she said.

Mattie's stomach screwed tight again. "Why do we have to wait there?" he asked.

"Because I'm very busy," Miss Maple said. "And I have to make an important call so you can't stand here."

"Oh," Mattie said. "And why do we have to see the headmaster?"

Miss Maple smiled. "Because he'll want to meet you, of course."

She made it sound like a good thing. Mattie liked that. He was used to being a Good Kid. Adults liked him—that probably meant *this* adult would like him. He would have to make sure of it if he wanted to get out of Munchem Academy and back to after-school snacks with Manfred and *Como Pasa El Tiempo* marathons with his mom. In fact, the prospect made his chest feel light—the very first time he'd felt happy since he'd arrived.

Mattie gave Miss Maple his most enthusiastic grin. "Okay!"

Carter rolled his eyes. "C'mon, Fifi."

"Be good, boys!" Miss Maple trilled as she picked up the phone. Mattie turned around to tell her he would try his best, but Carter grabbed his arm and dragged him into the headmaster's office.

Munchem Academy Rule

RESPECT YOUR ELDERS

THIS IS THE PART WHERE OTHER BOOKS CLAIM MATTIE LARIMORE'S life gets much worse—and they're right—because *this* is the part where Mattie Larimore meets Headmaster Rooney. Headmaster Rooney enjoys Scrabble, the smell of shoe polish, and stringing students up by their ankles until their little faces look like swollen purple grapes. He's not allowed to do that anymore, of course, but that doesn't stop him from remembering those good old days when teachers could throw things at students and schools had dungeons.

Yes, everyone knows schools never had dungeons—well, there was this one school that . . . actually, never mind. Best not to even mention it. Anyway, everyone knows schools never had dungeons, but Headmaster Rooney likes to think they did. That's the funny thing about the past: everyone remembers it differently, and sometimes, they don't remember the way it was at all.

Luckily, this book has recorded everything perfectly, so we know that Mattie and Carter Larimore had to wait for Headmaster Rooney to return from stringing up some student by his ankles. Or whatever headmasters do in their spare time.

As far as Mattie could tell, Headmaster Rooney liked to collect things in his spare time. The headmaster's office was filled with everything adults enjoyed: heavy wooden furniture, lots of thick carpeting, and pictures of Headmaster Rooney with other people.

Lots of other people.

Mattie peered closely at the nearest photograph and thought Headmaster Rooney looked much happier than the guy he was hugging. In fact, as far as Mattie could tell, Headmaster Rooney looked happier than the person he was hugging in all the pictures.

"Should we sit down?" Mattie asked his brother. There were two plushy chairs in front of the big desk just like in their dad's office.

"Not if you want to live," Carter said.

Mattie spun around. "What?"

Bang!

The office door flew open and smacked into the wall. Both boys jumped as Headmaster Rooney charged into the room. He was much taller and thinner and redder than he looked in the pictures. The headmaster's head seemed to be only inches from the ceiling, or maybe it was just all his hair. It was pouffed and red. Very, very red.

"Boys!" Headmaster Rooney shouted. "It's the first day of school and you're already in my office? Unacceptable."

Mattie felt a bolt of alarm. This was not the way he wanted this first meeting to go. Not at all. "But—but Miss Maple told us—"

Carter kicked him. Hard. Mattie gaped at his brother and then at Headmaster Rooney. Surely the headmaster saw that and would do something.

Apparently not. The headmaster didn't even seem to have heard Mattie's protest, much less noticed how Carter had used Mattie's shin as a kickball.

Headmaster Rooney stomped around his desk, his feet making shushing noises on the fluffy carpet. "And do you know why you're here at Munchem? Because you're bad! Because you've disappointed your poor parents!"

Headmaster Rooney put both fists on his desk and leaned forward with such force that the picture frames on the desk teetered. "And do you know *why* you're bad?"

Mattie didn't, but he did want to know why Headmaster Rooney answered all of his own questions.

"Because you lack discipline!" Headmaster Rooney shouted. His eyes bugged out, and his face went purple. Mattie didn't mean to, but he took a step back. And then another.

Headmaster Rooney's head snapped toward Carter. "And now you've dragged your brother into it, haven't you, Carter?"

Mattie cringed. It was bad enough he'd gotten himself into trouble, but now Headmaster Rooney was mad at Carter too? If this bothered Carter, however, Carter didn't show it.

He squinted at the headmaster. "I didn't make Mattie steal that train."

"But did you inspire him to do better? To *be* better?" Headmaster Rooney demanded, his voice climbing in pitch and volume until he sounded like one of the preachers at Mrs. Larimore's favorite church. "Of course you didn't!"

If Carter was supposed to say something here, he didn't, and, for a very long moment, no one said anything. The only sound was the ticking of the headmaster's wall clock and someone yelling in the distance.

Headmaster Rooney narrowed his eyes at the boys. "Now," he said, "on to the reason for our discussion: in addition to your regular studies, you will be attending regular video conference sessions with your father."

There was a very small, very pitiful whimper to Mattie's left. He glanced at Carter, but the noise couldn't have come from his brother. Carter was staring at Headmaster Rooney like he was sleeping with his eyes open. Plus, Carter wouldn't have whimpered. Carter didn't know how to. Carter—

"Am I boring you, Mattie?" Headmaster Rooney asked in a voice that slithered like a snake.

Mattie snapped his attention back to the headmaster. "No, sir."

"Good." Headmaster Rooney crossed his arms and glared at the brothers. Or perhaps it wasn't a glare. Perhaps it was the only way he knew how to look. Mattie couldn't decide. He did know Headmaster Rooney's expression made Mattie feel squishable, like a bug about to be stomped by a boot.

"Now," Headmaster Rooney continued, one hand reaching into a desk drawer and pulling out a basket. He waved it under Carter's nose. "You know the drill."

Carter sighed and dropped his cell phone into the basket.

"And you?" The headmaster shook the basket at Mattie.

"I don't have one."

"Good," the headmaster said as he returned the basket to the drawer and locked it. "As you both know, no electronics are allowed at Munchem Academy, so using my computer for your video conferences with your father is a very special privilege. It is important to him that you take over his business when you grow up. And anything that is important to your parents is important to us at Munchem. Do you understand?"

"Yes, sir!" both boys said.

Headmaster Rooney smiled, his teeth very perfect and very white. "That's right. So, in order for you to fulfill your father's expectations, you will both attend your weekly sessions with him in my office."

The headmaster patted the computer monitor at his desk

and gave both boys an even wider smile. "Consider it an independent study."

Headmaster Rooney said "independent study" the same way someone else might say "Happy birthday!" or "You've got snakes!" Mattie was pretty sure it sounded more like "extra classwork," but he wasn't going to complain. Bottom line: even though the headmaster made the whole thing sound exciting, Mattie knew anything involving his father was likely to be long, tedious, and possibly his best opportunity for demonstrating that he had learned his lesson and needed to come home. Immediately.

"That's a great idea!" Mattie said.

Headmaster Rooney put one hand on Mattie's head. "Yes, it is, son. Yes, it is." The headmaster's eyes cut to Carter, who might have been making a gagging motion, but Mattie couldn't be sure. "You could learn a lot from your brother here, Carter."

"Definitely, sir," Carter said.

"Do you have any questions?" the headmaster asked as he shuffled papers on his desk. He moved some to a pile on the right and some to the left and then moved them back. Mattie did have questions. He had several, actually, but he wasn't sure if the headmaster wanted to hear any of them.

Mattie took a deep breath. "When do we get to go home?"

"When will you be good?" the headmaster asked.

"Starting now?"

Carter hiccuped like he was swallowing a laugh, but Mattie

didn't look at him. He couldn't. Carter might be happy here, but Mattie wasn't. His panic tasted like old pennies in his mouth.

Headmaster Rooney considered both boys for a long moment. "I'm sure your parents will attend the school dinner at the end of first term. Good grades, good behavior . . . a good report from me—maybe your parents will reconsider."

Maybe they would! Mattie's heart double-thumped. If he was perfect, they might let him come home!

"And on a final note," Headmaster Rooney said, "I will have you know Munchem Academy is the world's greatest reform school."

Mattie pictured what it would be like to be back in his own bed and his own room and his own school and said, "Munchem is the greatest!"

"Are you mocking me?" Headmaster Rooney asked. He came out from behind his desk, eating up the space between them with just two strides of his long, long legs. "Are you?"

"No."

"No, what?"

"No, sir."

Headmaster Rooney put both hands on his knees and leaned down toward Mattie. Then he realized how short Mattie was and he leaned down some more. "And do you know *why* Munchem Academy is the greatest reform school ever?"

Mattie waited, but since Headmaster Rooney didn't answer he whispered, "No, sir."

"Because we have discipline!" Headmaster Rooney stood up and rubbed his lower back with one hand. "And because I feed vicious rumors about the other schools to parents. Now. Are we clear?"

Mattie hesitated. Was he supposed to answer? He was supposed to answer the last question, but the ones before—

"ARE WE CLEAR?!"

"Yes!" both boys said. "Yes, sir!"

"Good," Headmaster Rooney said and smiled at Mattie. "I have a good feeling about you, son." Mattie grinned, and the headmaster scowled. "Well? What are you waiting for?" he demanded.

"Um . . ." Mattie panicked. "I don't know?"

"Get out!"

Munchem Academy Rule

5

NEVER JUDGE A BOOK BY ITS COVER
OR A CLASSMATE BY HIS GRADES;
THEY'RE PROBABLY MUCH WORSE THAN THEY SEEM

IT JUST GETS WORSE AND WORSE FOR MATTIE LARIMORE. NEW school plus boring business lessons with Mr. Larimore plus Headmaster Rooney equals . . . actually, I have no idea what that equals. I never paid enough attention in math. Headmaster Rooney is considered creepy on three continents, and in all Mattie Larimore biographies. In fact, most Mattie Larimore scholars agree that Headmaster Rooney is creepy because of all his yelling and the way spittle collects in the corners of his mouth when he's yelling and then the way the spittle sprays onto your face when he's yelling at you.

It's also the way he chews with his mouth open, splattering food onto anyone unfortunate enough to sit near him, but that isn't recorded in this book because *this* book has standards, excellent ones at that, and also because this book has to keep up with Mattie and Carter, who are currently running.

In fact, Mattie and Carter did not stop running from Headmaster Rooney's bellowing until they reached a sunny courtyard behind the house.

It wasn't like anything Mattie had seen on the Web site. The stone angel by the pockmarked wall looked pained, the carved benches were fuzzy with moss, and the hedges were unkempt. Their branches stuck up in all directions, like fingers reaching for the sun.

Or for Mattie.

The grass was all overgrown too, tugging at the boys' sneakers. No matter where Mattie stepped, one or two blades kept reaching up his pant leg, making his shin itch. It was not a nice place to catch your breath, but Mattie really needed to stop. The problem was, Carter kept going.

"Wait!" Mattie grabbed his brother's arm. "Where are you going?"

"To my room," Carter said. "To see my friends."

"But . . . but . . ." Mattie shifted from foot to foot. "Miss Maple said you were supposed to show me to my room."

"It's that way." Carter pointed in the opposite direction, toward a stone archway that led back into the mansion. The corners were dusty with shadows. "Go through the back door and take the stairs on your left. You live on the second floor."

Mattie could hear his voice rising. "But *which* room?" he squeaked.

"There's only one suite at the top of those stairs. Look, it's easy. You're on the second floor," Carter said, counting off the arrangements on his fingers. "The girls live on the east wing. Upperclassmen live on the north wing's third floor. Be glad of that," Carter added. "It keeps them away from us."

Mattie squeaked again, but no words came out. He tried to take a steadying breath—just like his mother's yoga instructor was always doing—but he didn't feel steadied at all. Mostly, the smell of dead grass made him want to sneeze. His eyes watered.

Carter sighed and pointed toward the stone archway again. "It's not like you can miss it."

Mattie leaned in and gripped Carter's arm a little harder. "But aren't you going to walk with me?"

"No way." Carter picked up Mattie's hand like it was a bug and flicked it away. "Let me give you some advice."

Mattie straightened up. Carter never gave him advice. Well, there was that one time Carter suggested Mattie brush his teeth with a brick, but Mattie didn't count that.

"Yes?" Mattie asked his brother eagerly.

"Don't kiss up to Rooney," Carter said. "It won't get you anywhere, and it'll make the other kids hate you."

"But . . ." Mattie didn't know what to say after "but." He couldn't think past the embarrassment heating his face and the anger tightening his chest. He wasn't kissing up. He *wasn't*.

What did Carter know about being a good kid anyway? More importantly, what did Carter know about getting out of Munchem? He was back for his second year, and Mattie wanted to be gone by tomorrow.

Mattie put his fists on his hips. "You can make fun of me all you want, Carter. It's called 'playing the game.' Dad talks about it all the time, and you'd get a lot further in life if you'd learn how to do it."

Carter laughed and laughed. He laughed so hard he slumped in half and tears leaked from his eyes. "Well, if that's the way you want to play it, then go ahead. Be my guest, *New Kid*."

"New kid." The two words gave Mattie the shivers.

Mr. Larimore didn't just love big things, he loved the best things. He liked to say he was "obsessed with the best!" And because Mr. Larimore was obsessed with the best, Carter and Mattie had been to six schools in four years. They both knew what being the New Kid meant. It meant never knowing your way around. It meant no one talked to you. It meant it would be very hard to look like you didn't belong at Munchem Academy because no one at Munchem Academy was going to pay enough attention to you to realize you didn't belong.

Mattie felt a little faint. "But you have to help me!" he protested. "What about being brothers and looking out for each other?"

"What about it?" Carter asked.

Mattie crossed his arms and tried to look mean. "I know how this works, Carter. I've read the books. There are whole movies about this stuff. We're supposed to take on the world together."

Or was that a line from *Como Pasa El Tiempo*? Mattie wanted to think about that, but Carter didn't give him time.

"Listen up, Lassie," Carter said, straightening his book bag and eyeing a pair of girls walking on the other side of the courtyard. "Around here, I don't know you."

Mattie's mouth dropped open. He always felt short staring up at his brother, but, right now, he had never felt so small. "But you *do* know me."

"You ever heard Dad say it's a 'dog-eat-dog world'?" Carter asked.

"Yeah, I've heard it," Mattie said at last, digging the toe of his white sneaker into the faded green grass until he hit dirt. "I don't know what 'dog-eat-dog' means, though."

Carter sighed. "It means you're on your own, Pluto," he said and walked away.

Mattie stared after his brother and did indeed feel very much on his own. Luckily for Mattie, however, he was about to meet the Spencers. In this story, "the Spencers" stands for Eliot and Caroline Spencer. Eliot and Caroline are Mattie Larimore's future best friends and partners in crime so this first meeting is clearly very, very important.

Or not, because the first time Mattie and Eliot met, Mattie

thought Eliot was ridiculous, and Eliot thought Mattie was hysterical. Which was a word Eliot had learned from his father for describing Eliot and Caroline's mother that seemed to mean "when your voice gets high and screechy, I get to call you names."

To be quite frank, Caroline didn't think much of Mattie or Eliot during this meeting either, but neither boy asked Caroline's opinion because neither boy had yet learned that they should *always* ask Caroline's opinion—especially when dealing with explosives and bank vaults and Silly Putty, but that's another story and has no place here.

Part of Mattie wanted to run after Carter. The rest of him stood his ground. Or tried to anyway. Ants had found Mattie's left foot and were tunneling into his sneaker. Mattie stomped around and around and decided he'd do this without Carter.

"I don't need him," Mattie mumbled as he scratched his ant-chewed ankle. He faced the arched stone doorway that led back inside and thought what he really might need were some rubber gloves . . . and maybe a face mask . . . and some bleach, because the world's greatest reform school was *filthy*.

Manfred, the Larimore family's butler, would not approve of Munchem. There were cobwebs in the corners, dust in the stairwells, and fingerprints on every window. As Mattie climbed the stairs to the second floor, hoping he was going the right way, he wondered how on earth cleaning could prepare him for being an adult.

Then another slate tile slid from the roof, hurtled past the window on Mattie's left, and crashed to the ground below amid the cheers of four older students. Mattie stared at the students and realized he didn't care about dirt or cleaning. He just wanted out—and maybe that's why he didn't notice the ceiling panel above his head slide to one side. As Mattie leaned closer to the smeary window, a thin, blond boy dangled from the hole in the ceiling and dropped—*whap!*—to the floor right behind Mattie.

"Ahhhhh!" Mattie screamed and put one hand over his heart—although as soon as he realized that was something Mrs. Larimore did all the time, he dropped his hand. "Why would you do that?" he demanded.

The blond boy shrugged. "Why wouldn't I?"

Mattie hesitated. It wasn't an entirely unacceptable response, he thought—and then he wondered how he could possibly think that.

"What were you doing up there?" Mattie finally asked.

The blond boy shrugged again. He had shadows under his eyes like he hadn't been sleeping, and there was a smudge of dirt on his nose. "I'm doing whatever I want. The teachers are trying to pull Eric Benson out from under the bleachers."

Mattie's stomach curled with unease. "Why's he under the bleachers?"

"Because Doyle stuffed him in there. I'm Eliot Spencer, by the way." He stuck out his hand and Mattie took it. But

Mattie had to close his eyes to do it. Eliot smelled musty, like the inside of a grandmother's purse, and his hands were covered in grime.

"I'm Mattie Larimore."

Whap! A dark-haired girl hit the floor next to Eliot and rolled smoothly to her feet. "I'm Caroline Spencer," she said, even though Mattie hadn't asked.

Remember how Mattie and Eliot never asked Caroline anything until they learned the hard way? This would be called "case in point."

Mattie and Caroline stared at each other. Caroline was short like Mattie, but wider. She had a wide face, a wider smile, and a spike of dark hair above her head that looked like an exclamation point.

Eliot jammed a thumb in Caroline's direction. "She's my sister."

"Not by choice," Caroline said.

"Nor mine," Eliot returned.

"I get that," Mattie said and then felt bad because he didn't really regret having Carter as a brother. Not exactly. Well, possibly. "You don't look like brother and sister," Mattie said at last.

"I'm adopted," Caroline told him. "You don't have to look alike to be family, genius."

Mattie glared at Caroline. Caroline glared back. Mattie knew he should be angry because Caroline meant the "genius" comment as an insult, but it was still better than being called Astro or Scooby, so he was torn.

He *did* know Caroline was a bit frightening. Maybe more than a bit.

"What are you in for?" Eliot asked.

"In for?" Mattie echoed. Eliot made Munchem sound like prison, which was sort of cool and sort of terrifying.

Mostly terrifying, Mattie decided. "I stole a train," he said at last.

Caroline gasped. "You stole a *train*?"

"It was an accident," Mattie said.

"You stole a train *accidentally*?" Caroline was aghast, and when Caroline was aghast her nose wrinkled like she smelled something bad. "How do you steal a train *accidentally*?"

"Poor judgment?" Mattie guessed.

"Little tip," Eliot said, shaking his head. "Don't tell people around here you stole stuff 'accidentally,' okay? You will not like the results."

"Okay," Mattie said.

Eliot nodded. "You know what I did? I broke into my school's security system and rigged the fire alarm to go off during my math test."

"Wow," Mattie said because he couldn't think of anything else and Eliot was staring at him expectantly.

Mattie wanted to ask Eliot why he didn't just study for the math test in the first place. In fact, Mattie was very busy thinking about how Eliot must be smart if he could hack into his school's security system and how smart kids could make really good grades if they wanted to, when Mattie realized Eliot and Caroline were still staring at him.

Was he supposed to say something else? Mattie crammed both hands into his pockets and thought really hard. "Your parents must've been super mad," he said finally.

Eliot shook his head. "Not so much."

"They were angrier that he started doing it for everyone else too," Caroline said.

"And charged them for it," Eliot added. "I made twenty dollars off every person who wanted to get out of a test. You know how much money that is?"

Mattie thought about it. "No."

"A lot," Eliot said. "Only I didn't get to keep any of it because my parents made me give everything back and then they sent me here."

Mattie perked up. "So you're new too?"

"No. I came last year."

Mattie felt deflated. He looked at Caroline. "What about you? What did you do?"

"She let a bunch of laboratory animals loose," Eliot said.

"You did?" Mattie's eyes widened and his mouth hung open. "Like rats or something?"

"Monkeys." Caroline crossed her arms and squared her shoulders like a superhero overseeing her city. "Animals should be free. They don't like being experimented on."

"They don't like living in the Bloomingdale's department store either," Eliot told his sister.

Caroline rolled her eyes. "They looked pretty happy to me."

"They jumped on all the beds in the home department! They used *all* the pillows!"

"Haven't you always wanted to do that?"

"That isn't the point!"

"That's *exactly* the point!"

Caroline held her palm inches away from Eliot's face. "I can't deal with you when you're being like this," she announced and stomped away, kicking up swirls of dust with her shoes.

Eliot glared after her before turning to Mattie. "Boost me up, okay?"

Mattie blinked. "Oh, you mean . . . ?" He looked at the shadowy hole in the ceiling. It looked scary and interesting at the same time. "What were you doing up there?"

"Nothing." Eliot put one hand on Mattie's shoulder and motioned for Mattie to bend down. "You know how this works, right? You've boosted people before?"

"Um," Mattie said. Actually, he didn't know because he'd never done it. Carter never asked him for help, and the grown-ups usually boosted Mattie. He'd never done it the other way around, but maybe—

Eliot rolled his eyes. "You know what? I'll boost you.

You're smaller anyway. Just grab the ceiling tile and pull it over the hole as you come down. Got it?"

"Okay," Mattie said, balancing one foot on Eliot's linked hands. He paused. "You're not going to drop me, are you?"

"I won't if you hurry," Eliot said.

That seemed like the sort of promise Carter would make, but Mattie stepped on Eliot's hands anyway and Eliot hoisted him up, leaning both of them against the wall for support and . . .

It worked! Mattie's head poked through the hole. He was in some sort of attic space. The air was cold, the floorboards were gritty, and it smelled exactly like Eliot smelled, like an old lady's purse. It was also dark and Mattie couldn't see a thing.

"Where's the—" Mattie scrabbled around until his fingers found the ceiling tile. He tugged it closer. But not before he caught a quick glimpse of lights in the dark. Why were there tiny lights in the attic?

Then his feet went out from under him and both boys crashed to the floor.

"You said you weren't going to drop me," Mattie complained, rubbing his aching hip.

"You took too long," Eliot responded. He lay on the floor and studied the ceiling. As Mattie fell, he had slid the panel into place, and now the hole was perfectly plugged.

"You're good at that, Mattie," Eliot said and rolled to his feet. "We're going to do that again. Later."

Mattie wasn't sure he liked the idea, but he *did* like the fact that Eliot wanted to include him. And that Eliot had used his real name instead of New Kid. Maybe this was what his dad meant when he said Mattie "should concentrate on the big data."

"So what grade are you in?" Eliot asked.

"Sixth," Mattie said.

"Oh!" Eliot rocked back on his heels. "That means we're roommates."

Mattie grinned. It should have been a forced grin because Mattie was now dirty, Eliot was clearly out of his mind, and plugging holes in Munchem's ceiling was probably frowned upon, but at the moment, Mattie was feeling pretty good.

He was feeling useful. Capable.

Mattie kind of liked that. In fact, he liked it so much that he forgot about being nervous as he followed Eliot down the hallway. It was long and narrow and framed by windows on both sides. At the very end there was a single door.

"This is our room," Eliot said. Mattie stopped and took a deep breath. This was a moment he needed to prepare for, a moment to savor. Only Eliot pushed him along and they crammed through the single red door together.

MEET ALL SITUATIONS WITH OPTIMISM

ELEVEN YEARS OF LIVING WITH THE LARIMORES HAD PREPARED Mattie for saying things that made adults laugh at dinner parties, nodding during lectures, and always picking the first desk in the first row. It had not prepared him for three other roommates who looked at him as if he had tracked mud into their room.

Although, if he had, Mattie had no idea how anyone would be able to tell. Room 14A's floor was dirt-colored, or maybe it was just dirt. He couldn't tell.

"Lookit," said a freckle-faced kid sitting on a broken-handled trunk. He had dust bunny brown hair and freckles bright as fresh-cut ham. "It's the new kid."

New kid. Mattie rubbed the back of his neck. It felt like

it was on fire, and he knew why, because there was another problem with being the new kid. You didn't have a name. You were just New Kid and, if Mattie didn't do something quick, he was going to be New Kid until another new kid arrived. That could be tomorrow or next week.

Or two years from now!

He had to do something. Something fast! Something smart! Or else—

"Hey." A much taller boy in a Munchem blazer appeared in the bathroom door. He pointed at the farthest bed. "You get that bunk, New Kid."

Too late.

Mattie sat on his New Kid bed. It even had his red trunk sitting at the foot of it, waiting for him just like Miss Maple said it would be. Suddenly, all of his How to Escape Munchem Academy Plans didn't matter because Mattie was stuck here and Carter wasn't speaking to him and he was New Kid from now on and—

"I've never had a Mexican roommate," the freckle-faced kid said.

Mattie stared at him. "I'm not Mexican," he said slowly. "I'm American."

"You don't look it."

Mattie could feel his face twisting in confusion even though he knew—he *knew*—he shouldn't make this bigger kid feel stupid. Making bigger kids feel stupid was the first step toward a future of wedgies and arm burns. "I have dark hair and eyes because my mom's Dominican," Mattie said at last.

The freckle-faced boy snapped his fingers. "So I was right."

"Ignore Bell," the tall boy said. "I'm Kent."

"Nice to meet you," Mattie said. "I'm—"

"The New Kid," Kent finished for him. "We got that. What are you in for?"

"Oh." Mattie's hands started to sweat. He remembered what Eliot said about not telling the others he stole the train "accidentally," but admitting he stole a train on purpose felt worse, and admitting he stole a train to prove something to Carter made Mattie's stomach want to hurl.

Or maybe that was because all the boys of 14A were staring at him.

"Um," Mattie said at last. "I stole a train."

"A train?" Kent tilted his head to one side. "You stole a train?"

"I didn't mean to!" Mattie blurted. Eliot smacked one hand across his forehead like he couldn't believe what he was hearing. "It was an accident!"

"Huh," Kent said. "Modesty. I like it."

"Modesty?" Bell asked. "What's he have to be modest about? He's not that great."

Everyone nodded.

Kent pointed his chin toward the other boys. "I'm here for fighting. Eliot's in for fire alarm stuff."

"And I did something disgusting in public," a loud voice said. Everyone in the room tensed and stared at the doorway. Slowly, his stomach sinking toward his toes, Mattie turned around and realized the voice belonged to the biggest kid Mattie had ever seen.

"I'm Doyle," the big kid announced. "Who're you?"

"I'm the new kid," Mattie said. He couldn't help it. Doyle was just so *huge*. Like could-kill-Mattie-in-his-sleep-and-bury-him-in-the-courtyard-where-no-one-would-ever-find-him huge. Doyle was as wide as he was tall and had shaved his blond hair so close to his skull that he looked bald. Kind of like a baby. A really, really ugly enormous baby that wanted to pound Mattie into the dirty carpet.

Mattie swallowed.

"Well, New Kid," Doyle said, coming so close to Mattie the tips of their sneakers touched. "If anyone asks, I've been here all afternoon. You understand?"

Mattie blinked and blinked again. He couldn't understand anything. All he could think about was Eliot saying something about Doyle stuffing some kid under the bleachers. *Doyle.* How many Doyles could there be at Munchem? Mattie was pretty sure there weren't going to be many and now he was *rooming* with Doyle?

Mattie started to wheeze.

"Hey!" Doyle shoved Mattie's shoulder. "Is this one stupid?"

"Kinda early to tell," Kent said.

"I'm not stupid. I'm eleven," Mattie managed and then wondered if he really might be stupid. It was starting to seem entirely possible. He held his breath, ready to run for his life if Doyle should try to squish him.

Doyle sighed. "Kent? Take care of this."

For a moment, Mattie thought Doyle had just ordered Kent to take care of *him*, but then he realized Doyle didn't mean that at all. He meant for Kent to take care of Doyle's bed.

It was disgusting. The covers were streaked with dusty smears. The bedspread was coated in orange crumbs, which perfectly matched the orange fingerprints on the pillows. And then there was the wet spot on the mattress by the headboard.

Was that *drool*? Mattie shuddered, but Kent didn't seem to notice as he shook out the pillows.

"Get dressed," Kent said as he smoothed Doyle's bedspread. "The Rooster's going to do room checks—"

"The Rooster?" Mattie interrupted.

"Headmaster Rooney," Kent explained, staring at the wet spot on the bed. Mattie thought he saw Kent gag. "He'll be here in twenty minutes, and if you get us in trouble, there *will* be payback."

"Definite payback," Bell agreed.

They made it sound like something they were looking forward to. Mattie managed a nod and shuffled toward his trunk. He took out all the things Manfred had packed for him: his new navy pants, his new white shirt, his new red sweater vest.

Mattie put them on the bed and then, because his knees were wobbly, he sat on the bed.

It was more comfortable than he expected it to be. In fact, sitting on the New Kid bunk was a bit like sitting on his bed at home.

It made hot tears creep into the corners of his eyes.

Which, if Mattie were honest (and he was trying to be extra honest because he wanted to get out of Munchem), were really badly timed.

The last thing he needed was his new roommates watching him cry. Mattie closed his eyes and took a deep breath just like his mother's yoga instructor was always telling her to do and . . . *yes*. Yes, he was better. Mattie thought about his new room. He thought about his roommates. Bell had freckles. Eliot liked to fall out of ceilings. Kent was Doyle's friend. And Doyle . . . well, Doyle seemed like he enjoyed kicking people.

Mattie took another breath, and felt his spine unknot. Yep, he definitely felt better. He felt—

Thwap!

Something soft and smelly smacked him in the nose. Mattie's eyes flew open. "Oh, God!" was all he could manage because a sock was now lying in his lap, and it smelled horrible. Like dead fish and mall bathrooms and rotten things lying in the summer sun.

Worse, the terrible stench clung to the skin between his eyes so that every time he breathed through his nose he smelled it, and every time he breathed through his mouth he tasted it.

"Welcome to 14A," Doyle said as Bell and Kent laughed.

Mattie laughed too. "Good one," he said.

He considered throwing the sock back at them, but because Mattie wasn't stupid, he put the sock on the floor next to his bed instead. He had twenty minutes to change. The other boys might think he was playing along because he didn't want to make them mad and that was fine.

Because Mattie had other ideas. He was getting out of here and he knew exactly how he'd do it. Project A: Charm the Teachers was about to begin.

Munchem Academy Rule

DON'T PUT THINGS
WHERE THEY DON'T BELONG

TO MATTIE'S ETERNAL CREDIT, PROJECT A: CHARM THE
Teachers did indeed begin. It started with Mattie smiling at
every teacher in the hallway, it continued with Mattie agreeing with everything the teachers said, and it ended a week
later when Mrs. Hitchcock smelled something horrible during
morning study hall.

Mattie smelled it too. His eyes began to water. The stench
was like flaming garbage and week-old underwear and dirty
turtle tanks, and it made Mrs. Hitchcock gag.

"Which one of you did that?" she demanded, eyes darting from
student to student, but the students were writhing in their desks
and no one would admit anything. Mattie tried to breathe through
his sweater sleeve, but now he just smelled wool and stench.

"Tell me!" Mrs. Hitchcock shrieked, smashing one hand against her nose. "Tell me right now or—"

HummmmmNAH!

The classroom's air conditioner cut on, billowing cool air and stink over everyone. People starting choking.

"It smells like bathrooms!" someone cried.

"It smells like girls!" someone else shrieked.

"No, it doesn't! It smells like boys!"

"It smells like it's coming from the air vent," Mattie said, because it did. The stench ballooned over them as soon as the air conditioner started. Mattie had a bad feeling he knew what was in there. Well, not precisely *what* was in there, but he'd smelled a similar joke before.

It had been last summer. Mr. Larimore had cranked the air conditioner in his big black SUV and the vehicle had been filled with the stench of Manfred's fish dinner. It had been stuffed underneath the hood, pressed into the air vents. Their father had sworn. Their mother had cried. Mattie had gagged. And Carter? Well, Carter had taped the whole thing on his cell phone.

His brother was behind this. Mattie was sure of it.

Still holding her nose, Mrs. Hitchcock approached the air conditioning unit wedged into the narrow window. She crept closer . . . and closer . . .

And reeled backward, gagging.

"You!" Mrs. Hitchcock snapped her fingers at Mattie. "Take a look."

"Teacher's pet," Doyle whispered.

Behind him, Doyle's best friend, Maxwell, snickered. "Good one, Doyle!" he whispered, which was what Maxwell usually said because Maxwell always agreed with Doyle. Mattie still couldn't figure out if that was because he really thought Doyle was awesome, or if Doyle had simply swirlied Maxwell so many times he thought everything was awesome.

"Let's see you look happy about this, New Kid!" Doyle added, kicking Mattie's shin as he passed.

Mattie winced and limped to the front of the classroom. He was sorry when he realized that Mrs. Hitchcock's selecting him had less to do with Mattie being her favorite as much as it did with Mattie being the smallest kid in the class and the only one who could fit both arms into the metal window unit.

Mattie undid the front screws (loose), pulled back the grill panel (also loose), and, while holding his breath, looked inside.

Mrs. Hitchcock took a step toward him. "It's . . ."

"It's a dead possum," Mattie said, or at least he tried to say it. Mattie had his arm across his nose and mouth again. It didn't really help. Nothing helped. The fish dinner had almost been better. The possum was too dead, too stinky, and too smushed. It had a tire track across its back, and a perfect black "C" drawn between its eyeballs.

C for Carter, Mattie thought. Carter knew Mattie had study hall in this classroom. If Mattie were half as bad as his brother, he would stick the dead possum in Carter's bed as payback.

Only Mattie wasn't.

Or at least he wasn't *yet*.

Instead, Mattie turned and smiled at Mrs. Hitchcock. "It's a dead possum," he repeated, and Mrs. Hitchcock fainted.

After finding the dead possum, the teachers didn't seem particularly interested in homework or smiles or even how Mattie agreed with them that the dead possum was indeed disgusting.

They were interested in work—specifically, the teachers were interested in making the kids clean.

In addition to the new possum stench in Mrs. Hitchcock's classroom, there were old fingerprints on the windows and dust in all the hallways and the bathrooms had the greenest and crustiest toilets anyone had ever seen.

It was Mattie's job to clean them.

Well, not *just* Mattie's job; it was the job of all the students at Munchem Academy. Whenever they were bad, whenever they made a mistake, whenever they needed improvement, the teachers made them clean.

"Because cleaning is good for the soul!" Mrs. Hitchcock

would repeat. Mrs. Hitchcock taught reading and floor washing, which meant she always smelled a bit like old books and a lot like bleach. Her gray hair fanned around her head in tiny, tight ringlets and, because it was raining today, the ringlets were higher and tighter than ever before.

"Cleaning will make you good!" Mrs. Hitchcock continued as she paced the hallway, seemingly oblivious to how her clumpy, black shoes smudged all the places Mattie and the other children washed. They'd been cleaning for three straight weeks, and Mattie figured he must be extra good by now.

Munchem Academy definitely wasn't anything like Wicket Prep. At Mattie's old school, the teachers used natural cleaners made of vinegar and oranges. At Munchem, the teachers used bleach and spit. At Wicket Prep, the students studied mildew for biology. At Munchem, the students mostly inhaled it.

"I don't remember seeing this on the Web site," Mattie muttered to Eliot, who wasn't really washing the floor so much as swirling the dirty water around and around with his equally dirty rag.

"I'm glad it's not," Eliot said, slopping his cloudy water onto the bit of floor Mattie was washing. "My parents would've sent me here years ago."

Mrs. Hitchcock strolled past them, leaving oily shoe prints on the tile. "For this term's project, you will each be responsible for an essay detailing your journey at Munchem Academy.

You will explain what kind of person you've become thanks to Munchem, what you've learned along the way, and you will read it at the end-of-term dinner."

Eliot made a gagging noise.

"It sounds nice," Mattie whispered to him. It didn't actually, but he was trying to be positive.

"It sounds like stuff the Rooster will put on the Munchem site to make it look awesome around here," Eliot said, and Mattie nodded because it did indeed sound like something the headmaster would do. But it didn't seem that hard. Surely he could come up with something—*anything*—about how he had changed.

Mrs. Hitchcock strolled in their direction again, shoes squishing in the water. "After all, Munchem Academy is the world's greatest reform school!" she announced, making the words sound peppy like the students should repeat them and clap.

Mattie thought he would totally repeat them and clap if it would help him look reformed.

Good?

Clean?

Mattie definitely wasn't clean. All the grime turned the students' skin gray. "Like zombies," Carter had said that morning at breakfast—although he hadn't said it to Mattie. He'd said it to his roommates.

Carter still wasn't talking to Mattie, but it wasn't as

noticeable as Mattie had feared. This was mostly because the kids at Munchem stuck together. If you shared a dorm, you ate together, had classes together, took your free time together, which meant the other boys from 14A had to hang around Mattie. They didn't actually *talk* to him, of course, but they were still around and Mattie could pretend. The headmaster called it enforced team-building.

Doyle called it a death march.

Mattie dipped his sponge again, his eyes wandering to Doyle, who was currently spitting into Caroline Spencer's bucket of sudsy water. Caroline didn't usually clean with Mrs. Hitchcock, but she was in trouble because she had let all the frogs loose from their cages in the science department. Mrs. Hitchcock spent extra time stepping on Caroline's work— and Doyle's too now that Mattie noticed it. Doyle looked over at Mattie and Mattie quickly looked away.

Too late.

Doyle flicked something small and slimy from the bottom of his bucket to the top of Mattie's ear. Mattie sat up straight.

"Mr. Larimore!" Mrs. Hitchcock shrilled, stomping toward him. "Hands on your work, sir!"

Mattie's hands were, in fact, clasped to his ear where they had found the small and slimy thing and were trying to wipe it away.

Doyle snickered as Mattie slowly put his palms on the floor. "Yes, Mrs. Hitchcock," Mattie said. Doyle laughed harder. He could hear the waver in Mattie's words. Everyone could. The two girls next to him elbowed each other and giggled.

Their teacher stamped her foot. "Everyone get back to work," she demanded and walked over to check Caroline's progress. Mattie concentrated on the floor in front of him.

"Don't worry about it," Eliot whispered, crawling alongside Mattie as he pretended to clean the baseboard. Eliot smelled like old-lady purses again, and Mattie wondered if he'd been up in the attic with the blinking lights.

"Doyle's just being Doyle," Eliot said.

But Doyle was always being Doyle and he was always getting away with it. For the world's greatest reform school, the kids didn't seem very, well, *reformed*. They seemed to be as bad as ever—like they were proud of it. And then there was the dirt situation.

"Where does it all come from anyway?" Mattie whispered to Eliot, pivoting so his back was to Mrs. Hitchcock and both boys faced the baseboard. "We clean and clean and it always gets dirty again."

Eliot scratched his nose with the back of his hand. "Who knows? It's like the dirt comes up from the air vents." Eliot sat up a little and glanced around. "Do you smell something burning?" he asked.

Mattie shook his head. The only thing he smelled was bleach and Doyle's occasional burp.

"I definitely smell something burning," Eliot muttered.

"Maybe it's one of Caroline's stupid frogs. Maybe it got stuck in the heating vents and is getting fried. It would serve her right for being such a pain."

"That's disgusting," Mattie said.

Eliot rolled his eyes. "You think everything is disgusting. Live here a little longer and you won't care anymore."

Mattie really, really disagreed with that, but he didn't want to argue with the only person who was nice to him at Munchem. Instead, Mattie concentrated on the green film caked on a nearby air vent. It seemed especially difficult to get off. Maybe Eliot did have a point about all the grime and dust wafting up from the ventilation system. Maybe—

Hooooorrrrrk!

Plop.

Mattie froze. He stared. Doyle had hawked a loogie onto Mattie's hand. It shivered like Jell-O and looked . . . well, it looked disgusting. Mattie held out his hand and wished it were attached to someone else.

Mattie shook his hand, his arm, his whole body, and—*plop!*—the loogie dropped to the wet floor. It shivered again and all Mattie could do was stare. He was horrified.

And angry.

Sometimes when Mattie was horrified and angry, he was known to do things he wouldn't normally do—things like throwing his sponge. Right in Doyle's face.

It was satisfying for precisely three-quarters of a second,

and then everyone gasped and Mattie realized what he had done and Doyle realized what Mattie had done.

Mattie looked at Doyle, looked at the sponge, looked at Doyle, and felt a high-pitched *eek!* climbing up his throat.

"You are so dead," Caroline said. She was right. Mattie should've been dead. Doyle should've squished him flat and buried him in that overgrown courtyard with the ants and the itchy grass where no one would've ever found him. Except for the ants.

But Doyle didn't get a chance. Headmaster Rooney suddenly banged through the hallway's double doors.

"Doyle!" Rooney barked, charging toward them with such force his shiny shoes squeaked like evil mice against the wet tile.

"I know what you did!" *Squeak! Squeak! Squeak!* "I know all about it!" *Squeak! Squeak! Squeak—Splash!*

Headmaster Rooney had stepped in Caroline's bucket. He slid to a stop and shook his left foot, showering Caroline and another kid with dirty water.

"Admit it," the headmaster roared at Doyle. "Admit it and it'll go easier for you!"

"Maybe you should admit what you've been doing!" Doyle stabbed a finger in Rooney's direction. "I know about the basement!"

The headmaster's face went purple. A vein on his forehead throbbed. "How *dare* you!" Rooney shrieked and seized Doyle's upper arm, hoisting him onto the balls of his feet. "Detention! Now!"

Rooney dragged a struggling Doyle down the hallway.

Mattie slumped with relief, realizing he had been clenching his fists until his fingers were numb. He forced himself to relax. Everyone was still staring after Doyle and Rooney. But Mattie's brain was stuck on what Doyle said: *I know about the basement.*

What basement? Mattie didn't think Munchem had a basement and, even if it did, who cared? Why would a basement make the headmaster so angry?

Bell let out a long, low whistle and dropped his rag into his bucket. "I've never seen the Rooster so mad," he whispered.

Kent nodded in agreement, then Kent and Bell turned to Mattie.

"You know Doyle's going to kill you, right?" Bell asked Mattie.

"Nah," Kent said. He was kneeling in a patch of sunlight that made his black hair extra shiny. "Killing's too easy. Doyle will rip his arm off and club him with the wet end."

Everyone nodded like this was the most natural thing in the world. Although, considering it *was* Doyle, it was probably natural to assume Mattie was going to be clubbed by his own arm.

"Why'd you do it?" Kent asked.

"Yes." Caroline narrowed her eyes at Mattie like she was seeing him for the very first time. "Why?"

Mattie swallowed. He didn't really know and that worried him. A lot. Throwing the sponge had been rather like stealing that train—it was just something that came over him, like all his frustrations took over.

His mother had episodes like that too, but usually only when she was purchasing a new hat or a car. Mrs. Larimore had never stolen a train, and she certainly had never tossed a slimy, wet sponge in someone's face.

Well, at least as far as Mattie knew.

Stealing that train hadn't been particularly satisfying, but throwing that sponge at Doyle? That was kind of sort of possibly *very* satisfying, and that worried Mattie. He was supposed to be getting better.

What if he was getting worse?

Mrs. Hitchcock—who up until that moment had been clutching her throat and staring after the headmaster—jerked to life. She swung around on the students and pointed a shaking finger toward them.

"Back to work!" she shrilled. "All of you need to get back to work!"

The students faced the floor again, cleaning with more enthusiasm than before. The boys of 14A moved closer together, scrubbing the same four tiles over and over.

"What do you think they're going to do to him?" Eliot whispered.

"Nothing good," Kent said, and all the boys shuddered.

Well, all the boys except for Mattie.

Mattie was relieved. It wasn't that he *wanted* Doyle to get in trouble. It was more that Mattie liked where his arms were attached to his body.

"Maybe by the time Doyle gets back," Mattie ventured, trying the words out to see if they had any truth to them. "Maybe he will have forgotten all about what happened."

Caroline snorted. "Doubtful. It was a bold move, though. I'm impressed."

"Thank you?"

Kent studied Mattie for several seconds. "What's your name again, New Kid?"

Mattie went still. "It's Mattie. Mattie Larimore."

Everyone nodded.

"You're still dead," Caroline reminded Mattie and went back to her own cleaning.

Mattie looked at Eliot, who frowned. "It's been nice knowing you, Mattie."

EMPLOY GOOD MANNERS AT ALL TIMES

MATTIE TRIED TO ENJOY HIS ARMS WHILE HE STILL HAD THEM.
He used them to shield his face during gym class, where he
never managed to dodge the ball. He used them in the cafeteria line to help push his tray along the counter. Later, he used
them to cover his eyes from the lamplight because Eliot wanted
to stay up reading, and Mattie wanted to sleep one last night
with all of his body parts still together in one place. By the
next morning, he was sick with waiting.

But Doyle never showed. He wasn't at dinner that night, and
he didn't return to room 14A at bedtime. At first the boys wondered if maybe Headmaster Rooney really did have a dungeon,
but everyone knew it was a joke. When Doyle didn't return by the
end of the week, however, they began to think maybe it wasn't.

"I mean, where could he *be*?" Eliot asked as they sat down for dinner. Caroline was already at their table, peeling an apple. Everyone else sat with their roommates. Caroline refused to. Last week, when Mattie had asked her why she didn't get along with the other girls, she'd shrugged.

"It isn't that I mind managing people," Caroline had said. "It's that I mind when they don't do what I tell them to."

"That's not really the point of roommates," Mattie had told her.

"Isn't it?" Caroline had asked. She'd looked utterly confused—rather like she did now sitting at their table. "What are you talking about?" Caroline now wanted to know. Her hair was extra high and dark today like a tornado was swirling above her head.

"Doyle," Mattie said glumly. "He still isn't back."

"You should be happy about that," Caroline said and took a bite of her apple.

Mattie studied Caroline, and Caroline studied Mattie. She was right and Mattie knew she was right, but Mattie didn't think Caroline should seem so smug about it. He pretended to be interested in the next table instead.

Unfortunately for Mattie, the only people at the next table were Marcus and Jay. Normally, Mattie wasn't big on watching people eat, but looking at the two of them now, Mattie couldn't turn away. There was something just so *strange* about them.

To be precise, it was the way Marcus and Jay were eating. It was almost in unison, like they were doing an act or an ice-skating routine. They would slice bite-sized pieces of broccoli from their plates, put them in their mouths, and chew them eight times before swallowing. Then they did it again. And again.

Mattie sat up and glanced around, trying to decide if anyone else had noticed, but he couldn't tell. Eliot and Caroline were arguing, Kent was spitting food on Bell, and Carter was looking the other way.

Mattie slouched down again and played with his food because not staring at Marcus and Jay reminded him about his countdown to being armless—and that will make anyone lose his appetite.

"Are you going to eat that?" Eliot asked. Mattie pushed his tray toward him. He knew he shouldn't stare, but he kept thinking about how Marcus had said that weird word on his first day of school. What was it again? Yoohoo? Booboo?

Mattie sat up. "Yobbo!"

"What?" Eliot's mouth was full and bits of food sprayed the tabletop.

"Yobbo," Mattie repeated. "Do you know what it means?"

Eliot shrugged. Caroline sighed. "It means hoodlum."

"Oh." Mattie considered Caroline for a long moment. "How do you know that?"

She rolled her eyes. "How do you not?" The boys kept

staring at her, and Caroline sighed again. "It's a British word. I learned it watching *Doctor Who*."

"Oh." Mattie studied Marcus again, wondering why on earth he would've said "yobbo." Miss Maple said Marcus was a good kid. Maybe it had something to do with that? Mattie tugged at his jacket and wondered how Marcus got his sleeve so smooth. Manfred would probably know. Mattie thought he might write him and ask—

"Mattie? Are you coming?"

Mattie jumped. Eliot and Caroline were ready to go, holding their empty trays and waiting for him.

"Yeah," Mattie said and jumped to his feet. "I'm coming."

Thanks to Caroline's Free the Frogs Project, she still had extra cleaning to finish, so the boys were on their own as they trudged to 14A.

Mattie had to admit the stairwell looked pretty good since Mr. Scratch's seventh graders had cleaned it. In fact, Mattie was so focused on how he could almost see the grain in the wooden floorboards that he almost didn't see the person standing in 14A. The person was . . . *ironing*?

Yes. He was ironing. The sight was so strange that Mattie took a step forward and froze. He knew that shaved head. He knew those enormous hands. Doyle!

He was *back*!

And he was ironing?

Mattie felt that high-pitched *eek!* start creeping up his

throat again, but Doyle only smiled at him and went back to pressing his socks. For a long moment, no one said anything; then Eliot leaned in to Mattie.

"Tell him you're sorry," Eliot whispered as Doyle removed a sock from the ironing board he'd propped between his bed and Bell's bed.

"Tell him what?" Mattie couldn't comprehend what Eliot was saying. There was a whine in his head now and his armpits were sweating. Doyle was still ironing. The whole dorm smelled like fabric softener and pumpkin.

Like pumpkin muffins, to be perfectly precise.

Mattie gaped and stared. There was a muffin tin on Doyle's bed and a toaster oven sitting on a table by the window. Was Doyle *baking* something? Where did Doyle get a toaster oven? Mattie didn't know. Mattie could only stare and make gulping noises.

"Tell him you're sorry," Eliot repeated. "And tell him you'd like to keep your arms."

Mattie turned to goggle at Eliot because he very much wanted to keep his arms, but how exactly was he supposed to beg for that? He never got the chance to ask, though, because Eliot planted his fist into Mattie's back and propelled Mattie forward.

"So. Doyle." Mattie edged a little closer to the door in case he needed to make a run for it. "About what happened before . . . with the bucket . . . and the sponge. I'm really sorry about that."

Doyle looked up, his light blond eyebrows knitted together in confusion. "What bucket and sponge?"

Mattie cringed. Doyle wasn't really going to make him spell it out, was he? Mattie waited and Doyle waited and Mattie knew he was going to have to say it. "We were cleaning in Mrs. Hitchcock's class and I hit you in the face with a dirty sponge."

Doyle's face relaxed into a faraway smile. "Oh."

"I'm sorry I did it," Mattie said quickly. "Please don't rip my arms off."

"But we're friends," Doyle said as he started ironing another pair of black socks. Judging from the holes in the toes, they looked like Eliot's. "Why would I rip off your arms?"

"Because . . . because . . ." Mattie wanted to say, *Because you're Doyle and that's what you do*, but somehow it didn't feel right. Then again, none of this felt right. Doyle was being completely weird.

Mattie glanced at Eliot. He was studying Doyle closely too. Had he noticed Doyle was acting strange as well? Or had he noticed Doyle was ironing Eliot's socks? Mattie figured it could be either. Eliot took the pen from behind his ear and put it in his mouth, chewing hard like he always did when he was thinking.

Mattie leaned closer. "What's Doyle doing?" he whispered.

"It appears he's ironing my socks," Eliot said.

"But why?"

Eliot shrugged and chewed the pen harder. "You should ask him."

Mattie considered Doyle's massive shoulders, his meaty hands, and his sausage-sized fingers—which held the iron in a surprisingly delicate fashion—and decided he was much better off not asking. "No, thank you," Mattie said to Eliot.

Eliot spit out the pen. "I didn't think so. What do you think happened to him?"

"Maybe it's magic," Mattie said. He was only half joking. He couldn't think of a single logical reason why Doyle would go from, well, being Doyle to being whatever he was at the moment. Nice? Considerate? Pleasant?

All of the above?

"There's no such thing as magic," Eliot said and tapped the pen against his chin. "Magic is just science no one understands yet."

"Okay." Mattie nodded. "So how does science explain the new Doyle?"

"I have no idea."

That made two of them, Mattie thought.

"Hey, Doyle," Eliot said and Doyle looked up, holding the iron away from the socks. "So where have you been? Detention?"

Doyle broke into a wide smile. "Oh, no. No. Not detention. I got tutoring from Headmaster Rooney."

Mattie perked up. "What kind of tutoring?"

"Special tutoring."

"To teach you how to iron socks?" Eliot's tone was approaching snotty and Mattie thumped him. Doyle didn't seem to notice the tone or the thumping, though. He unplugged the iron and turned to face the two boys with the same pleasant expression on his face.

"I want to tell you the good news," Doyle began.

"Wait." Eliot shifted from foot to foot. "I think I've heard this somewhere before."

Doyle smiled. He sat on his bed (perfectly made), adjusted the cuff of his school pants (perfectly pressed), and folded both hands (perfectly manicured) onto his knee.

"I learned how to be good," Doyle told them. "I'm going to get to go home after the end-of-term dinner. My parents are so happy and I'm so happy and we're all so happy."

"That *is* a lot of happy," Mattie muttered and, this time, Eliot thumped him. Mattie ignored it because all he could think of was how Doyle was going home. *Home.* Mattie swallowed around the lump that suddenly formed in his throat. They had three more months before end of term, and Mattie wasn't sure he was going to make it.

"So, like, how'd you learn so quickly?" Mattie asked, daring to scoot closer. That's when he smelled soap. Doyle had showered. *Doyle.*

"Headmaster Rooney helped me." His smile was full of teeth. Soap or no soap, Mattie took a step back. "We went to his office together and the other teachers were there and everyone helped me figure out how to be good. Makes sense, huh?"

"Total sense," Eliot said.

"Yeah," Mattie agreed, but inside he was gaping. Sense? It didn't make any sense. "So," Mattie said slowly, "what did they tell you? How'd they teach you how to be good?"

"It's a secret," Doyle said with another dreamy smile.

"A secret?" Mattie echoed.

"Yeah, a secret." Doyle smiled like this was his favorite subject. "I'm not supposed to tell secrets."

Mattie and Eliot exchanged a quick look. "Yeah," Eliot said, nodding. "You're definitely not supposed to tell secrets."

"Nope," Doyle agreed. "It's going to be a surprise."

Eliot's pale eyebrows shot up. "A surprise? That's cool. Maybe you should tell us where you've been so we know not to go there."

Doyle scratched his neck, his eyes moving side to side like he was searching for an answer.

"You know," Eliot continued, "because if you tell us where you've been then we'll know not to go there and then we can still be surprised."

Doyle stopped scratching. "Oh! Good idea! They keep it in the headmaster's office."

It? Mattie scowled. Now he knew Doyle was nuts. What kind of secret could you keep in an office—especially a secret that could make someone good?

Ding! Doyle's whole face broke into another toothy smile.

"My muffins!" Doyle galloped to the far side of the room and crouched over the toaster oven.

Ironing, baking, and bathing. This wasn't just weird. This was . . . Mattie didn't know what this was, but he knew "weird" wasn't a big enough word to cover it.

"Ironing his socks," Eliot said to himself. "The teachers are gonna love that."

Mattie thought the teachers would love the fact that Doyle was showering more, but he nodded anyway. Honestly, it had never occurred to Mattie to iron his socks. What other opportunities had he missed?

"I need Doyle's secret," Mattie said.

Eliot snorted. "Why? It's not like you need help being good, unless there's a train involved. Is there a train coming to Munchem? Are you worried about a relapse?"

"What's a relapse?"

Eliot chewed hard on his pen as he thought about this. "It's when you do something again and again because it's fun."

"Oh. Well, I'm not stealing a train again. I want to go home."

"What's at home?" Eliot asked.

Mattie blinked. "Home is home," he said, and when Eliot kept staring at him, Mattie tried to explain again: "It's not here. It's better."

"Huh." Eliot took the pen out of his mouth. "Mine's not."

The boys watched Doyle fuss over his muffins, his great

big baby head bobbing to some tune only Doyle could hear.

"I wonder what kind of help they gave him," Mattie muttered.

Eliot laughed. "Maybe they got a copy of the *How to Be Good Manual* and read him chapters."

Mattie scowled. A *How to Be Good Manual*? That was stupid. No one would have something like that. Except Doyle did say his secret to becoming good was in Headmaster Rooney's office. Maybe it *was* some sort of manual.

Or something.

Obviously, it really helped Doyle—and Mattie could use help too. At the rate he was going, he was never going to get out of Munchem.

"I want to find out what Doyle's been doing," Mattie told Eliot.

Eliot watched him closely. "Are you saying you want to sneak into the Rooster's office?"

Mattie's stomach dipped like he was riding a roller coaster. "No, of course not."

"Because that would be wrong." Eliot was still watching Mattie, but now his eyes were bright and interested.

"Very wrong," Mattie said. "I'll think of something else."

"Like what?" Eliot asked in a tone that said he knew very well Mattie wouldn't think of something else because what else could he think of? If the secret was in the headmaster's office and Mattie wanted the secret . . .

"Face it, Mattie." Eliot looked at him. "What do you have to lose? You're already stuck here."

Mattie stared at Eliot and thought of all the reasons he should never ever sneak into the headmaster's office—reasons like it was wrong, it was scary, and if Rooney caught them he would string them up by their ankles. They were all excellent reasons and yet they somehow still paled in the light of one reason: Mattie really wanted Doyle's secret.

"How bad do you want to know?" Eliot asked.

Bad. Maybe more than anything Mattie had ever wanted before. Until now, Mattie had always been able to figure out how to be good. It had been a matter of smiling and agreeing and holding open doors. But now it seemed to mean pressed socks and baked goods. Or did it? If Mattie learned Doyle's secret, he would know for sure.

Doyle turned from the toaster oven, holding a tray of muffins. "Would you like some?"

Mattie and Eliot exchanged a look. They were both thinking about the headmaster's office and they were also thinking about muffins, but their look said the same thing: How hard could a little breaking and entering be?

Munchem Academy Rule

PAY ATTENTION

OTHER BOOKS MIGHT SAY THIS LITTLE BRUSH WITH BREAKING
and entering was Mattie Larimore's Great Beginning, but
really it wasn't. It was more like Mattie Larimore's Brush with
Mattie Larimore's Great Beginning.

In later years, Mattie and Eliot wouldn't be troubled by
something so trivial as how to break into Rooney's office. By
then, they would have the Eiffel Tower Job under their belts
and the Tragic Toothbrush Incident on their resumes. But
for now, this was Mattie's first experience with breaking and
entering.

At the moment, however, Mattie and Eliot weren't thinking about where breaking and entering might lead them—they
were thinking about how to get into the headmaster's office

without getting caught. They thought and they thought and they pretended to do their homework, but neither of them could concentrate while Doyle was making another batch of pumpkin spice muffins. They smelled too good.

"What if we used disguises?" Mattie suggested the next morning. The boys were walking downstairs to the cafeteria, their shoes sticking to the floor.

It had been so nice before, Mattie thought to himself as they pushed through the heavy double doors into the cafeteria. Long tables with long benches stretched the length of the room. Teachers paced the perimeter, watching the students, and students sat on the benches, watching the teachers. The cafeteria workers watched everyone.

"What would we disguise ourselves as?" Eliot asked as they picked up plastic trays from a teetering stack at the end of one table.

"Parents?"

"You are way too short for that."

Mattie sighed because it was true. "What about a distraction?"

Eliot considered it, his blue eyes narrowed in concentration. "That could work. We could set off fireworks near the woods and, while Rooster is investigating, we could break into his office."

"Do you have fireworks?"

Eliot's shoulders slumped. "No. Do you?"

"No."

They went through the breakfast line in miserable silence. Mattie put scrambled eggs and whole wheat toast on his plate. He started to put strawberry yogurt on his plate too, but he noticed Mrs. Hitchcock watching him, her veiny hands wrapped around a clipboard. Her eyes narrowed when Mattie reached for the gooey sweet stuff. Mattie panicked. He grabbed plain Greek yogurt instead, and Mrs. Hitchcock smiled at him and made a little mark on her clipboard.

Mattie smiled back even though he hated plain Greek yogurt.

"That stuff's gross," Eliot said.

"It's good for me," Mattie told him and hoped Mrs. Hitchcock heard. If he was going to eat the stuff he might as well get credit for it.

Eliot rolled his eyes as they took their seats at the table. "I know how to break into computers," Eliot said, digging into his scrambled eggs. "I don't know how to break into offices."

Mattie thought for a moment then said, "Your sister knows how to break into cages."

"No way. We are *not* asking Caroline."

"Ask me what?" Caroline sat down next to them. Even though it was breakfast, her tray was filled with salad, salad, and more salad. She stuffed a forkful of lettuce into her mouth.

"Nothing," Eliot said and took an equally huge bite of

his scrambled eggs. He chewed with his mouth open.

"You're disgusting," Caroline told him. She turned to Mattie. "What do you want? I haven't done my good deed for the day yet. If you're lucky, I'll do something for you. If you're very, very lucky, it will be something you like."

"Um . . . we need help with a problem."

"What kind of problem?" Caroline wanted to know.

Mattie sighed. He knew this was going to sound crazy even before he said it. "I need to get into the headmaster's office and find the *How to Be Good Manual* so I can read it, memorize it, and go home."

Caroline cocked her head. "A manual about being good?"

"I'm sure they call it something different," Mattie said. "But that's what we're calling it."

"How will you know it when you see it if you don't even know what it's called?"

Mattie sighed again. He was starting to regret telling Caroline anything. "I just will, okay?"

Caroline studied the windows across from them as she considered this. A roof tile plummeted past and, outside, someone screamed. "If there is a book like that," Caroline said in a faraway tone, "I want to use it for my essay. I can't think of five hundred words on how Munchem taught me how to be a better person. I bet that book would help."

Mattie squirmed. "I don't know that it's a book exactly."

She shrugged. "Whatever. I'll do it."

"You'll help us?" Mattie sat up straight. "Really?"

"Why?" Eliot asked.

Caroline scowled and stabbed her salad with her fork. "Because I was going there anyway. The Rooster confiscated Beezus and I need to get him back."

"Who's Beezus?" Mattie asked.

"Not Beezus again!" Eliot said at the same time.

Caroline pretended she didn't hear her brother. "Beezus is my pet rat," she told Mattie. "The Rooster found him and confiscated him because of Rule Ten."

"What's Rule Ten?" Mattie wanted to know.

"No pets," Caroline said.

"Beezus is not a pet." Eliot scrunched up his face. "He's a rat! And he looks like he's melting."

"It's called *molting*," Caroline said, narrowing her eyes at her brother. "And his hair only falls out when he's stressed."

Eliot's expression was triumphant. "Then he must be stressed all the time!"

"Rule Twenty-Seven: No electronics of any type," Caroline said, putting both elbows on the table and glaring at her brother.

Eliot shut his mouth. He concentrated on cutting his bacon into tiny pieces.

"Now," Caroline said and wiped her hands twice before putting the napkin on the table. "I'm very good at breaking into locked-up places, as I'm sure Eliot told you."

"You don't like me talking about you," Eliot complained.

"It's not that I *don't* like you talking about me," Caroline explained and took another bite of salad. "It's just that I prefer you use terms like 'genius' and 'visionary' when describing my work."

Eliot pointed his fork at her. "Letting animals loose is *not* work."

"Do you want my help or not?" Caroline asked.

"Yes!" Mattie said quickly, waving one hand between the brother and sister. "Yes! We want your help!"

Caroline sniffed and spent a moment rearranging the carrots on her salad. "Do you *need* my help?"

Mattie stared at her and then looked at Eliot. Eliot rolled his eyes. Mattie turned back to Caroline. "Yes. We *need* your help."

She brightened, her smile as wide as her face. "Good. Remember that. You came to me. You needed me."

"Okay," Mattie said even though he was starting to wonder if he should have opened his mouth at all.

"We'll break into the office tonight."

"Tonight?" Mattie's question escaped on a squeak, and Caroline shook her head like he was an enormous disappointment. Actually, at that moment, Caroline and Eliot were both looking at Mattie like he was an enormous disappointment. They might look different, but their expressions were exactly the same.

"Tonight," Caroline repeated, and Mattie didn't realize until now that her smile could get even wider and whiter. "We're going to break in tonight and I know just how we're going to do it."

Munchem Academy Rule

NO PETS ALLOWED

MATTIE COULD BARELY CONCENTRATE ON HIS CLASSES. HE didn't notice when Doyle's best friend, Maxwell, put thumbtacks on Mr. Karloff's seat. He barely noticed Mr. Karloff's screaming shortly thereafter. All Mattie could think about was Caroline and Eliot and how he might be getting out of Munchem.

Or how he might be getting into even more trouble.

Mattie spent their study hall session working on his essay. He'd titled it "How Munchem Academy Made Me a Better Person," but it certainly wasn't good to break into the headmaster's office, and Mattie couldn't seem to write himself around it. The guilt sat on his chest, making it hard to breathe, and by the time they were supposed to meet Caroline, Mattie felt a little nauseous and a lot shaky.

It wouldn't have been hard to convince Kent and Bell he had to go to the nurse's office, but Eliot decided to say they'd been assigned extra cleaning. Mattie thought the excuse was pretty good—the other boys certainly seemed to buy it. Or maybe they just didn't care.

Either way, Eliot and Mattie waited for Caroline in the dark by an oak tree with a trunk so wide that they couldn't get their arms around it even if they tried. Which they didn't because birds were sleeping in the branches and one pooped on Eliot.

"This would be so much cooler if I had a computer," Eliot complained as he tried to shake the white bird poop off of his sweater vest. The bird poop didn't budge. "It's not like a spy movie at all."

"That's because we're not in a spy movie," Mattie said.

"What is he complaining about now?" Caroline walked out of the dark like she was a part of it, like even her hair was made from shadows.

"Nothing," both boys said. It was too dark to see Caroline's eyes, but Mattie and Eliot knew she was rolling them.

"Are you ready?" she asked.

"Yes!" Mattie stuffed his sweaty hands in his pockets. "How are we going to get in?"

"The window."

Mattie studied Caroline very carefully. Even in the dark, he could see she hadn't brought anything with her. "How are you going to open the lock?" he asked. "Don't you need a tool or a hair pin or something?"

"Oh." Caroline waved one hand. "The lock's been broken for a week now. I saw the work request on Miss Maple's desk. We can just let ourselves in."

"'Just let ourselves in'?" Eliot echoed. "You could've told us that!"

"True, but then you wouldn't owe me a favor."

Eliot made a gurgling noise, and Caroline turned to Mattie. "Are we doing this or not?"

"We're doing it," Eliot said and started down the path. His sister skipped along behind him and Mattie followed, his stomach twisted tight with nerves.

"Wait!" Mattie tugged Eliot's and Caroline's sleeves, dragging them to a stop. "What if the lock's been fixed? You said the work request was a week old."

"Oh, um . . ." Caroline seemed to be looking anywhere and everywhere except at Mattie and Eliot. "Freeing the biology lab frogs was messier than I anticipated. There were some casualties. The janitors are still cleaning up."

Eliot started to say something, and Caroline jabbed two fingers into his chest. "Not a word, Eliot. Not. A. Word."

Eliot seemed to have quite a few words, but he shut his mouth anyway and the three of them scuttled along in the dark until they reached the outside wall of the administration wing. Caroline counted windows to figure out which window belonged to the headmaster's office and then, once she was sure, motioned for the boys to go ahead.

"Boost me?" Mattie asked.

Eliot shrugged. "Nothing like a spy movie," he muttered, but he let Mattie step on his knee anyway. They both wobbled as Mattie fumbled with the window. The latch was broken, as Caroline had said it was, but Mattie still had to use both hands to pry the glass panels open. They swung outward, toward them. Eliot tried to step back. They teetered once . . . twice . . . *crash*.

Mattie spit bits of grass from his mouth.

"Ladies first," Caroline said and stepped on Mattie's shoulder to climb through the window. Eliot and Mattie scrambled after her and, for a long moment, all three of them just stood in the headmaster's office.

"We did it," Eliot breathed and Mattie nodded. They were inside the headmaster's office. They were alone. The plan was working. They grinned at each other and their teeth were stripes of white in the dark.

"Would you two hurry it up?" Caroline huffed. She was at the bookshelves, inspecting Rooney's pictures and checking the cabinets underneath the shelves. The cabinet doors swooshed open and shut, open and shut as Caroline searched then, finally, "Beezus!"

Something—presumably Beezus—went *squeak squeak!*

"Put him back!" Eliot whispered at her. "Rooney will know someone's been here. You'll get in trouble."

"Will not." Caroline stood up, leaving the cage and cabinet doors open. She cradled something in her arms and, as Caroline drew close to him, Mattie finally saw Beezus.

"That thing is *ugly*," Mattie said. In his defense, it was true. Beezus was quite ugly, but Mattie probably didn't look very beautiful to Beezus either. Beauty is often a question of perspective. What's beautiful to one person isn't always beautiful to another, but who knows what rats find beautiful. Cheese, maybe? A nice bit of carrot? Human flesh?!

Maybe, because at that moment Beezus was actively trying to bite Eliot's finger as Eliot shook it in his sister's face. "You can't take him with you! You'll only get caught again!"

Squeak! Squeak!

Caroline held Beezus up to her ear. "What's that, Beezus? Yes, I think he's quite annoying as well."

"Stop it! That stupid rat doesn't talk!"

Caroline nodded as though she were listening to someone else and Eliot didn't exist at all. "He *does* smell! I've told him that several times and he doesn't believe me."

The only thing Mattie smelled at that moment was orange wood cleaner. Rooney's desk must've been recently cleaned. There was a cup of pens, a calendar, and a Post-it note to Miss Maple about ordering more paper clips.

Headmaster Rooney should check Miss Maple's purse, Mattie thought.

"What would Doyle be doing here?" Mattie asked.

Eliot held up a jar of paste. "Eating paste?"

It did seem like something Doyle would do, but Mattie didn't think it would help him impress the teachers. Mattie took another long look at the jar's sticky, crusty lid. He really hoped it wouldn't impress the teachers. He had no desire to put that in his mouth even if it did get him a trip home.

Eliot joined his sister at the bookshelves, and Mattie turned in a small circle, studying the window, the desk chair, and, finally, the closet behind the desk. The door eased open with just the slightest tug on the handle.

He poked at the coats inside. "Rooney must get cold a lot."

Eliot stood next to him. He checked the pockets of each coat, but came up empty-handed. "Why would Headmaster Rooney want an orange plaid jacket?"

He held up the orange plaid jacket in question. They took a moment to contemplate not only why Headmaster Rooney would wear such a thing, but why *anyone* would wear such a thing.

"Grown-ups," Caroline said at last. She said it so determinedly, and in a way that was so completely Caroline, that there was nothing left to be said and all three of them shuffled out of the closet and returned to searching the office.

They found nothing.

Well, that wasn't entirely true. After all, Caroline did find Beezus, but Mattie didn't find anything about Doyle and absolutely nothing that looked like a *How to Be Good Manual*.

When the Spencers wanted to leave, Mattie had to drag himself after them.

What good were criminal acts if you didn't get what you wanted? Mattie thought about asking the Spencers, but they were busy. Eliot had pushed open the window and was checking outside. The light from the full moon illuminated the whole courtyard in silver and black. It still looked empty, but it was hard to tell what might be hidden in the overgrown grass and the crooked trees.

"Ready?" Eliot asked. Mattie nodded and put one foot on Eliot's knees just as there was a rustling in the grass like something was thrashing through it.

"What's that?" a voice cried out.

They froze, straining at the window.

"Teachers!" Mattie squeaked just before Eliot dropped him. They lay on the floor of the office, staring at each other. "Hide!"

But where? Underneath Rooney's massive desk? Too obvious. It would be like hiding under the bed in a scary movie. Behind the plushy chairs? Too stupid. The three would be instantly spotted. So that left . . .

"The closet!" Mattie whispered. Mattie and the Spencers lunged for the headmaster's closet door and shut themselves inside, getting a face full of woolly jackets and tasseled scarves. They backed up until their shoulders hit the wall behind them, until something small and hard and round crammed into Mattie's spine.

It felt like a doorknob.

Mattie grabbed it with both hands and the smooth, cool knob turned. Why would there be a door inside a closet?

"Hey!" Mattie whispered, nudging Eliot with his elbow.

"Why is this window open?" The voice from the dark was now closer, *much* closer. It sounded like it was right outside the office, under the window Mattie and the Spencers had used. "Is someone in there? Come out! Right now!"

"We're going to get caught!" Eliot exclaimed—although, to be fair, it was a little hard for him to exclaim considering he couldn't lift his voice above a whisper.

"We're not going to get caught!" Mattie wasn't sure why he said this because he was pretty sure it wasn't the truth. Actually, he was positive it wasn't the truth, and the small voice inside his head—the one that was usually right—also agreed it wasn't the truth. They were totally going to get caught unless . . .

Mattie gripped the doorknob harder. "Through here!"

Eliot grabbed him. "Are you *crazy*?" he whispered. "We don't know where that goes!"

Mattie did know that if they didn't do something, they were going to get caught. And it was amazing how desperation brought out something that might have possibly always been waiting inside Mattie for just such a moment, because he yanked open that hidden door like he knew exactly what he was doing.

It fell open to reveal a square of shadows.

And stairs.

The stairs went down, down, down into the dark, and all three of the kids drew closer together. "I am *not* going down there!" Caroline whisper-yelled at Mattie.

"No one's asking you!" Eliot returned.

"Mr. Karloff?" trilled a female voice outside the closet. It sounded like Mrs. Hitchcock. "I think I heard voices!"

Eliot glared at Caroline. Caroline glared back at Eliot. Mattie started to sweat.

"Voices?" Mr. Karloff responded. "Where did you hear voices?"

"Over *there*!"

The friends gulped. Mrs. Hitchcock could have meant over there by Headmaster Rooney's wastepaper basket. She could have meant over there by his picture of a politician who looked more like a beady-eyed hobgoblin than someone engaged in the politics of a nation.

Which is to say the politician looked exactly as he should look.

But Mattie, Eliot, and Caroline knew the teacher didn't mean any of those places. She meant the *closet*.

Mattie didn't stop to think. He didn't stop to argue. He just grabbed Caroline and Eliot by their arms and hauled them into the dark.

NEVER GO OUT OF BOUNDS

MATTIE CLOSED THE LITTLE DOOR JUST AS A FINGER OF YELLOW office light crawled across the closet floor. He pressed one ear to the door, listening as the teachers pawed through the coats, making the metal hangers bump into the wall.

"We need to have your hearing checked," Mr. Karloff said. "There's nothing here."

"Let me look," Mrs. Hitchcock said. The hangers went *thump thump thump* as she banged around in the closet. "Perhaps you're right," she said at last. "Unless they went through the door?"

Caroline gasped and Eliot used both hands to cover his sister's mouth. The three of them stared at each other as footsteps drew closer.

And closer.

Mr. Karloff was on the other side of the door. Mattie felt his eyes bug. He looked at Eliot, at Caroline, and, finally, at the door handle. There was a little button on it like . . . a lock.

Mattie stabbed one finger into it and there was the softest *click.*

"Did you hear that?" Mrs. Hitchcock asked. "Could they have started without us?"

"I didn't hear a thing," Mr. Karloff grumped and the door shook as he rattled the handle. "See? It's locked. Rooney would never leave it open."

"True," Mrs. Hitchcock said, but she didn't sound as if she believed it. "We should get going. They'll be expecting us."

Expecting them for what? Started what without them? Mattie wondered. The door stopped shaking and Mattie carefully pressed his ear to the wood again. He could hear shoes scuffing against the floor and more hangers thumping into the wall.

Whump!

Mrs. Hitchcock slammed the closet door with such force it made Mattie's eardrum shudder. He rubbed one palm against his sore ear and faced Eliot and Caroline, surprised he could see them at all. The stairwell—which had looked so dark before—was now faintly lit with small electric bulbs that flickered and flickered but never seemed to go out.

Mattie could see the stairs went far down into the ground.

He could also see Eliot and Caroline were ready to pound each other. He knew because Carter also had the same look right before he pounded Mattie.

"I thought you had this planned," Eliot whispered to Caroline.

She threw up both hands. "How was I supposed to know the teachers were patrolling the grounds?"

"Did you let anything else loose?" he demanded.

Caroline had to think about it.

"Look," Mattie whispered. "We can't go back. They're searching the other rooms. They'll catch us in the hallway if we try to leave."

"Maybe we should wait here until morning," Eliot suggested.

Caroline huffed. "Then the Rooster will catch us."

"Well, what do *you* suggest we do, then?" Eliot asked Caroline.

"We go down," Mattie interrupted. "I mean, they're stairs, right? They have to go somewhere."

And, technically, Mattie was right. Stairs usually do go somewhere. They go off cliffs or off the sides of pirate ships. No, wait. That's a plank. Planks go off the sides of pirate ships. Anyway, the point is: stairs go somewhere and sometimes, as in this case, they go into a very unappealing basement. At least, Mattie assumed it would be an unappealing basement. It could just as easily be a storage room with more Headmaster Rooney pictures.

"Why would you have a hidden door?" Eliot asked. "Because it leads somewhere you don't want anyone to go."

"There has to be another way out," Mattie said. He meant to sound confident, more like Carter, definitely more like Mr. Larimore, but, instead, he sounded like Mattie, which is to say the words turned out a bit squeaky.

Caroline groaned and marched down the stairs, stiff-legged. Her Beezus brown hair snapped from side to side. The boys exchanged a quick glance and followed her, going down, down, down into the basement.

Except it wasn't really a basement. Or, at least, it wasn't a basement like people usually think of basements, because Mattie and Eliot and Caroline walked down one hundred stairs and reached a massive, enormous, completely gigantic room!

Yes, *fine*, a basement can be massive and enormous and completely gigantic. It can especially be massive and enormous and completely gigantic if your parents have made their for-tune from a reality television series or if they sell that cement fancy ladies inject into their wrinkles.

But this room was at Munchem Academy, and Mattie had never seen anything like it. The basement's walls were so far away that Mattie couldn't see them, and the ceiling was so high that Mattie could only see shadows above them, and every-where he looked there was machinery.

"This is stuff my dad makes," Mattie said, putting one hand on a cable as thick as his wrist. It was warm to the touch even though the air was cool. "I've seen those wires and that electrical paneling at his factory."

Everyone paused to look at those wires and that paneling and, once they were done, Eliot put his hands on his hips and shook his head. "Who knew you could fit so much underneath a school? It really makes me rethink Munchem's whole deal. I mean, they're supposed to be teaching us not to lie and yet look at all of this."

Eliot spun in a small circle, his arms spread wide to indicate everything around them. There was a lot to take in. There were smokestacks reaching for the ceiling and cables hanging like jungle vines.

Mattie really wanted to swing on one. It was very unlike him, and he took a deep breath until the feeling passed. Thankfully, it did, but Mattie's hands were still sticky like he'd been eating candy and his heart was still thumping like he'd been running even though they were creeping along, trying to be quiet.

"What are they doing down here?" Mattie asked at last. Caroline and Eliot shrugged.

"I want a closer look," Eliot said, approaching the nearest electrical panel with outstretched hands.

"And I want to get out of here," Caroline said, grabbing her brother by his collar and hauling him toward her.

Mattie nodded. "She's right. We need to find an exit."

Eliot grumbled, but agreed. Mattie started to guide the Spencers carefully around the pipes and wires and cables—

although is there any other way to pick your way through things that could electrocute you?

Okay, perhaps they couldn't *all* electrocute you, but they could trip you and that's rather unpleasant.

Being electrocuted is worse, though, and you should keep that in mind.

"What are they powering it with?" Eliot craned his head back and stared at curls of steam or, maybe, smoke spiraling above them.

"Hamsters," Caroline said with a nod.

Eliot glared at her. "You can't power anything with hamsters."

"You can if you have enough hamsters."

Mattie tried to picture the thousands of hamsters running on the thousands of spinning wheels that it would take to power a machine of this size. "I think Eliot might be right, Caroline."

Caroline crossed her arms and rolled her eyes. "Boys," she said in a tone that might also be used to call something stupid. The boys ignored her.

"Maybe it's the heating and cooling system," Eliot said as he examined a network of pipes that twisted past them. "Look, here are the power lines."

Mattie nodded and motioned to their right. "This is a water pipe."

Caroline pointed a single finger ahead of them. "And those are teachers."

Munchem Academy Rule

NEVER TOUCH ANYTHING
WITHOUT PERMISSION

HAVE YOU EVER HEARD THE EXPRESSION "OUT OF THE FRYING pan and into the fire"? I'm sure you have, but if you haven't, consider Mattie's situation to be a perfect illustration of what happens when you're running from one set of teachers and you plunge headlong into another set of teachers.

The moral of the story? Teachers are everywhere. They don't stay in their classrooms or coffins or wherever teachers are supposed to stay when they're not teaching.

But back to Mattie and Caroline and Eliot, who were about to get caught. Again.

"Hide!" Mattie whispered, his eyes darting to find a hiding place.

"Where?" Caroline whispered, her eyes darting also.

"Here!" Eliot grabbed them both—much like Mattie had grabbed him before—and yanked them to their knees. They scrambled underneath a wide metal cabinet that seemed to enclose only red and yellow wires. Eliot was fascinated. Mattie and Caroline were not. They held their breath as footsteps approached.

Scuff. Scuff. Scuff.

Two sets of shoes passed them—one pair of sensible pumps and one pair of sensible loafers. They were teacher shoes and they didn't stop and they didn't hesitate. They actually seemed kind of in a hurry.

"Where are they going?" Mattie whispered to Eliot, but Eliot didn't notice because he was trying to unscrew a yellow wire. Mattie smacked his hand.

"I just want to look!" Eliot protested. Caroline smacked them both.

"If they're going that way," Caroline said, pointing one finger in the direction the teachers were headed, "then we should go that way." She pointed in the opposite direction. Beezus squeaked his agreement.

Mattie agreed too, but when he nodded, he knocked the back of his head into the metal plating. "Let's go," he said. He had crawled almost all the way out of the hiding spot before realizing Eliot was still playing with the wires.

"Eliot!" Caroline kicked him. "Come on!"

Eliot grunted, but he did follow them. They wriggled along

on their bellies, leaving student-sized smears in the dust. They crawled over pipes that were as thick as pythons and under long dangly lines of copper wiring. They crawled and crawled and popped out on the other side of *somewhere*.

Or possibly the same place they were before. Mattie wasn't sure. There were more pipes, more cables, more wires, and yet it all looked the same.

"Where are we?" Caroline asked. She had dust down the front of her sweater and pants and some on her nose. She looked at Mattie like he was supposed to have answers.

"How am I supposed to know?" Mattie asked.

"Sssshhhh!"

Mattie and Caroline turned to see Eliot on his hands and knees, peering through a tangle of cables. His butt wagged from side to side as he followed whatever was on the other side.

"Look!" Eliot whispered.

Mattie and Caroline glanced at each other, shrugged, and joined him. And, at first, it didn't look like anything. There was another set of stairs leading to a platform, some sort of conveyor belt leading away from the platform, and two huge smokestacks pumping smoke up into the ceiling.

"I don't see—" Mattie started to say, until he did see. He saw exactly what Eliot was seeing: Mrs. Hitchcock and Mr. Karloff were walking up the platform steps. Headmaster Rooney and a student that looked an awful lot like Albert Maxwell were right behind them.

Then the student turned and Mattie realized it looked like Albert Maxwell because it *was* Albert Maxwell.

"Is this what they were talking about?" Mattie whispered and Caroline elbowed him to be quiet.

"Headmaster Rooney, you have to do something about him!" Mr. Karloff shrilled. The older teacher had always reminded Mattie of a mall Santa out of uniform. His enormous stomach bounced with the effort of his shouting. "He kicked a sixth grader today!"

"And he stole all of the answers to my book report!" Mrs. Hitchcock announced.

"You can't prove that!" Maxwell returned.

"You can't prove that you didn't!" Mrs. Hitchcock countered and everyone fell silent because that was true.

"My fellow teachers," Rooney boomed. "It's time for Maxwell to change, don't you think?"

Nods and murmurs all around indicated that, yes indeed, the teachers did think it was time for Maxwell to change. Maxwell, however, seemed undecided.

"Do you know what comes next?" Rooney asked the teachers, who squealed and jumped up and down like someone was passing out Halloween candy.

"We should get out of here," Mattie said. Between the tangle of enormous pipes and the noise from the machine, Mattie was pretty positive they couldn't be seen or heard, but he wasn't sure he wanted to know what came "next."

Actually, Mattie was *sure* he didn't.

The Spencers waved him off. "Two more minutes," Eliot said.

"I just want to see this," Caroline said and held Beezus up so he could get a better view. Beezus looked about as thrilled as Mattie.

"Considering our great success with Project Marcus and Project Jay," Headmaster Rooney continued, spreading his arms wide, "and considering our even greater success with Project Doyle, I think we should begin Project Maxwell."

The teachers cheered and Maxwell swallowed. "Wha—what do you mean?" he asked.

Headmaster Rooney clapped Maxwell on the shoulder. "I mean, dear boy, that we're going to make you into the perfect student we've always known you could be."

And before Maxwell could ask what on earth Rooney meant, Mr. Karloff tackled him. He tied Maxwell's hands behind him and his feet together and then lifted Maxwell onto a long, low table.

Mr. Karloff held Maxwell's arms, Mrs. Hitchcock held his feet, and Headmaster Rooney cackled. It wasn't helpful unless you considered scaring Maxwell to be helpful, in which case it was incredibly helpful because Maxwell was now whimpering.

Headmaster Rooney grabbed a huge switch along the machine's side. It took two yanks before he could tug it downward, but once he did, there was a deafening groaning. The machine huffed smoke into the air like a dragon and then the long, low table began to move.

"It's a conveyor belt," Eliot announced happily, pointing in case Mattie and Caroline couldn't see for themselves, which they clearly could.

"Your brother has issues," Mattie said to Caroline, who shrugged like she already knew.

"Don't fight it!" Headmaster Rooney called to Maxwell as the conveyor belt chugged him into the machine's wide opening. "This won't hurt much."

Maxwell was swallowed into the machine. The smokestacks puffed harder and all the lights turned orange. Something screeched so loudly it should have been a cat, but it was the machine.

Or possibly Maxwell.

It was hard for Mattie to tell anything at that point.

The teachers and Headmaster Rooney trotted to the other side of the conveyor belt and peered into the opening. Mrs. Hitchcock took a handkerchief and dabbed her eyes like Mattie's mother did at weddings.

"It's just so beautiful," she yelled to Mr. Karloff, who nodded and patted her shoulder as if he understood perfectly.

Mattie was glad someone understood because he certainly didn't. The air around them smelled like burning hair and Mattie wanted to cover his nose and mouth, but he couldn't move. He couldn't take his eyes off the gigantic engine grinding and grinding above them.

"I can see him!" Mrs. Hitchcock yelled. The teachers leaned in, looking down the conveyor belt expectantly.

And yet the only thing that appeared was Maxwell. The conveyor belt slowly trundled along until he reached the teachers. Headmaster Rooney untied Maxwell's arms and feet and offered him a hand to sit up. Maxwell did so and the first thing Mattie noticed was that Maxwell's clothes were different. He wasn't wearing his uniform. He was wearing a long-sleeved white shirt and white pants. He looked like he had on pajamas or hospital scrubs.

Maxwell stood and Headmaster Rooney, Mrs. Hitchcock, and Mr. Karloff backed up to stare at him. Mattie kind of understood because Caroline, Eliot, and Mattie stared too. Something weird was definitely going on. Mattie wanted to know why Maxwell's clothes were different. What was so special about a machine that made you dress like you were ready for bed, he wondered.

The engine continued to grind and grind and then suddenly another set of shoes appeared. The shoes were attached to legs, which were attached to a torso, which were attached to . . .

"Maxwell?" Caroline whispered.

That's who it looked like. He was wearing the same red Munchem sweater, the same blue Munchem pants. The conveyor belt brought the boy closer and closer, finally stopping in front of the teachers just like it had before. Mrs. Hitchcock and Mr. Karloff untied Maxwell and helped him to his feet, which seemed like a very good idea because this Maxwell kept swaying. The other Maxwell kept smiling.

But was it Maxwell? Because Maxwell was Maxwell . . . *right*?

"That boy looks just like Maxwell," Caroline said softly.

"He *is* Maxwell," Eliot insisted. He was leaning forward, squinting like he was trying to focus his eyes. "It has to be some sort of trick."

Except it wasn't. Eliot just wanted it to be. They all wanted it to be a trick because if that thing wasn't Maxwell, if it was some sort of . . .

"Clone," Mattie breathed. "They made a *clone* of Maxwell— like in the movies."

Caroline gasped. "Like with sheep!"

"Like I've always wanted to!" Eliot said.

Caroline and Mattie glared at Eliot. He shrugged. "What? I always have."

"It's a new day, my friends." Headmaster Rooney wrapped one bony arm around Clone Maxwell's shoulders and turned him so the teachers could see them both. Everyone clapped. Eliot leaned into Mattie and Mattie leaned into Caroline.

"Behold the future of Munchem!" Headmaster Rooney continued. "We will have the greatest students ever because we will *create* the greatest students ever!"

BE GOOD

THE TEACHERS CONTINUED TO CLAP, AND CLONE MAXWELL clapped the hardest. Original Maxwell didn't clap at all. Original Maxwell collapsed in a pile of legs and arms and cradled his head like it hurt.

Mr. Karloff hooked one arm around Original Maxwell and pulled him to his feet. "This would be so much easier if we just put the bad kids down," he told Mrs. Hitchcock.

Put them down? Mattie wondered. Like *killed* them? He glanced at the Spencers and saw the Spencers were just as confused or maybe they were just horrified. After all, sometimes confused and horrified look astonishingly similar.

Mrs. Hitchcock pulled her cardigan tight around her. "It wouldn't be easier," she said to Mr. Karloff. "It would be *messier.*"

"We need to get out of here," Mattie whispered again.

"Smartest thing you've ever said," Caroline whispered back.

"I want a closer look," Eliot breathed. Mattie and Caroline ignored him. Mattie looked around for another exit while Caroline kept a firm grip on her brother's shirt collar.

"There!" Mattie pointed to the wall beyond the teachers, where another stairwell led up. Mattie leaned against the pipe they were hidden behind, peering at the teachers as they filed behind Headmaster Rooney and the Maxwells and marched across the platform.

"Where are they going?" Eliot wanted to know.

"I don't care," Caroline answered. "As long as they're going the opposite direction that I'm going. I don't want another Caroline running around."

"Neither do I," Eliot said.

Mattie agreed, but he didn't say anything. He was too busy trying to decide how they should get to the stairs. By the time the last teacher disappeared, Mattie had a plan.

"C'mon," Mattie said. Caroline and Eliot followed Mattie so closely that they repeatedly stepped on Mattie's heels as they squeezed behind two rumbling generators, scurried under a rusty platform, and ducked around a tangle of blue Larimore Corporation cables.

"Get to the stairs!" Mattie pushed Caroline and Eliot ahead of him. The three did indeed reach the stairs, which they climbed and they climbed until the stairs turned into a ladder and the ladder turned into more stairs and, finally, Caroline's head bumped into something hard, flat, and metal.

"Ow!" Caroline said, rubbing the top of her head.

"What is it?" Eliot whispered.

"It's . . ." Caroline's voice trailed off. The sound of metal scraping against metal sent a chill down Mattie's back. Suddenly, pale moonlight shone down on them and the air turned cooler, fresher. "It's like a manhole cover," she said and poked her head through the opening. "C'mon."

They took the last few steps up and spilled onto thick grass. Eliot and Caroline struggled to replace the cover. Mattie knew he should help, but he couldn't seem to catch his breath. He lay on his back and looked at the stars and realized he had never been so scared in his life.

"Where are we?" Caroline asked again. Mattie was ready to tell her again that he had no idea, but Eliot spoke up first.

"We're in the south meadow," he said and pointed to their right. Caroline and Mattie both turned. "See? There's the science wing."

Sure enough, Eliot was right. The school's science wing sat in the dark like a fat black dog.

"Good," Caroline said. It wasn't cold, but she was shivering. "That means I'm only a few minutes from my dorm." She started to turn away, but Mattie grabbed her sweater.

"Wait," he said. "Don't we need to talk about this?"

"I think some things are better left undiscussed," Caroline informed him.

"That isn't even a word," Eliot said.

"It is now."

"Stop it!" Mattie snapped. "This is serious. Remember how Rooney said that thing about Project Doyle? What if Doyle's a clone too? That would explain everything."

"I think it complicates more than it explains," Caroline said.

"Ignore her," Eliot said. "I know what you mean. It's actually very exciting, though, Mattie. Think of the possibilities: if you had your own clone, you would never have to do homework again."

"Or eat your bratwurst," Caroline added.

"Or go to the dentist," Eliot finished.

Caroline cocked her head to one side. "Well, I would still go to the dentist."

"I probably would too," Eliot agreed.

"Enough about the dentist!" Mattie stomped his feet and waved his hands to get the siblings' attention. They stared at him like he was a lunatic. "They *cloned* Maxwell and Doyle and we don't know what happened to the *real* Maxwell and Doyle."

"I'm not sure I want to know," Eliot said.

"Agreed," Caroline said. "Besides, I like the new Doyle. He gave me pumpkin muffins this morning at breakfast."

Mattie gaped. "But we can't let them get away with this!"

Caroline shook her head. "Honestly, Mattie, what do you really think we can do?"

"We can—" Mattie stopped. Caroline was right. What could they do? They were just kids. Who would believe them? Even now, Mattie could barely believe it himself.

"We could call the police," he said at last. "We could show them this entrance and then they'd find the machine."

"I think you have to have paperwork or something for that," Eliot said.

"It's true," Caroline added. "They're always asking me for probable cause when I try to get the police to come to the laboratories."

"What's probable cause?" Mattie asked.

"I think it's a reason the police should come help you," Caroline said.

Everyone went quiet as they thought about that. Unfortunately, no one could think of a reason the police would come help them. The police would probably think they were making the whole thing up.

"It's best to just keep your head down," Eliot said and Mattie nodded in spite of himself because he knew that. He knew it because keeping his head down was a key part of being good and because Mr. Larimore often said the same thing when people from the Environmental Protection Agency came to his office.

"Good," Caroline said, her smile especially white in the shadows. "I'm glad that's settled. Now, if you two don't mind, Beezus and I are going to bed."

"Don't get caught," Eliot warned her.

"I won't get caught." Caroline tossed her hair and Beezus squeaked. "But you probably will."

"Will not."

"Will too."

"Will—" Eliot didn't get to finish because Caroline was already gone. She stomped into the dark until all they could see was nothing and all they could hear was muttering and then, finally, even the muttering was gone.

"We have to get back to our room," Mattie said quietly. He was talking to Eliot, but he couldn't take his eyes off the opening in the ground, and he couldn't stop thinking about the machine that lay behind the opening in the ground.

"Yeah," Eliot said and scratched his stomach. "We should get back, but I had fun. We should do this again."

Mattie stared at Eliot and didn't care that his mouth was hanging open and that his eyes were huge. Eliot was clearly insane and, when dealing with insane people, one does not have to worry about appearing normal. In some ways, Mattie found it rather freeing.

"I'm never doing that again," Mattie said. "I've learned my lesson."

"Oh, yeah." Eliot wiped his nose with the back of his hand.

"I always forget that you're a good kid. That's probably going to keep you pretty safe around here."

"What do you mean?"

Eliot stretched both arms over his head as he yawned. "I mean you don't have anything to worry about. It's not like they're going to clone the good kids."

"Yeah," Mattie said and then immediately his heart double-thumped—because even if Mattie didn't have anything to worry about, Carter did.

NO, REALLY, BE GOOD OR ELSE

IN FACT, THE MORE MATTIE THOUGHT ABOUT CARTER AND clones and how bad kids were getting turned into clones, the more Mattie realized he had to tell his brother. The trouble was how?

Mattie had no idea. He followed Eliot as they crept back to their dorm and made up a list of ways to tell Carter the truth:

1. Tell him at breakfast

2. Give him a note

3. Skywriting

"Skywriting?" Eliot gaped at Mattie, his breath exhaling in a hard puff. "Where would you get a plane? Wait! If you warn

Carter with skywriting then Rooney will know you know and then Rooney will also know he has a problem . . . you know?"

Mattie was afraid he did. "Fine." Mattie frowned. "I'll put everything in a note."

"You really think Carter will believe a story about cloning because you wrote it down?"

"Not really." Mattie also knew his brother wasn't the kind of kid who would believe he needed to clean up his act or risk being cloned. Not to mention, there was the little matter of what would happen if the note fell into a teacher's hands.

Mattie shuddered. That wouldn't be good, but he had to try.

"I'll tell him at breakfast," Mattie said at last. It sounded reasonable and simple.

Too bad something so reasonable and so simple could make his stomach squeeze and squeeze.

The morning started out like any other morning. The boys in 14A woke up. They brushed their teeth. They acted like there wasn't anything going on underneath their school, like the only thing they had to worry about was whether the pudding at lunch would have a green skin on it again. Everyone got dressed. Everyone went down to the dining hall.

It was cold that morning. As Mattie and the others walked through the courtyard on the way to breakfast, their breath puffed in wispy clouds above their heads. The long grass was crunchy under Mattie's feet and the benches were sparkly with frost. They looked almost pretty for things that would freezer burn your butt if you sat on them, Mattie thought.

"Would you hurry up?" Eliot asked him. Mattie hurried. He followed Eliot, Eliot followed Doyle, and Doyle led the way, grinning.

"After you, Mattie," the clone said, holding the door open so Mattie could pass.

"Thanks, Doyle," Mattie mumbled as he hurried past. The dining room smelled like eggs and burned toast and bleach. Students stood in clumps between the rows of tables and teachers kept telling everyone to sit down. Mattie was silent as they pushed through the breakfast line. He took a tray from the teetering stack. He took an orange juice from the sweating cooler. He didn't notice Mrs. Hitchcock making notes or Mr. Karloff muttering observations into a small recorder. Mattie was too busy hunting for Carter. Luckily, it wasn't hard to find him. His brother was sitting a few tables away, surrounded by his friends.

It was now or never. Mattie put down his tray and started toward them.

"What . . . what are you doing?" Eliot grabbed Mattie's sleeve. "Those are eighth graders!"

"Yeah, and that one's my brother." Mattie shook Eliot off and marched toward the big kids. Three older girls drew away, revealing the students still sitting at the table. Mattie saw his brother again. Carter's hair was spiked in just the way their mother hated. His uniform jacket was wrinkled and there were small feathers on his collar.

From his pillow? Mattie wondered, but he didn't get to wonder for long because Marcus and Jay turned to stare at him.

It was like they knew what Mattie was going to say, but they couldn't know.

Could they?

Mattie gulped. "Um, Carter?"

Carter didn't turn around. He stabbed his eggs with a little extra force, though. "What is it, Pippi?"

"Good morning, Mattie!" Jay boomed. He leaned across Carter to grab Mattie's hand and shake it, reminding Mattie of the time the mayor came to their house.

"Morning, Jay," Mattie said. "Um, Carter? I need to talk to you."

Carter sighed and swiveled to face Mattie. "Talk."

"Can we do this, um, privately?"

"'Can we do this, um, privately?'" A pretty brown-haired girl mimicked Mattie's question, but she made it even higher and squeakier. Carter started to laugh and stopped himself.

"Cool it, yeah?" he asked, and she quieted. Carter stood

up and shook his head like he couldn't really believe he was doing this.

Neither could Mattie. He tried not to bounce along next to Carter as they walked to the edge of the cafeteria. Generally, Carter never went anywhere with Mattie.

Carter leaned against the wall and crossed his arms. "What?"

Mattie blinked and blinked again. How was he supposed to say *You have to get good or Headmaster Rooney is going to turn you into a clone?*

"You have to get good, Carter, or Headmaster Rooney is going to turn you into a clone!"

Carter stared at him. Mattie mentally kicked himself and sneaked a glance around Carter's shoulder. Marcus and Jay were staring at them, but Mattie was pretty sure they were too far away to hear anything.

Mattie took a deep breath. "They're cloning students," he explained. "Or maybe just turning them into robots. I don't know. I couldn't get close enough to see, and I really didn't want to get that close anyway, but Headmaster Rooney told the teachers that all the bad students were going to be turned into good students thanks to the machine."

Carter was still staring, but now his mouth was hanging open. "The machine?"

"Yeah." Mattie nodded. Students were starting to file out of the cafeteria. The homeroom bell would ring soon. They needed to go, and Mattie couldn't let Carter leave. "It's a huge machine. It's in the basement. I found it by—never mind. All that matters is I found it and you're in danger if you don't start being good."

"Like you?"

Mattie shrugged, suddenly uncomfortable. There was something about the way Carter's eyes had narrowed that worried him. "I don't know. I guess? I don't want anything to happen to you."

Someone behind them called Carter's name. Was it Jay? Marcus? Maybe the clones had super hearing too? Mattie was too scared to turn around. Carter looked up and waved.

"Haven't you noticed Jay and Marcus seem different? *Weird?*" Mattie asked. He sounded desperate—he *felt* desperate. Carter raised his eyebrows.

"You don't want anything to happen to me?" he asked at last. "That's just so special. I had no idea you cared so much."

Hope and relief made Mattie's chest loosen. "Of course I care. You're my brother."

Carter shook his head. "It's just that Dad always taught me not to need anyone and gosh, Mattie, do you think we could be friends *and* brothers?"

"I would love that!" Part of Mattie was suspicious. Carter was taking this awfully well. But the rest of Mattie? The rest of Mattie couldn't stop grinning. He'd always wanted Carter to pay attention to him. He'd always wanted Carter to like him, to be friends—

"That's so great!" Carter continued. "Do you want to braid my hair first or yours? Maybe afterward we could give each other manicures and talk about our feelings."

Mattie deflated. "You're making fun of me."

"You're smart."

"You're *still* making fun of me. This is serious, Carter."

Carter snorted. "Seriously ridiculous, Snoopy—"

"Stop calling me dogs' names!"

"Then stop being so stupid," Carter said with exasperation. "There aren't robots in the basement. You're insane. How much cleaning solution have you been sniffing?"

"Carter, I'm telling you the truth! The machine is under the school. There's a doorway in Rooney's closet and—"

"Now you're *really* making stuff up."

"Carter, I saw—"

"Leave now." Carter reached into the back pocket of his pants and pulled out a rolled-up car magazine. He thwapped it against his palm. "Either you leave now, Toto, or I'm going to make you pay."

"Carter—"

"I *will* whack you on the nose, Scooby!"

Mattie opened his mouth, shut it, opened it, and shut it.

"That's what I thought," Carter said.

Above them, the homeroom bell rang and the remaining students began to rush the cafeteria doors in a crush of Munchem red and white.

"Hey, Carter!" It was Marcus or maybe Jay. They talked so similarly and were standing right next to each other. Mattie could feel his stomach sink into his knees when he realized they had been watching them. Waiting.

To drag Carter into the basement?

Mattie's eyes bugged.

"C'mon, Mattie." A scowling Caroline appeared at his side. Mattie couldn't tell if she was scowling at him or at Carter or at the whole world. It was hard to tell when it came to Caroline. "We're going to be late," she said to Mattie.

"Let's go!" Marcus called, waving Carter over.

Carter turned away from Mattie and Caroline. "See you around, Buttons," he said, strolling toward his friends. Jay and Marcus gave Carter high fives as they pushed into the crowd. Carter didn't look back, but Marcus did.

His eyes flashed robot red and then, just like that, he was gone, lost in the crowd of students.

Mattie grabbed Caroline's arm. "Did you see that? Tell me you saw that!"

"See what?" Caroline asked, but her voice shook, and Mattie knew Caroline was lying.

BE AWARE OF YOUR SURROUNDINGS

BUT FOR ALL OF MATTIE'S WORRY, CARTER SPENT THE NEXT month being good—not really the kind of good Carter could put in his essay about how Munchem changed him, but good for Carter. He didn't skip class. He didn't backtalk the teachers. He stayed away from roadkill.

Mattie was starting to feel really good about his brother's future.

Or he was until Caroline came to get him before study hall. "I'm going to kill your brother," she hissed as she slid into a chair at their table. Mattie and Eliot glanced at each other. It wasn't the first time a girl had vowed to kill Carter, but Mattie still didn't know what his response was supposed to be.

"I'm sorry?" Mattie guessed at last.

Caroline's dark eyes narrowed. "Carter stole a bunch of chickens."

"From where?"

"I have no idea! Is he going to free them?"

Knowing Carter it didn't seem likely, but Caroline's grip was choking him, so Mattie nodded. "I'm sure . . . almost positive."

"Mattie? I want to know about the chickens," Caroline said. "You have to find out where Carter got them. Don't forget."

Like that was something anyone could forget. In fact, right now, the only thing Mattie could think about was: Carter had found chickens and Carter had plans for them.

"What do you mean you have *plans* for the chickens?" Mattie panted as he scurried after his brother. He'd found Carter between the east wing and the west wing, and the bell for study hall was still ringing. And yet they were still rounding the back of the school, sticking close to the dead gardens. Mattie was following Carter, and Carter was following the tumbledown wall that circled the flower beds.

"Are you talking about, like, a menu or something?" Mattie pressed. "Are you going to cook the chickens?"

"Go away, Henrietta," Carter said and hopped over a low

spot on the wall. His red backpack jostled, and the chickens inside squawked.

Mattie did not go away. He tugged at Carter's sleeve. "What would Mom and Dad say?"

His brother stopped, blew out a long sigh, and turned. "Why do you always do that?"

"Do what?"

"Worry about Dad. You worry what he thinks. You worry what he'll say. You even agree with him—all the time."

Mattie paused. He wasn't sure how asking Carter what their parents would say about the chicken situation equaled agreeing with Mr. Larimore all the time. He *did* know it seemed important to his brother.

Carter was staring at Mattie like Mattie had something important to share, something Carter might actually want. Mattie desperately *desperately* wanted to give his brother the answer he needed because Carter had never needed anything from Mattie before—*ever*—and Mattie wanted to know what that felt like.

"We're supposed to agree with Dad," he said at last and, even before Carter rolled his eyes, Mattie knew it was the wrong answer.

Carter's face wound tight like he was going to thump Mattie, but he didn't. He just shook him off. "Whatever," Carter said. "You'll agree to anything to stay on their good side. Kids like you do anything to make other people happy."

Mattie stared after Carter. He didn't . . . he *never* . . . maybe he did. Mattie watched his brother walk away from him and wondered if maybe he *was* a kid who'd agree to anything to stay on someone's good side. What if he *was* the kid who would stand for anything as long as it kept other people happy?

Mattie wasn't sure he liked that.

Actually, Mattie was quite sure he didn't like that, and if it hadn't been for the little matter of Headmaster Rooney cloning bad students, Mattie might have left Carter alone with his chickens. He might have let his brother risk getting caught.

Mattie might have, but he didn't.

"Carter," Mattie said, scrambling after him. "Carter!"

Carter didn't stop. He hustled around the back of the dining hall, skirting the clay gray toadstools that lined the wall.

"You can't do this!" Mattie tripped on a bit of broken stone and stumbled into his brother. "You can't keep getting in trouble. Headmaster Rooney will turn you into a—"

Carter swung around on Mattie. "If you say clone one more time . . ."

Mattie opened his mouth, closed it, and then opened it again. "Fine! But whatever you're planning, *don't do it*. Please? For me?"

Carter stared down at Mattie. "You know what? You just lost puppy privileges, Coco." He spun on his heel and walked away. "No more walkies. No more fetch. No more belly rubs."

"Not funny, Carter!"

But Carter was already around the corner. Mattie raced after him and found his brother by the dining hall's far windows. Carter had one shoulder against the brick wall and both hands on the window frame. Two yanks and the window swung open.

"What are you doing?" Mattie asked.

Carter ignored him. Instead, Carter unzipped his backpack. Three chicken heads popped up. They were fluffy chickens, the kind with long white feathers and angry red heads. They were also painted with the numbers 1, 2, and 4. Carter picked up Number 1 and it clucked.

"Why are they painted?" Mattie asked.

Carter continued to ignore Mattie. He opened the window a bit more and into the dining hall went Number 1.

"What are you doing?" Mattie grabbed for the chicken, but it was too late. It landed on the glossy wooden floor with an indignant squawk that echoed in the empty dining hall. "You can't do this!"

"I just did, Ginger."

And into the dining hall went Number 2. Number 4 was next. It flailed a bit, catching Carter in the face with its wings. Carter coughed and tossed the chicken through the window—perhaps a bit harder than necessary. Number 4 landed with a healthy *ploomp* on the floor.

Mattie pulled himself up to peer through the glass. Numbers 2 and 4 were now standing on the closest table, pecking at a few crumbs left over from breakfast. Number 1 was staring into space, like it was very deep in thought.

Mattie pressed his nose closer to the window and wondered what on earth chickens thought about. He knew he shouldn't ask, but he couldn't help himself. "Where's Number 3?"

Carter zipped up his backpack and grinned. "That's what everyone's going to ask. C'mon."

"Where are we going?"

"Up."

Up? Mattie couldn't imagine what that meant, but he followed Carter back the way they'd come and suddenly realized what his brother meant.

"Up in the trees?" Mattie asked. Three ancient oaks bordered the dining hall's other side. At some point there must have been a dozen more trees, but time and weather had ground them down and now the rotting trunks stood like broken pillars.

The remaining trees, however, were almost as tall as the school's roof. Their leaves were Munchem red and faded gold and even if the boys just climbed to the lowest branches they would still be able to see through the dining hall's windows. As Mattie watched, two more roof tiles plummeted to the ground. The school was molting worse than Beezus.

"Move it, Misty." Eliot gave Mattie a shove.

"Won't they see us?"

"Adults never look up," Carter said and gave Mattie another

shove, sending Mattie higher. "You need to remember that."

Mattie hooked his arms around a branch and pulled until he could swing his legs up. "Now what?" he asked, clutching the trunk. From here, he could see the Munchem grounds stretch on and on—almost to the cemetery, almost to the crooked gate.

Carter hoisted himself onto the branch next to Mattie and leaned forward eagerly. "Now we wait."

They didn't have to wait long before Mrs. Hitchcock appeared. The boys couldn't see their teacher until she pushed through the dining hall doors—and the teacher certainly couldn't see the boys hiding in the tree. But, to be perfectly frank, Mrs. Hitchcock might not have noticed Carter and Mattie if they had been standing right in front of her because she was a quart low on coffee.

Her eyes were puffy, her focus wasn't the best, but Mrs. Hitchcock's grip on her stained coffee mug was true and fast.

Or it was until she noticed Number 4.

And dropped her mug.

And screamed.

At least Mattie assumed it was a scream. From out here, he could only hear the faintest *Aiiiieeeee!* but he was pretty sure it was a scream, just as he was pretty sure Number 4 didn't like the sound of the scream because it took off, feathers flying. Numbers 1 and 2 followed. Headmaster Rooney burst through the doors and skidded to a stop. He blinked at the chickens and at the still-shrieking Mrs. Hitchcock.

Aiiiieeeee! the boys heard again. Carter laughed. He laughed so hard he wheezed like a broken accordion. He laughed so hard he almost fell out of the tree.

Headmaster Rooney, however, was not laughing. Rooney was running. He ran after Number 4, and Number 4 ran after Numbers 1 and 2. As they streaked past the closest window, Mattie heard Rooney yell, "For God's sake, woman! There are four of them! Find the other one!"

Carter knew perfectly well there wasn't another chicken and that Headmaster Rooney and Mrs. Hitchcock would just waste their time looking. Carter wiped tears from his eyes as Rooney dashed after Number 1 and missed, and dashed and missed, and dashed and missed. Carter laughed harder and harder and then, very suddenly, Rooney stopped running. He stood up straight. He stared right. He stared left. He stared out the window and Carter stopped laughing.

"Time to go." He scooted off the branch and hit the patchy grass below at a dead run. "You better move it, Fido."

Munchem Academy Rule

TAKE YOUR RESPONSIBILITIES
SERIOUSLY

CARTER LAUGHED THE WHOLE WAY BACK TO THE GARDENS. HE laughed the whole way across the courtyard. He even laughed the whole way up the stairs. In fact, Carter was *still* laughing when they reached the administrative hall.

Mattie, however, wasn't laughing at all. They were awfully close to being late for their tutoring session with Mr. Larimore. Mattie wasn't sure where tardiness fell on Headmaster Rooney's plans for cloning students, and he didn't want to find out. He dragged a snickering Carter all the way to Headmaster Rooney's office, where they both stood in front of Miss Maple's desk and waited for her to return. It didn't take long.

"Hello, Mattie! Hello, Carter!" Miss Maple wore pale blue high heels today. They matched her eyes. When she walked in them her feet moved so smoothly it was like she was on wheels.

"I'm sorry I'm late," Miss Maple said. "There was the most *dreadful* commotion in the dining hall. Someone let four chickens loose! Can you imagine?"

"No," Mattie said as his stomach dipped toward his feet.

"No," Carter added as he wiped tears from his eyes. He stood up straighter as Miss Maple passed.

"You better hurry if you want to be on time for your father," Miss Maple told them as she sat down at her desk and heaved her purse onto the chair next to Mattie. Maybe that's why he looked down—because it was close to him, because he could, and because, well, why not? Mattie looked down and saw Miss Maple's purse was bursting with calculators and graph paper.

And pens.

She must really like pens, Mattie thought just as her manicured hand heaved the bag away.

"Did you lose something, Mattie?" Her voice was chilly, sounding nothing like it had ever sounded before.

"No, Miss Maple."

"You're going to be late." She looked at Carter, who was looking at Miss Maple with that stupid, glassy expression he got whenever she was around. "You two better get inside. I have important things to do."

"Yes, Miss Maple," they both said and hustled into Rooney's office. They sat at the big wooden desk where the computer had been turned to face them. Mattie sat in the closest plushy chair and squished around trying to get comfortable. It didn't work. His feet didn't reach the ground and his back started to hurt immediately and then there was a smell, like hair burning.

Mattie shuddered.

"You aren't seriously cold, Martha?" Carter asked. Sweat had popped up on Carter's forehead and Mattie understood why. Headmaster Rooney had the heater on full blast, and both of them were already hot.

"No! It's just . . ." Mattie trailed off, unsure what to say next.

"Do not start with that robot stuff again," Carter warned.

"But you have to believe me! Look—" Mattie jumped off his chair. "I'll show you the door and then—"

Mattie reached the closet door in two bounces. He grabbed the doorknob, he turned it, and it was locked. Mattie tugged once, twice. His heart sank.

Carter came to stand next to him. "It's right behind here," Mattie told his brother, who nodded like he understood and then flicked Mattie's ear. Hard.

"Ow!" Mattie rubbed his ear. "I just—"

Carter flicked him again. "You just what?"

"Nothing," Mattie said at last.

"Exactly." Carter turned back to the desk and tapped their names into the computer, notifying their father that they had arrived. A large image filled the screen.

Mattie leaned forward. What was that? It was shiny and kind of white—it was an eyeball!

"Well, boys, what do you think?" Mr. Larimore boomed. Their father sounded delighted so Mattie was pretty sure he knew the answer.

"It's cool, Dad!" Mattie hesitated. "Where are you?"

"I'm in my office! This is Larimore Corporation's latest invention! Computer eyeglasses!"

Mattie sat back and kicked his feet a few times as he thought about this. Their father's eyeball was huge and glassy and gross, taking up almost the entire computer screen.

Every time it rolled, Mattie thought he was going to be sick.

"I think you have a crusty in your eye," Carter said.

An equally enormous finger appeared and fished around in the corner of the eyeball. Mattie *knew* he was going to be sick.

"Thanks to these glasses, I can have a conversation with you two while sitting at dinner with your mother and get both things done at the same time. It's genius!"

It was something, Mattie thought. He wasn't sure if it was genius though.

It made him think of all those Larimore wires and pipes and cables underneath the school. The more Mattie thought of them, the more his stomach clenched. Maybe he shouldn't have told Carter. Maybe he should've just told Mr. Larimore.

Mattie sat up. "Dad?"

"Yes, Mattie?"

It was now or never, Mattie thought. And for the first time he realized his mistake with Carter: he had just jumped right into it. But he wouldn't do that this time. Nope, this time Mattie would ease his dad into discussing the clones . . . robots . . . whatever they were.

"Do you ever worry about how people use our products?" Mattie asked.

"What do you mean?" Mr. Larimore asked the question innocently enough, but Mattie could see how his father's eye went glinty. Flinty. For some reason, it made Mattie think he wasn't going to get an answer to his question.

"Wrap it up, Eleanor," Carter said under his breath.

The eye cut to Carter and narrowed. "Did you have something to say, Carter?" their father demanded.

Mattie squared his shoulders and tried again. "What if someone were to buy something we make and use it to hurt someone else?" he asked.

His father's eye blinked. "Well, Mattie, that's a very interesting question. Now let me ask you a question."

Mattie sat up. Mr. Larimore rarely asked anyone's opinion on anything. Mrs. Larimore said it was because Mr. Larimore always knew his mind. She said he hadn't changed it in the twenty years she had known him.

Mattie's father cleared his throat, making the huge eyeball water and tear up. "Mattie, would you blame a pencil for misspelling a word?"

"Well," Mattie said slowly. "I guess not. It's not the pencil's fault. It's the person writing with it."

"Exactly!" Mr. Larimore's eye rolled. It seemed happy. "You blame the person *using* the pencil. At Larimore Corporation, we create products. Whatever people decide to *do* with those products is not our fault."

"It isn't?" Mattie asked.

"Of course not!" The eyeball blinked again. "So you understand now? Are we clear?"

Mattie stared at his father's eyeball. It didn't feel clear at all. In fact, it was just like Caroline said before, it kind of made everything *more* complicated, but Mr. Larimore was waiting for Mattie to say yes and Mattie usually would say yes, but . . .

"There are robots in the basement, Dad!"

The eye blinked and Carter sighed. Mattie ignored him and leaned forward, gripping the arms of the chair with both hands. "They're replacing the kids with robots or clones—I don't really know which it is, but it's happening and you have to do something because Carter's going to be next."

The eye swung toward Carter and narrowed. "Why is Carter next?"

"Because of the chickens!"

"WHAT?"

Mattie started to sweat. That might've been the wrong thing to say. He decided to switch subjects. "They're using Larimore Corporation materials to make robot children!"

The eye stared at Mattie and then turned slowly to Carter. "How long has he been like this?" Mr. Larimore asked Carter.

Carter hesitated. "Not long. It's not his fault. Some kid probably told him about *The Stepford Wives* and you know how his imagination—"

Mr. Larimore blinked. "The one where they turned all the wives into robots? That was a terrible movie."

Carter shrugged.

"Maybe I should speak to Rooney," Mr. Larimore wondered. "Maybe Mattie should be seeing a psychiatrist."

"You can't talk to Rooney!" Mattie jumped to his feet. "He's behind it! Please, Dad! Please, please, please believe me!"

His father made a choking noise, and the skin at the corner of the giant eye began to spasm. "Stop it! Stop it at once, Mattie! You're hysterical. Do you know what that means?"

Mattie slumped in his chair. "It means you get to call me names."

"No, it means your voice is high and screechy, and you're making no sense!" Mr. Larimore's voice rose until the computer's speakers crackled. Mattie and Carter both winced. "I'm disappointed in you, Mattie. I expect this nonsense from Carter, but not from you. What do you have to say for yourself?"

Mattie had nothing to say. Why was disappointing his parents so much worse than making them angry? Why was it that whenever he tried to do the right thing it ended up being the wrong thing? Why wouldn't anyone believe him?

But, of course, Mattie couldn't say any of that so he

continued to say nothing until the giant eyeball flicked away from him.

"Now on to today's subject," Mr. Larimore said with a harrumph.

Next to Mattie, Carter groaned.

The eye snapped toward him. "I heard that, Carter."

"Heard what?" Carter asked.

The eye narrowed. "Today's subject is about customers: how you get them and how you keep them."

Mattie lifted his pencil to his notebook and found himself studying it even as he asked, "And how do you do that, Dad?"

"You have to win them over," Mr. Larimore explained. "Sometimes people don't know their own minds so you have to tell them what to do, protect them from themselves."

Mattie studied his father's eyeball and then studied his brother's face. Carter had that look again, the one where he seemed to be sleeping with his eyes open. It was only a matter of time before Mr. Larimore noticed and Carter got in trouble. Again.

Carter was definitely not a customer, but he did need protecting. Maybe Mattie's brother didn't know his own mind. That might be okay, though, because Mattie definitely knew his own mind, and he knew he didn't want his brother to get made into a clone.

So how was he going to save him?

Munchem Academy Rule

YOU BREAK IT, YOU REPLACE IT

BUT NO MATTER HOW HARD MATTIE THOUGHT, HE COULDN'T come up with a way to save his brother. Carter had stalked off as soon as Mr. Larimore's eyeball disappeared from the screen, leaving Mattie to power down the computer and collect his book bag. Mattie was so lost in his own thoughts that he didn't see Caroline in the hallway outside the headmaster's office until they were nearly toe to toe.

Caroline had a tiny smudge of dirt on her cheek and smelled like a hamster cage. She eyed Rooney's office door with interest. "What were you doing in there?"

"I have to video chat with my dad," Mattie explained as he tugged the door shut. The little desk by the office was empty. There was no sign of Miss Maple or her purse anywhere.

"My dad's teaching me how to run our family business."

"I'm sorry," Caroline said and reached into her red Munchem sweater to scratch herself.

Mattie stared and then realized Caroline wasn't scratching herself; she was scratching Beezus. The rat was tucked under her uniform. It wiggled with joy as she scratched, making the front of Caroline's sweater twitch.

"Why are you sorry?" he asked at last.

"It doesn't sound like much fun," Caroline explained as Beezus crawled up her side. "It doesn't sound like you either."

"It doesn't?"

"No."

Mattie thought about this. He knew—he *knew*—he shouldn't ask Caroline anything else, but sometimes he just couldn't help himself. "Why doesn't it sound like me?"

"Because it doesn't."

"My parents think it does."

"My parents think I should work for their company too," Caroline said. Underneath her sweater, Beezus climbed higher. His head poked out from underneath her collar, and he nuzzled the ends of her dark hair. "But I don't want to work for them. I want to be a scientist."

"I thought your parents had a lot of laboratories."

"That's their kind of science. I don't want to make better eye shadow and lipstick. I want to study why diseases do what they do."

"Like eat people's faces?"

Caroline nodded. "Pretty much." She considered him for a minute, squinting like she was thinking through a math problem. "You really want to run your dad's company?"

Mattie relaxed. He might not know what to do with the clones in the Munchem basement, but he knew how to answer this question. In fact, he'd been answering it for as long as he could remember. "My parents think it's best for me."

Caroline petted Beezus's head before he disappeared inside her sweater again. "But what if they're wrong?"

Mattie blinked. "But they're not. Our parents know what's best. Ask them. They'll tell you."

"But what if they *don't* know?" Beezus was crawling around inside Caroline's sweater again, making it look like she had a twitchy potbelly.

Mattie started to explain how Caroline was wrong—enormously wrong—and realized he couldn't. He didn't have the right words, and Mattie always had the right words. It was one of the things that made his parents so proud.

"Who do you want to be when you grow up?" Caroline asked as Beezus's tail poked over her sweater's collar. It curled around her chin and under her nose.

"I want to make my parents proud," he said finally.

Caroline scratched her cheek. "Oh, is that the same thing?"

"You never make any sense, Caroline. Do you know that?"

Caroline shrugged. "It makes sense to me," she said and

pushed past him to go wherever Caroline was headed. Probably the science building, Mattie thought. Mr. Karloff was supposed to get a new order of frogs.

Mattie spun on his heel and went in the other direction—down the dusty hallway with the ugly portraits, up the stone steps, and through the overgrown courtyard. At first, Mattie stomped because he was mad (although he didn't quite know why), then he stomped because he had ants in his shoe (although he should've known to pick his feet up).

By the time he reached the door to 14A, he was grouchy, sweaty, and itchy. He was also locked out of the dorm, but Mattie didn't know it until he tugged on the door handle. It wouldn't budge. He banged on the door and a mouse nest dropped on his head.

Mattie kicked the wall, and when that didn't make him feel any better, he kicked it again. He *still* didn't feel better, but it did leave a nice Mattie-shaped shoe print on the cream paint, and the door bumped open. It hadn't been locked. It had only been jammed, and unjamming it was ever so briefly satisfying until the realities of science homework set in.

Mattie sat at the small desk by his bed and tried to concentrate. He finished his science homework. He finished his math homework. He tried to finish his essay, but only managed to write a couple of paragraphs about how Munchem had taught him the value of a stiff toothbrush when scrubbing crusty toilets.

Which wasn't the point. Clearly. Mattie crumpled the note-book paper and tossed it in the trash. He wasn't getting any-where. Caroline's words kept echoing through his head like they were looking for places to grow. The words were worse when Mattie tried to go to sleep.

He couldn't stop thinking about them, especially what Caroline had said about *him*. All that stuff about Mattie know-ing what Mattie wanted? He knew. He'd always known. He wanted to be a good kid. He wanted to make his parents proud.

He also wanted Carter to like him, and Mattie wasn't sure he could have both. Actually, he was quite sure he couldn't have both.

Maybe that's what he should say in his essay. Munchem Academy helped Mattie realize what he wanted.

Only in order to make Carter happy, Mattie would have to cool it about the machine and Headmaster Rooney and what Headmaster Rooney was doing to the students.

Mattie wasn't sure he could do that.

Honestly (and Mattie tried always to be honest), he wasn't sure he could stay quiet at all. Because what kind of a person did *nothing* when they could do *something*?

Mattie sat up in his New Kid bunk. He could barely see. Room 14A was still dark, and the boys' beds were lumps in the shadows, but Mattie knew what he needed.

Well, *who* he needed.

Mattie kicked his legs out from under the covers and put his bare feet on the floor. They stuck a little to the dirty carpet—maybe more than a little—but he ignored that. Mattie tiptoed to Eliot's bed and shook his friend's arm.

"You awake?" Mattie whispered, putting his face inches from Eliot's.

"I am now," Eliot whispered back.

"I need your help." Mattie took a deep, deep breath. "I have to break Rooney's machine."

Munchem Academy Rule

NEVER THINK OUTSIDE THE BOX

IN LATER INTERVIEWS WITH *ROLLING STONE*, THE *NEW YORK Times*, and, of course, the *Quality Thief's Quarterly*, Eliot Spencer would say this was one of his favorite childhood memories of Mattie Larimore, World's Greatest Thief. He also would say it was one of his scariest memories because, at the time, Eliot knew nothing about their future jobs. He didn't know that one day he would bungee jump down an elevator shaft with Mattie or race dirt bikes through a forest in Russia.

All Eliot knew at that moment was that Mattie wanted to break that marvelous machine. It was an interesting idea, Eliot would remember. Even if Eliot kinda sorta hated doing it because Eliot had always loved computers—especially the gears and gadgets and wires that made them. All those little things that made something so much bigger than they were. Eliot liked that. He liked that a *lot*. He still does.

And the opportunity to see all those gears and gadgets and wires again? Well, even at eleven years old, that was an opportunity he wasn't going to miss.

So when Mattie woke Eliot up in the middle of the night, breathing minty toothpaste breath on him and shaking Eliot's arm so hard his teeth rattled, Eliot sat up. "You want to break the machine?" he whispered.

Mattie nodded. Kent snorted. And Doyle made a little squeak, which could've been a fart, but it sounded more like a computer chirp. Both boys froze, waiting and listening until Eliot finally kicked off his covers. "C'mon."

"Where?" Mattie whispered.

Eliot pointed to the door and Mattie's eyes bugged. "We're not allowed out there!"

"You're too scared to sneak out of our room, but you want to sneak into the basement again and—" Eliot broke off as Doyle chirped again. The boys stared at Doyle and then they stared at each other.

Mattie's eyes went even rounder. "Fine. Let's go," he whispered. They tiptoed across Room 14A, flinching every time Kent snorted and Doyle squeaked. Mattie eased the door open and Eliot followed him into the dim hallway.

"Do you hear anything?" Mattie swiveled his head from side to side. He was sweating and his heart was thumping and even his whispers seemed too loud.

"No," Eliot whispered. "Bathroom. Go to the bathroom."

Mattie wanted to run, but he managed to continue tip-toeing. The lights from the courtyard below them made the fingerprints on the windows look like ghost prints. Then Eliot stepped on something squishy.

Leaning against the chipped sink in the bathroom, Eliot picked at his feet while he waited for Mattie to explain. "You want to break the machine?"

"It's the only way to save my brother and the other students. Will you help me?"

"You want to go back into that creepy basement?"

Mattie took a deep breath and then nodded. "Yeah."

"And risk getting caught?"

"Yeah." Mattie waited. Eliot had that faraway look he got whenever he was thinking hard. Mattie hoped he wasn't thinking about more reasons why they shouldn't do this. Mattie wasn't sure how much longer his courage would last. The small voice inside his head knew this was the right thing to do. It *was*.

So why was it also the *wrong* thing to do? Mattie had always been taught never to destroy someone else's stuff and never ever to go against grown-ups.

"Can I keep whatever we break off?" Eliot asked at last.

Mattie thought about this. It didn't seem like it would matter, but . . . "Why?"

Eliot shrugged one shoulder. "I have my reasons. Yes or no?"

"Okay."

"Cool," Eliot said, rubbing his palms together. "So, how are you going to break it?"

Mattie had no idea. Both boys thought. The silence stretched on and on, which began to bother Mattie more and more. "You should always say something," Mrs. Larimore had told him again and again. "Even if you have nothing to say at all, you should always say something. That's what good manners are, filling up the silences during dinner."

Maybe that's why Mr. and Mrs. Larimore talked so much. They couldn't stand the silence, and they didn't understand that words were supposed to matter. They just threw them away and maybe that was okay because the more and more Mattie thought about it, the more and more he wondered if words really didn't matter. It was actions. It was what he *did* that actually mattered.

And that was scary because to talk about something was easy, but to do something about it was infinitely harder, especially when one was thinking about doing something to a machine that cloned students.

The problem was, how did one go about breaking a machine that big, that protected, that *complicated*?

Fortunately for Mattie, he suddenly had an idea. Maybe even more than an idea because he knew the Larimore Corporation equipment and he knew its weaknesses. There were the cables that broke when overstretched and the wires that sparked when overheated. Mr. Larimore had meetings about them sometimes.

A lot of times, now that Mattie thought about it.

But right now he concentrated on Eliot. "We passed two generators on our way out, right?" Mattie asked.

"Yeah. I think they were the main power sources," Eliot said, studying Mattie with a puzzled expression on his face.

"Then that's where we need to be," Mattie said. "I'll need a distraction and a wrench. Maybe a few wrenches." He thought about it. "Definitely a few wrenches. Big ones."

"What are you going to do with those?" Eliot asked.

"Drop them in the generators' reactors and jam the gears."

Eliot crossed his arms and considered Mattie with squinted eyes. "That doesn't sound like it will work."

"It will," Mattie said. "I saw an engineer do it at one of my father's factories. He was trying to show how the company's generators were vulnerable to attack."

"Who would attack a generator?" Eliot asked.

"People like us."

Eliot nodded like he guessed that was true enough.

"We can do this," Mattie said. "We just need the distraction and we need the wrenches and I can do the rest. I just have to, you know, get started."

They studied each other. Getting started suddenly seemed awfully difficult.

Eliot blew out a long sigh. "You know who's good at distractions, right?"

Mattie thought about it. He was pretty sure he knew the answer, but he wasn't sure he wanted to admit it and, when he looked at Eliot, he knew his friend felt the same way.

"No," Mattie said at last. "Who's good at distractions?"

"Caroline."

Munchem Academy Rule

PLAY WELL WITH OTHERS

"IT'S TRUE," CAROLINE SAID THE NEXT MORNING AT breakfast. Her dark hair was even more tangled than usual, rising up in a snarl above her head. "I *am* really good at distractions. It's a talent actually."

"Well, we need to borrow your talent," Mattie said and then thought for a moment. He wasn't thinking very fast. Staying up all night had made his brain muddy. "Actually, we need to borrow some tools too. Like a couple wrenches or heavy-duty screwdrivers."

"Borrow?" Caroline squinted at them and ate a mouthful of salad. "Are you going to give them back?" she asked through half-chewed lettuce.

Mattie squirmed. When she put it like that . . . "No," he said at last. "We're not."

Caroline brightened. "Oh, then you mean *steal* some tools. My mother says you should always be specific. You might want to remember that, Mattie."

Eliot spoke before Mattie could. "Do you know where we can get some or not?"

"Ugh, why are you so grouchy?" Caroline pushed a bit of carrot under her sweater. It was awfully disgusting until Mattie realized it was for Beezus.

Then it was only sort of disgusting—or possibly more disgusting.

"And I *do* know where you can get some tools," she continued. "But I'm not telling you."

Eliot made a spluttering noise. "Why not?"

Caroline glared at him. Mrs. Hitchcock and her clipboard walked past them, eyeing everyone's tray. Caroline gave the teacher a wide smile. "And that's why I've resolved to be good from now on!" she said loudly.

Mrs. Hitchcock made a notation on her clipboard and kept moving. Caroline turned back to Mattie and Eliot. "I'm not helping because you only talk to me when you want something," she said.

Mattie blinked. "That's not true."

"Not you," Caroline said, looking at her brother. "Him."

"It's totally true," Eliot said, and thought about it for a moment. "Sorry."

"Why are you sorry?"

Mattie and the Spencers wheeled around. Doyle. He was standing right behind them, only inches from Eliot.

Mattie gulped. How had he not heard Doyle approach?

Worse, how much had Doyle heard?

"Uh, Doyle," Eliot stammered. "How you doing?"

"Fine." Doyle's eyes slid to Caroline. "Muffin?"

The clone shoved a basket of muffins under Caroline's nose and waggled it. Mattie wanted to ask where Doyle had found a basket and then realized he also wanted to know where Doyle found the eggs, flour, and pumpkin spice for the muffins.

Caroline leaned across the table to get a closer look at Doyle. She studied his shoes, his uniform, and, finally, his face.

Doyle didn't seem to mind the attention, but he also had no idea Caroline was looking at him with the same focus she usually reserved for Beezus.

He also didn't seem to notice Caroline held her fork like she just might be tempted to stab something.

Caroline dragged her eyes down to the basket and took a great big sniff. "Pumpkin?"

"Yes," Doyle said with a smile so wide Mattie could see the backs of his teeth. They were alarmingly white.

"Where did you get the muffins?" Caroline asked, tucking a strand of hair behind her ear. Or, possibly, reminding Beezus to stay put. "Did you steal them?"

Doyle stopped smiling. "Stealing is wrong, Caroline."

Caroline took a muffin and gave Mattie a long look. "That's

true, Doyle. That's very true. I'll take a muffin, but it's not for me. It's for Beezus."

"Who's Beezus?" Doyle asked.

"Her imaginary friend," Eliot said before Caroline could reply. Doyle looked at Mattie. Mattie looked at Doyle.

"Muffin?" Doyle asked and shoved the basket into Mattie's chest.

Hard.

Did Doyle know what they had been talking about? The idea made Mattie's knees start to puddle, and he summoned his best smile. "Uh, no thanks, Doyle. Why don't you ask Mrs. Hitchcock? I bet she'd love some."

Doyle perked up and scurried toward Mrs. Hitchcock, who was watching Maxwell the Clone eat his breakfast. Mattie and the Spencers relaxed, and then Bell sat down. His tray clattered onto the tabletop and bits of sausage fell off.

"Hey, Caroline!" Bell grinned. "Did you see? They have chicken nuggets for breakfast!"

Caroline gagged. Eliot rolled his eyes. Mattie winced. Poor Numbers 1, 2, and 4, he thought.

"Shove off, Bell," Eliot said, leaning a little away from his sister. Mattie didn't blame him. With every bite Bell took, Caroline looked a little closer to hurling.

Bell took another big bite. "Do you know what we learned in science yesterday? Humans can live without their heads for hours. They run around and everything."

"That's *chickens*," Caroline said, clamping one hand against her mouth. She definitely looked close to barfing—and maybe crying. "Not *humans*."

Bell chewed harder. "Nope, I'm pretty sure it's humans."

"I have to go now." Caroline stood up, followed by Mattie and Eliot.

"I'm not sure which is creepier," Caroline whispered as they walked between the tables. "The fact that Doyle made muffins in your dorm or the fact that he barely blinks."

"Or the fact that any one of us could end up just like him," Eliot whispered back.

"No way will it happen to me." Caroline tossed her hair. "I never get caught."

"Then how'd you end up here?" Mattie asked.

Caroline glared at Mattie. Mattie tried his best to glare back. She giggled. "Fine. The other girls aren't talking to me anyway. I'll help."

"You will?" Mattie sagged with relief.

"Yep." Caroline fed her hair—Beezus—a piece of muffin. "But you can't ditch me after this."

"We won't," Eliot said quickly.

"And you have to do what I say."

"We will," Mattie agreed.

Caroline smiled. "Good, then prepare to be amazed."

Mattie wasn't sure what was so amazing about breaking into the janitor's closet. Honestly, the only thing he found truly amazing (if he could even call it truly amazing and Mattie wasn't sure he could) was the fact that he hadn't thought about breaking into the janitor's closet until now.

"Why didn't I think of this?" Eliot complained.

"Because you're not me," Caroline told him. Beezus squeaked in agreement. Or worry. Mattie couldn't be sure. He did know *he* was worried.

The Spencers and Mattie were huddled by the second floor's red lockers—recently polished and repainted thanks to Mrs. Hitchcock's misbehaving fourth period class—and even though the hallway was deserted, Mattie was worried a teacher was going to come along at any second. They would be busted for sure. Eliot and Mattie were supposed to be in study hall. Caroline was supposed to be, well, somewhere that wasn't on the second floor, crouching by shiny lockers and staring at the janitor's closet.

"The janitor's still in there," Mattie reminded Caroline as they watched shadows shuffle back and forth under the door.

"His *name* is *Rupert*," Caroline said, narrowing her eyes at Mattie. "And I know he's still in there. We have to get him out."

They fell silent as they thought about this. Eliot scratched the back of his head. "I guess I could go throw up outside—or maybe on the stairs? I had two milks at breakfast. It wouldn't be that hard."

Mattie took two steps back. "What?"

"Ugh." Caroline made a face like she might throw up now. "You have no idea what my childhood has been like. He's disgusting. He can do it on command."

"Hey! It's effective! No one argues with barf!"

"You're *not* throwing up, Eliot Spencer!" Caroline stabbed her finger between her brother's eyes. "That's disgusting! Plus it would make more work for Rupert."

"Then what's your plan?" Eliot asked. "Because we could've come up with this—" His sister cocked one eyebrow at him. "We could've come up with this *eventually.*"

"Eventually can be a really long time," Caroline said, petting Beezus as he tunneled under her sweater. "Besides, you can't do *this.*"

This? Mattie craned his head around Eliot to get a better look at Caroline. She was staring down the hallway, but her eyes were faraway like she was thinking of something else.

Something sad, Mattie thought with a bolt of alarm. Something *really* sad! Caroline's eyes were starting to fill with tears!

"Hurry up!" Eliot whispered.

"I *am* hurrying!" Caroline gave her brother a vicious shove. "It's not like I can just do this on command."

"That's kind of what we need you to do," Eliot retorted, but he retreated a step when he did.

Which was fortunate for Eliot because Caroline whipped around like she was ready to punch him.

"Why do you always have to—" She stopped dead, study-ing something above Mattie's head. "It's just like when Peanut had that allergy attack."

Eliot nodded hard. "Go with that. It's exactly like Peanut."

Caroline gave her brother a murderous look. Then she snif-fled, wiped her nose on her sleeve, and spun around. Mattie started to follow, but Eliot shook his head. "Watch and learn."

Caroline stomped across the hallway and banged on the closet door with her fist. The janitor—Rupert, Mattie reminded himself—yanked the door open and blinked down at Caroline. His mouth worked up and down, but he didn't say a word.

Mattie didn't think he *could* manage a word.

"They broke the cages again," Caroline wailed. "How will we get new frooooogggggggssss?" She dissolved into a howl and Rupert yanked a broom from behind him.

"Kids," he muttered. "Can't trust 'em. Can't trust 'em at *all*," he added and started to lock the closet door behind him.

Caroline sucked in another breath and howled even louder. Rupert winced. "Now, now," he tried. "Where's your teacher?"

Caroline honked into her sweater and pointed down the hallway toward the empty classrooms. Rupert's expression turned relieved. "Go find her, okay? You go find her."

Caroline nodded and watched the janitor hustle in the opposite direction. She waited until they heard Rupert's foot-steps on the stairs and motioned for the boys to join her.

"How did you know the cages were broken?" Mattie asked

nervously. Caroline looked a little wild. Her face was red and her hair hung in damp hanks across her cheeks.

"Because I broke them," Caroline said. "No more cages means no more frogs which means no more dissections."

"Oh," Mattie said because really what else could he say?

"You're the lookout, Eliot," Caroline announced. "Mattie, come help me find what we need." She scrubbed her arm across her face and then wiped her arm on her sweater. "Someday I'm going to make people do things by yelling at them."

With that, Caroline marched into the janitor's closet and disappeared behind a sagging cabinet. "Hurry up, Mattie!"

Mattie dashed after her. The closet was bigger than he expected, with shelves and shelves of paint and cleaners. It smelled like bleach and old wood. Mattie tried to breathe through his mouth as he searched the closest cabinet.

"What about this?" Caroline reappeared, holding up a large wrench like a torch.

"Exactly! Are there any more?"

Caroline turned back around and they searched the same metal bin, finding two more wrenches left under an oily rag. Mattie tucked them under his sweater as they walked out.

Caroline dusted off her hands. "What would you do without me?"

Mattie started to answer and heard Eliot hiss, "Someone's coming!"

Mattie froze. Who was coming? Rupert? A teacher?

No! It was Rooney! Mattie and the Spencers recognized his long, lanky shadow walking down the hallway. He was whistling.

"Go!" Caroline whispered, pushing Mattie and Eliot in the opposite direction. They tiptoed across the hallway and, once they were safely down the other side, Mattie and the Spencers took off, their feet slapping against the tile.

"Who's there?" Rooney yelled and began to run too. "Do you know you're out of bounds?"

"Uh, *yeah*," Eliot puffed. They hit the back hallway at a dead run. Maybe it was all the panic or maybe it was sniffing all that bleach, but Mattie felt like he was flying. He was moving faster than he'd ever sped in that stolen train. Once Rooney rounded that corner, Mattie and the Spencers were long gone.

Munchem Academy Rule

TAKE CARE OF YOUR FELLOW CLASSMATES

THIS IS WHERE OTHER BIOGRAPHIES CLAIM MATTIE LARIMORE took a turn for the worse, but as we already know, those biographies are wrong. This isn't where Mattie Larimore took a turn for the worse, it's only where Mattie Larimore's *story* took a turn for the worse. Much worse.

But naturally, Mattie and the Spencers had no idea what was coming. At this moment, they were nervous, but confident. They thought they had a plan—a good idea, if you will. This is a feeling you get when you do, in fact, have a good idea, but it can also happen when you have a bad idea and don't realize it.

Mattie Larimore and the Spencers eventually learned the difference, but it took several years. Of course by then, they had also learned just because something is a bad idea doesn't mean it won't be a good time.

Unfortunately for them, this was not going to be the case.

That night, Eliot and Mattie waited until Kent was snoring and Doyle was squeaking. Then after Mattie grabbed his backpack they crept out the door and across the darkened hallway and down the even darker stairs. It was easier than their first time sneaking out.

Well, Mattie thought while they crouched by a row of prickly hedges to let Mr. Karloff stalk past with his belly jiggling, it wasn't exactly easy to sneak out, but he was getting better at it. Even so, they were still a little late meeting Caroline at the wall.

"Are you always this slow?" she asked, her arms wrapped tight around her body. It was cold and Caroline's breath rose like smoke. "We have only fifteen minutes before Karloff comes back around. Hurry up!"

Mattie started to tell Caroline that bossiness might be one of the reasons her friends didn't want to hang out with her anymore, but Caroline was already gone, power walking for the back stairs. The boys followed and, together, the three of them made it down to the courtyard entrance, across the scraggly patch of grass, and down into the south meadow behind the dorms.

It was easy until they couldn't find the entrance to the basement. They *knew* it was around here somewhere, but the grass seemed taller and thicker than before. It rustled and whispered as Mattie groped around, kicking at the ground and feeling his way with his hands.

Whump.

"Ow!" Eliot popped up, pulling bits of grass from his hair. "Found it."

Mattie trotted to his side and both of them struggled to lift the metal cover. Mattie heaved it to one side and peered into the exposed tunnel. Did it seem darker down there than it did before?

"You first," Eliot said, nudging Mattie forward. Mattie gripped the straps of his backpack a little tighter and slid his foot around, searching for the first step.

Ah! There it was. And then, as if the stairs had detected Mattie's feet, small lights illuminated the steps. He could see now. Well, he could see *better* now. The light should've been reassuring, but Mattie's stomach was still clenched as tight as his fists.

"Mattie!" A voice whispered from behind them.

The friends froze. Caroline looked like she was ready to run. Eliot looked like he was ready to follow her. And Mattie . . . Mattie looked like he was going to pass out. There was a rushing in his ears and his feet felt like concrete as he slowly— *slowly*—turned around.

"What do you think you're doing?" the voice whispered, although it almost wasn't a whisper. It was really more of a whisper-yell. Like the whisperer didn't want to be heard, but was also really, really mad.

Mattie knew that whisperer. "Carter?"

Branches snapped like teeth as Carter shuffled out of the trees. There was a girl close behind him, and Mattie squinted as she stepped closer. Yuck. She was the same girl who had laughed at Mattie before and now her hand was wrapped around Carter's.

Even in the shadowy light, Mattie could tell her eyes were huge. She was horrified.

That made two of them.

"What are you doing?" Carter demanded. "You're not supposed to be out here."

"Technically, neither are you," Caroline said. Carter glared at her, and Caroline glared right back. Actually, Caroline looked like she was trying to will Carter to burst into flames with just the power of her mind, but Carter didn't seem to notice.

He wheeled around on Mattie. "I thought you wanted out of here, Mattie. I thought you didn't belong at Munchem—"

"I don't!"

"Well, it looks like you do to me." Carter crossed his arms and smirked like he was trying not to laugh.

"C'mon, Carter," the girl said. "I'm bored." She tugged on Carter's sleeve, but he shook her off.

"Not now, Amy," Carter said, still glaring at his brother. "Good kids don't break the rules, remember?"

Mattie pulled the straps of the backpack and felt the wrenches dig into his back. He *did* remember that good kids didn't break the rules, and he did indeed want to go home. But maybe more than anything, Mattie wanted Carter to stop looking at him like he was a very stupid puppy who had just piddled on the carpet.

"I have to break the machine before you get turned into a clone!"

Carter's eyes bugged. "There is no machine!"

Mattie let go of the backpack straps and balled his hands into fists. "It's under the school and Rooney is using it to make bad kids into good kids and if you don't shape up, you're going to be next and I'm not going to let that happen!" And, with that, Mattie took off running down the stairs. Carter swore and took off running after him, and then everyone else followed.

Well, everyone except for Amy, who was now stomping toward the school, vowing never to speak to Carter Larimore again.

Mattie was the first down the stairs. Caroline was faster than Carter, so she was right behind Mattie. And Carter was right behind her—or he was until Eliot kicked him and ducked ahead.

"Now you're both dead!" Carter fumed.

You'll have to catch me first, Mattie thought and, just like before, he went down, down, down into the basement. The stairs turned into a ladder and the ladder turned into stairs and everyone skidded to a stop when they finally hit the floor.

The whole basement smelled like burned hair.

"Phew!" went Mattie.

"Ugh!" went Caroline.

"Ouch!" went Eliot because Carter had finally caught up to him and had thumped him on the head.

"What the . . . ?" Carter sounded scared and horrified and amazed all at the same time.

Mattie knew exactly how his brother felt.

The basement was even more crowded with pipes and tubing and wires. Cables hung in loops from the ceiling and, somewhere, water went *drip, drip, drip*.

Mattie's stomach did a little flip and he clutched the straps of his backpack a little tighter. The machine wasn't running, and if the machine wasn't running then Mattie couldn't drop the wrenches into the generators. Well, he *could* drop them into the machine, but what if someone noticed them and took the wrenches out? Mattie's entire plan would be pointless.

"I think we might have a problem," Caroline muttered, and Mattie knew she was thinking the same thing.

Which meant that Mattie was going to have to come up with another plan. He took the wrenches from his backpack, stuffed them into the front of his sweater, and tried to think.

But unfortunately all Mattie could think about was how his knees were starting to shake and how all of his plans might fail and how Carter's mouth was hanging open because for *once* he couldn't argue with Mattie.

At least that was satisfying.

Or it was until Carter faced him.

"Mattie," Carter said in a low voice—usually the low voice he used whenever he was irritated or tired or irritated *and* tired and about to thump Mattie for annoying him. "Get back to the meadow right now or so help me—"

Mattie ran. He ducked under the new set of pipes and shimmied under another set of cables. He scuffed his knees, and someone grabbed his ankle, but he kicked.

And then he kicked harder.

"Ow!"

Apparently, he'd kicked Carter. That wasn't going to end well, but Mattie kept going, scrambling along on his hands and knees. The wrenches thumped against his chest. Mattie went right. Mattie went left. Mattie went left again, but it was the wrong left.

Caroline caught up with him and grabbed his sleeve, hauling him toward a set of yellow drainpipes. They squeezed under the bottom pipe and popped up on the other side.

"Look familiar, genius?" Caroline asked.

Mattie ignored her even though it did indeed look familiar. This was close to where they'd come in the first time. The generators were only a few steps away.

Mattie jumped to his feet, took the wrenches out of his

sweater, and looked over the side of the first generator. It was just as he'd remembered from the meetings at Mr. Larimore's company. The engineers had explained that the motor was controlled by an electronic box at the top, but the actual mechanical gears were located farther down a metal shaft. If he dropped the wrenches—

"Mattie," Carter panted. "Don't do this. You'll get caught and Rooney will think I put you up to it."

Mattie looked at his brother. Carter had dust smeared completely down his front and was wheezing. How he had fit under those pipes was beyond Mattie. "Don't you dare—"

Mattie dared. He tossed the first wrench and then the second and third.

Clang. Clang. Clang. Clang. The wrenches banged down the sides of the generators, falling deep into their gears.

"I'm going to kill you, Mattie," Carter said, starting toward him. "Forget getting out of Munchem. I'm going to bury you here."

Mattie ignored him and peered into the generators. *Hmmm.* He couldn't even see the wrenches now. What if they fell straight through?

WHAT IF IT DIDN'T WORK?

Mattie looked at Carter again and realized he might die for nothing.

Bang! Something metal smacked against something hard and everyone crouched down. Did a pipe fall? Or maybe a metal panel? Whatever it was, it was way heavier than Mattie's wrenches.

"What was that?" Caroline mouthed at Mattie, but Mattie couldn't answer. Mostly he couldn't answer because he didn't know, but also he couldn't answer because Carter had lunged for him and Mattie had to duck. Carter caught him anyway and they grappled around on the concrete until Caroline yanked on Carter's sweater. He looked at her, and she put one finger to her lips. Everyone was confused. . . . Then they heard a soft *scuff* against the concrete.

Mattie swallowed. The banging must've been the door from the other entrance swinging open. And the scuffing? Someone was walking through the basement.

Scuff. Scuff. Scuff.

Someone was walking toward them!

Mattie leaned down (not exactly a difficult thing considering Carter was practically sitting on his head) and peered between two cables. Shiny brown shoes attached to long, thin legs attached to . . .

Headmaster Rooney.

Mattie squeaked. Carter pinched him, and Headmaster Rooney stopped.

Everyone held their breath.

"Who's there?" the headmaster demanded. "Mrs. Hitchcock?"

Mattie's eyes bugged. They were in so much trouble. They only knew two ways out of the basement: through Rooney's office and through the meadow. They couldn't go back through the office. They'd get caught for sure.

But they couldn't go back the way they came either. They'd run right into the headmaster.

We are so busted, Mattie thought. This was terrible. He hadn't broken the machine. He hadn't saved his brother. He'd actually gotten everyone into even more trouble.

"Just wait," Eliot whispered. "The Rooster has to go to bed sometime, right?"

Mattie had no idea. It had never occurred to him the Rooster did anything besides prowl the hallways at Munchem and yell.

"I heard that!" the headmaster shouted. He spun in a tight circle, looking and looking. "Who's there? You better come out right now or I'll come in there and drag you out!"

Carter shifted his weight and Mattie's cheek smushed into the floor, coating it with dust.

This is how it's going to end, Mattie thought while he tried to spit grit from his mouth. He couldn't say he was surprised. Although reform school and machines and clones were new developments in Mattie's life, being sat on by Carter happened more regularly than Mattie wanted.

"I know you're there!" Headmaster Rooney shrieked. His face was turning pink, pinker, *red*. "Show yourself this moment!"

On top of Mattie's head, Carter sighed heavily and then

stood up. He dusted off his sweater. He straightened his shirt. He looked at his brother.

"Go back to bed, Mattie," Carter whispered.

"What?" Mattie whispered back, but Carter didn't answer. He walked past the other kids and climbed over the pipes and cables that hid them. He walked straight up to Headmaster Rooney like this had always been the plan. And, as Mattie stared, his brother turned himself in.

Munchem Academy Rule

WATCH YOUR BACK

MATTIE DIDN'T KNOW WHAT TO SAY. HE DIDN'T KNOW WHAT to *do*. Headmaster Rooney was shouting at Carter, and Carter was nodding. He was agreeing with him! He was going *with* him! The headmaster and Carter were—

Eliot yanked Mattie backward, toward the pipes and the tunnel. "We have to go!" he mouthed.

But Mattie had to do something. Carter and the headmaster were past the smokestacks now. They had to save him!

"We have to go!" Caroline whispered, tugging on Mattie's sweater. "Carter didn't want you to get caught!"

"We can't leave him!" Mattie tried to release himself from Caroline's grip. She wouldn't let go, though, and they wrestled on the floor until Eliot helped his sister and, together, the Spencers dragged Mattie toward the tunnel.

But not before Mattie saw Carter and Rooney disappear around the corner of the machine.

"If you get caught then Carter will have gotten in trouble for nothing!" Caroline gave Mattie a jerk.

Maybe a harder jerk than necessary. Mattie stumbled after his friends as they squeezed under the pipes, crept up the stairs, climbed the ladder, and reached the second set of stairs again.

Sneaking around required a lot of effort, Mattie thought as he wheezed up the last flight. They popped out on the south meadow where Caroline took several seconds to listen for anyone who might be waiting outside.

"It's okay," she said at last. "No one's there."

They panted up the last three steps and then collapsed on the grass. Mattie rolled onto his back and caught his breath as he stared at the stars. The grass smelled like damp dirt and dried leaves and something sweet that Mattie couldn't name.

He felt like crying. He'd gotten Carter into so much trouble.

Mattie sat up. The Spencers sat up. Everyone looked at everyone.

"I didn't mean for Carter to get caught," Mattie whispered. Tears were pooling in the corners of his eyes. "I didn't mean for that to happen."

The Spencers nodded. "It wasn't your fault," Caroline said, even though they were all pretty sure it was. "Maybe Carter will get off with a warning?" she added, even though they were all pretty sure he wouldn't.

"We'll think of something," Eliot said and stood, brushing grass bits from his pants.

They were lying, Mattie realized, but for some reason the lies didn't bother him, not like he would've expected. He needed the Spencers and their encouragement because it made the dark feel a little better.

Or it did until they heard another rustling.

Caroline's head whipped to their left. "Was that you?" she whispered.

"Who's there?" a voice rang through the dark. "Come out at once!"

It was Mr. Karloff! Mattie jumped to his feet.

Eliot grabbed Mattie and Caroline. "Run!"

Mattie ran. Eliot ran. Caroline ran faster than both of them. They took off up the hill, charging toward the garden.

"Where's the break in the wall?" Eliot panted as they raced along the stone wall. "Where's the—oof!"

Caroline shoved her brother over it. Eliot tripped, tripped again, and righted himself. Mattie jumped over the break in the wall and dragged himself through a rosebush.

"Ow! Ow! Ow!"

"You just *wait* until I catch you!" Karloff shrieked.

"See ya!" Caroline turned left and raced for her dorm. Mattie and Eliot turned right and raced for theirs. They tore through the courtyard and vaulted over the mossy benches. They skidded across the flagstones, past the angry angel, and—

Crash! Crash! Two more tiles hurtled to the ground, splintering in the grass as Mattie pounded past.

"It's like the school's *trying* to kill us," Mattie gasped. Eliot didn't answer. Eliot was too busy running with all his might. His knees pumped like pistons, and his cheeks puffed in and out. The boys pushed through the narrow doorway. They dashed up the stairs. They dashed down the hallway. They only stopped when they reached the door of 14A. Mattie knew they had to be quiet. They didn't want to wake the others, but Mattie couldn't stop panting and Eliot couldn't stop wheezing. The door whined softly when they opened it.

The boys stuck their heads inside, listening. The others were still asleep. Now if they could just tiptoe inside—

Scrape. Scrape. Scrape.

Footsteps! On the stairs behind them! Mattie and Eliot whirled around to listen.

Scrape. Scrape. Scrape.

Was it Karloff? Someone was definitely coming closer.

Mattie's eyes bugged. "Bed!" he whispered and motioned Eliot inside. The boys closed the door as quietly as they could and rushed for their beds. Eliot dove under his covers. Mattie tugged the blanket over his shoes. They squeezed their eyes shut, pretending to be asleep.

The door opened. Mattie kept the blanket wrapped tight around him and his eyes closed.

It was a good thing too because a long, thin shadow crept across the floor. The shadow froze, watching.

Waiting.

And after what felt like forever, it shut the door. They'd gotten away, but Mattie was still scared.

Munchem Academy Rule

LIVE UP TO YOUR POTENTIAL

IN THEIR BEDS AND UNDER THEIR COVERS, ELIOT AND MATTIE didn't know what to make of this new development. When it came to Carter, Mattie kind of considered himself an expert. He knew Carter Larimore was a bad kid. Carter stuck dead possums in air vents and called Mattie girls' names. He turned chickens loose on school grounds and laughed at teachers.

He did not turn himself in so other kids could go free.

Except he did. He *had*. And that wasn't like Carter at all.

Clearly, it was a lot to think about. Mattie rolled onto his side and the bed squeaked. He rolled onto his back and the bed frame shook. He rolled onto his stomach and Eliot kicked his mattress.

"You're making the whole bed shake!" he whispered and kicked him again. "Would you stop it?"

Mattie stopped it. He lay there until cold gray morning light began to leak under the curtains and the other boys began to stir.

"Eliot," he whispered.

"Yeah?" Eliot whispered back.

"Did you get any sleep?"

"No way."

"Good morning!" Doyle shot up straight in his bed, his smile wider than his face. "Would anyone like muffins?"

Mattie didn't think he was going to want any of Doyle's muffins ever again. He suspected Eliot would agree.

"Thanks, Doyle, but I'm going to go downstairs," Mattie said, trying very hard to sound casual. Like it was no big deal. Like Mattie wasn't thinking about how Doyle was a clone and Carter was in trouble again and everything was ruined.

"No muffins?" Doyle asked. He looked so sad that Mattie actually felt worse.

"No, sorry, Doyle," Mattie mumbled and jumped out of bed.

"Would you guys shut up?" Kent snapped. He pulled the covers around his head, which made Kent's dirty feet stick out. Doyle scowled at them.

Because he didn't like dirt anymore? Mattie wondered. Because he was considering washing them? Because he was debating turning Kent into a clone?

Mattie didn't know, and he didn't want to find out. He

threw on his clothes and hustled downstairs, Eliot close behind him. Mrs. Hitchcock and Mr. Karloff were already patrolling the cafeteria. Mrs. Hitchcock kept whispering things to Mr. Karloff, and Mr. Karloff would nod and then take notes on his clipboard.

They were staring very hard at Caroline.

And then they started staring at Mattie.

Mattie started to sweat. Did they know? Were they taking notes on who would be next? Did that mean *he* was next?

Mattie got in line and picked everything that a good kid should pick for breakfast. There was yogurt. There was fruit. There were absolutely no waffles with syrup or cereal with marshmallows. Mattie arranged everything on his tray and carried it to the table. He couldn't eat a bite.

"Have you seen Carter yet?" Eliot whispered as he sat down next to him.

Mattie shook his head. "It took days for Doyle to return so wouldn't it—"

The cafeteria doors swung open and the eighth graders walked in. There was Marcus. There was Jay. And there was Carter!

He was talking to Marcus, who slapped Carter's shoulder and laughed like it was the funniest thing in the world. The sight of Carter made Mattie go a bit woozy with relief. If his brother was here now, he couldn't have been cloned!

"Be right back," he whispered to Eliot and jumped to his

feet, running off after his brother. Carter grabbed a tray from the stack by the cafeteria line and disappeared into the crowd of students. Mattie stood on his tiptoes and tried to see past the students ahead of him. He'd almost given up when Carter appeared at the end of the line.

"Carter!" Mattie cried and ran to him. "Are you okay? What happened?"

His brother gave him a funny look. "What are you talking about?"

"Last night." Mattie followed Carter to his usual table. Marcus and Jay were still getting their breakfast so Mattie sat down. He watched his brother take out a napkin and arrange it carefully on his lap. "What happened with Rooney?"

"Oh. That." Carter took a bite of eggs. He chewed for a few seconds and then swallowed and dabbed his mouth with the napkin. "We had a talk about being out of bounds after hours. He was really disappointed in me and, honestly, I'm pretty disappointed in me too."

"You are?"

"Yeah." Carter took another bite, chewed, swallowed, and wiped his mouth. Mattie wondered when his brother had gotten so picky about his table manners. He wanted to ask, but got distracted by Doyle. The clone was watching Carter—and Mattie.

"I can do better," Carter said. "Headmaster Rooney thinks so too."

Mattie scowled. Was his brother joking? "Stop messing around," Mattie said, sliding a quick glance at Doyle. The clone was *still* watching. Could he hear them?

Carter cocked his head, fork suspended above his scrambled eggs. "I'm going to be a good kid from now on, Mattie."

Mattie sat very still. He blinked, and then blinked some more. "Carter," he said slowly, his eyes going from Carter's napkin to Carter's unusually clean jacket to Carter's equally clean tie. Mattie's stomach started to knot and squeeze. "You've never wanted to be a good kid."

"Well," Carter said, using his napkin to wipe his mouth, "I used to be like that, but then we came to Munchem and now I want to be good." He looked at Mattie and gave him a big grin. Over Carter's shoulder, Mattie could see Doyle grinning now too. "Make sense, Mattie?"

"Uh-huh," Mattie said because it suddenly made perfect sense. Carter didn't wipe his mouth. Carter didn't smile in the morning. Carter definitely didn't call Mattie by his real name.

Carter wasn't Carter. Carter was a clone.

SET A GOOD EXAMPLE FOR
OTHER STUDENTS

HIS BROTHER WAS A CLONE. MATTIE LOOKED FROM CARTER'S dark hair (which looked just like it always did) to his crooked smile (which also looked just like it always did) to his wrinkled jacket sleeve (which, admittedly, also looked like it always did).

Mattie looked at all of these things and felt his head go bubbly like it was filled with ginger ale. Even though Carter looked like Carter always did, he definitely wasn't Carter.

Not good, Mattie thought. This is so not good.

But Carter was smiling at him like everything was perfect.

"You look a little pale." Carter poured a bit of orange juice into his cup and offered it to Mattie. Mattie shook his head. He looked around for Doyle, but the clone was gone.

"Are you okay?" Carter asked.

"Uh, yeah."

"You don't look okay." Carter leaned forward and Mattie tried not to squeak.

"Was Rooney mad?" Mattie asked, mostly because he really couldn't think of anything to bring up.

Carter sagged. "He was awfully disappointed. I have so much more to give, and I wasn't doing my best. So, to show him how I'm turning over a new leaf and going to be good from now on, I helped him with a project in the basement."

"Wha—" Mattie swallowed. "What kind of project?"

"An amazing machine!" Carter's dark eyes gleamed with the sort of excitement usually reserved for killing things in video games and peeing off of balconies. "There were wrenches stuck in the generators. We had to work all night to get them out, but we *did* get them out. Isn't that great?"

"Really great." Mattie managed a smile, but sweat had broken out between his shoulders and in his armpits.

"The machine's a secret though, okay?" Carter continued, folding his hands in his lap. "You can't tell people about it. I'm only telling you because you're my brother and Headmaster Rooney says our mom wants us to start *acting* like brothers. He says it's the only thing she really wants."

"Okay."

"I'm telling you because I can trust you, right? You're a good kid and you're going to do better from now on, right?"

Mattie stared at his brother—at the clone—and tried to

swallow again. He couldn't. Carter's voice sounded almost singsong, so why did it feel like Carter was threatening him? Was Carter warning him? Be good or else?

"Okay," Mattie managed.

"I *knew* I could count on you." Carter unclasped his hands and returned to eating his breakfast. Mattie started to stand. His legs were rubbery and his eyes were getting scratchy—sort of like they did before Mattie cried.

But he wasn't going to cry now. He couldn't.

Even if it *was* his fault that Carter was now a clone and that the machine was still running and everything was ruined.

Mattie forced himself to take a deep breath.

"I trust you, Mattie," Carter said and forked more eggs into his mouth. He chewed them exactly eight times and swallowed. "I'm so glad we're brothers."

Funny how it was something Mattie had always, always, always wanted Carter to say, and now it just made him queasy. Mattie picked at the cracked tabletop until a splinter stabbed him under his fingernail.

"You're a good kid. You don't belong here. Headmaster Rooney says we're going to go home soon and make our parents so happy. It's just like you wanted, right?"

"Right," Mattie mumbled. It was exactly what he'd wanted since the first day they'd come to Munchem, but Mattie didn't want it this way. He didn't know how he was going to fix this, but he *knew* he had to. "I have to go finish my breakfast."

"Okay!" Carter grinned and flashed Mattie a thumbs-up. "Don't forget we have tutoring with Dad today!"

"What?" Mattie suddenly remembered the clone was right: they *did* have their weekly tutoring with Mr. Larimore during lunch. But how did Carter the Clone know that? "Oh, yeah," he added. "Thanks for reminding me."

"That's what big brothers are for! Make it a great day!"

"Yes. Great day. Right." Dazed, Mattie wandered back to his table and collapsed in a heap next to Eliot and Caroline.

"Eat something," Caroline hissed. "They're watching us."

Mattie started to ask who was watching—the clones? The teachers? But he was still too stunned. He stuffed toast into his mouth, and it tasted like cardboard.

"They cloned him," he whispered to the Spencers.

"Impossible!" Eliot gaped. "Doyle was gone for *days* before they brought him back!"

"Are you sure?" Caroline studied Carter for a long moment. "Maybe he's messing with you. Carter likes to do that."

"Even Carter can't pretend to be nice this early in the morning, not even for a joke."

The Spencers nodded because it was true, and for several moments they sat in silence. Caroline pushed her salad around on her plate, Eliot smooshed his toast into bits, and Mattie tried to breathe through the tightness in his chest. It was no good, though. The more he thought about his brother getting cloned, the worse he felt.

"It's my fault," Mattie mumbled. "If I hadn't run down there, he wouldn't have followed. If I hadn't—"

"Time for class," Mrs. Hitchcock announced as the bell rang. Carter actually clapped. Mattie cringed.

Caroline elbowed him. "I don't know, Mattie. Maybe it's better this way?"

Mattie snapped, "What?"

"Maybe he's happier."

"Carter is *not* happy being a clone," Mattie said fiercely even though Carter did indeed look awfully happy. In fact, Mattie had never seen his brother smile so wide before. *Was* he happier? Mattie picked up his tray and dumped everything into the trash.

"Weren't you hungry?" Mrs. Hitchcock asked. She had her clipboard again and made a notation. Behind her, Marcus and Jay stopped and turned in unison. Mattie felt like the whole cafeteria was staring at him.

Like the whole cafeteria knew that Mattie knew.

This was what Caroline meant when she said "they" were watching. The teachers were watching. The clones were watching. Mattie had to be careful.

"Um, just . . . not very hungry," he stammered.

"You aren't getting sick, are you?" Mrs. Hitchcock asked.

Mattie's heart double-thumped. Could that get him in trouble too? "No?"

"Good," Mrs. Hitchcock said and stalked away, leaving

Marcus and Jay to study Mattie with their creepy clone eyes. Which admittedly looked like regular human eyes, but now that Mattie knew what the boys were, he couldn't stop thinking about Jay and Marcus in terms like "creepy" and "scary."

And terrifying.

And—

"Time for class," Caroline sang and hooked her arm through Mattie's, dragging him with her. They pushed their way into the middle of the other students. Eliot was already ahead of them, making his way toward Mrs. Hitchcock's reading class. Caroline and Mattie followed, keeping their heads down. They didn't say another word to each other. Maybe because there was nothing left to say, but also because what *could* they say? Carter was a clone. And, also, Mrs. Hitchcock didn't like the students to talk.

Mrs. Hitchcock wore three sweaters and a scarf. She was cold—she was always cold—and with that many layers on, she looked like a round, faded Easter egg.

"Hurry up!" she said, snapping her fingers. Mattie and the Spencers picked desks near the back of the classroom. Caroline took out her favorite purple notebook, Eliot chewed on his pen, and Mattie concentrated on the most horrible realization winding around him. It squeezed tighter and tighter.

"You know what this means, right?" Mattie whispered as Mrs. Hitchcock began to write the day's lessons on the whiteboard. It was the cleanest the friends had ever seen it, and their teacher's bright green marker squeaked just like Beezus. "They're getting better at programming the clones. Faster."

Eliot gulped and nodded.

"You know what else?" Mattie continued. "Carter the Clone is way nicer to me than the real Carter."

"I believe that," Eliot said under his breath.

"But the real Carter saved us," Mattie reminded him. "He knew he'd be in huge trouble when he walked up to Rooney, and he did it anyway. He sacrificed himself."

"Also true," Caroline whispered.

The friends were quiet until Mattie couldn't be quiet any longer. He had a horrible feeling in his stomach and at the same time he wanted to jump to his feet. He wanted to do something.

"Guys," Mattie whispered as Mrs. Hitchcock squeaked her marker across the whiteboard. "If Carter the Clone is out here, where's the real Carter?"

The Spencers exchanged a quick look that said, *I have no idea.* It also said, *I don't like where this is going.*

Because the Spencers didn't like where Mattie's thoughts were going and Mattie knew it. He wasn't even sure if *he* liked where his thoughts were going.

Mattie took a deep breath. "I don't know where Carter is, but I have to find him."

Munchem Academy Rule

ALWAYS GO THE EXTRA MILE

NO MATTER HOW MATTIE EXPLAINED THE SITUATION TO THE Spencers, they were still apprehensive. Mattie understood. He tried to tell himself it would be sort of fun, like when he stole that train.

Except it wasn't, and no matter how many times Mattie thought it over, he couldn't make his stomach stop twisting.

Stealing that subway train had been about proving something—even if it had only proven that Mattie had extremely poor impulse control. Saving Carter was about *saving Carter*. It was desperate. It was scary. It made Mattie's knees go wobbly.

And yet he couldn't turn away. This was doing something wrong to do something right.

Unfortunately, that didn't mean Mattie knew what to do

about it either. Where could Headmaster Rooney be hiding the real Carter? In fact, the more Mattie thought about it, the more he wondered where Headmaster Rooney could be hiding *all* the real students. By Mattie's count, there was Maxwell, Jay, Marcus, Doyle, and now Carter—five students who would have to be kept somewhere.

But where was somewhere?

Mattie had no idea, but he kept thinking about it. In fact, he was thinking so hard about Carter and where Rooney might hide him that he wasn't concentrating at all during Mrs. Hitchcock's class.

Which meant when she asked him about *Holes*—a novel about a bunch of bad kids and even worse adults—Mattie had no idea what to say. Which also meant he got the whole class in trouble and they had to scrub Mrs. Hitchcock's floor until the bell rang.

By the time classes broke for lunch and study breaks, Mattie smelled like bleach and his head hurt. He trudged to the headmaster's office still thinking about clones and Carter and was almost to Miss Maple's desk when someone rushed out of the shadows.

"Mattie!"

Mattie tripped in surprise. His heart hammered hard against his ribs. "Carter! You, uh, startled me!"

And he had. The clone was so quiet! Almost like he had been trying to sneak up on him.

"Sorry!" Carter said, bouncing from foot to foot. "I'm so happy to see you!"

"You are?" For the briefest of seconds, Mattie was thrilled. But the dark-haired boy who looked just like Mattie's brother wasn't Mattie's brother at all, and the realization was as swift as Mattie's initial surprise. For a nanosecond, everything had felt kind of sort of perfect and now all Mattie could feel was disappointment so strong it was as if it could pull him through the floor.

Carter the Clone was grinning away. "Did you see the wallpaper I fixed?"

Mattie hadn't, but now that he thought about it, Munchem was starting to look less, well, less like a zombie movie set.

"Let's get tutored!" Carter yelled.

"Yay!" Mattie tried to match the excitement but failed. He sounded sullen. Actually, he sounded like Carter the Original.

Carter the Clone typed their password into the videoconferencing account and adjusted the settings. The computer screen flashed twice and their father's face appeared.

"Boys!" Mr. Larimore boomed.

"Hi, Dad!" the boys boomed back.

"Carter," Mr. Larimore said and the camera lurched drunkenly. "I must say I am quite impressed with the talking points you sent me."

Talking points? Mattie cut his eyes to Carter the Clone, who had such a pleasant smile he looked angelic . . . or brain-dead.

"I'm so glad you enjoyed them! I worked on them before breakfast. It was a great way to start the day!" Carter the Clone had a pen poised above his notebook. His legs were crossed. His hair was combed, which suddenly made Mattie remember *his* hair. He hadn't brushed it this morning. He raked one hand through it and felt the strands stand up with static.

"Yes, yes," Mr. Larimore continued, flipping through the pages. "I appreciate the effort you took to outline potential business discussion topics. I'm glad you put thought into this, Carter. Mattie?"

Mattie sat up. "Yes?"

"You would do well to think on this," Mr. Larimore said. "Your brother showed a great deal of initiative by preparing these talking points. Do you know what initiative is?"

Mattie was still sitting up, but he felt as if he'd shrunk. "No."

Mr. Larimore's eyes went bright. "Initiative is drive! Initiative is ambition!"

Put like that, Mattie thought, initiative seemed more like a way to show up other people.

"It's something *you* used to have, Mattie," Mr. Larimore continued. "Do you remember when you won all those service awards at school?"

Mattie did. It made his parents really proud, and it made Mattie feel really good. Although, now that Mattie thought about it, Carter had been pretty irritated. He called Mattie fairy tale princess names for a month. At the time, Mattie just figured that was Carter. Now he kind of wondered if Carter was eaten up with the same ugly feeling eating up Mattie at this very moment.

"Yes, I remember the awards ceremony," Mattie said at last. "I worked really hard for those medals."

Mr. Larimore rolled up Carter's list of talking points and tapped it against the camera. "Well, initiative is like that. Sort of. You get the point, right?"

Mattie nodded. Actually, he didn't, but it seemed safer and easier to agree. Plus, it made Mr. Larimore happy.

"I'm really glad to see you shaping up, Carter." Mr. Larimore studied Carter the Clone and Carter the Clone smiled even wider. Mattie began to chew his thumbnail. If he found the real Carter—*when* he found the real Carter, would Mr. Larimore be disappointed? Mattie was worried he might be.

"This is why I sent you two to Munchem," their father continued. "That Rooney *guarantees* his results! Now, let's get started. Today, we're going to discuss the law—because if you know the law, you can make the law work for you. There is tremendous power in knowledge, especially if other people don't know the loopholes you know."

Mattie perked up. Maybe it was because he couldn't stop thinking about the real Carter or maybe it was because loopholes made him think of hidey-holes and hidey-holes made him think about where Carter might be hidden.

Either way, Mattie leaned forward as an idea walked into his mind. "Dad?"

"Loopholes!" Their father pointed to a purple pie chart on the first page. "You have to know your loopholes!"

"Dad," Mattie repeated and his father stopped pointing and squinted at his computer screen.

"What?"

"If you had to hide something," Mattie said slowly. "If you had to hide something really, really important, where would you put it?"

"Offshore account—or maybe Switzerland." Mr. Larimore's mustache twitched from side to side as he considered this. "The Swiss are a lovely people. They really know how to mind their own business—especially when it comes to offshore accounts."

"Offshore accounts?"

"We're getting to that next week."

"Oh." That didn't sound like fun at all. Mattie tried again: "Where else would you hide something?"

"Plain sight." Mr. Larimore's mustache twitched from side to side again. "Where everyone sees it, but no one notices it."

Where everyone sees it, but no one notices it. That made about as much sense as the offshore account explanation. Mattie slumped again. He took out his notebook and pen and wrote down things like "utilization" and "speed tests," which didn't make sense either, but they were at least fun to say.

"I'm proud of you, Carter," their father said when they

finally finished. "Now get your grades up and we'll be in perfect shape!"

"Yes, sir!"

Mattie concentrated on putting his notebook away so he wouldn't have to see his father grin and grin. Carter was now the kid Mr. Larimore had always wanted, the kind of kid Mattie had always strived to be and Carter had never wanted to be and now was.

Or rather the clone was.

And their father didn't even notice the difference. No, that wasn't right. Mr. Larimore *did* notice. He just liked the cloned version of Carter better. It made him happier.

Mr. Larimore was happy. Carter the Clone was happy. Maybe even Mattie could be happy. Carter the Clone wasn't just the son the Larimores had always wanted, Carter the Clone could also be the brother Mattie had always wanted.

"And I want another set of talking points for next week," Mr. Larimore continued. "From both of you."

"Yes, sir!" the boys said.

"Good. That's what I like to hear. Your mother's getting ready for that dinner of yours and we'll see you soon." Mr. Larimore held up one finger and pointed it at the camera. "No screwups, right?"

"Right!" the boys said, and the computer screen went blank as their father signed out of his account. Mattie waited by Rooney's desk while Carter closed down the computer. The end-of-term dinner was right around the corner. Mattie needed to study for his finals, write his essay, and *find his brother*. Mattie sighed and Carter the Clone clapped him on the shoulder.

"Don't be glum, chum!" he said with a grin.

Mattie stared at him. If he hadn't already known Carter the Clone was indeed a clone, *that* statement would have totally given it away.

"Everything's going to be great now that we're both good," Carter told him as they left the headmaster's office.

Mattie smiled weakly. Carter wasn't so bad, actually. In fact, if Mattie didn't know Carter the Clone was indeed a clone, Mattie might actually like him. Mattie blinked. Had he really just thought that? He *had*. And it was kind of true. He did like Carter the Clone. He just wanted his brother too.

Mattie followed Carter the Clone down the dusty gallery filled with equally dusty oil paintings and wondered how this had become so hard. In the movies, the bad guys were always bad, the robots were always evil, and the right thing was always easy to spot.

Mattie knew the right thing was to find his brother. But Carter the Clone would make their parents happier than the real Carter ever would. The clones were polite. They knew what to say and when to say it.

Wait a second, Mattie thought. The clones knew all sorts of things about the people they were impersonating. What if they knew more than that? What if—

"Carter?"

"Yes?"

Mattie tried to sound casual as they turned toward the dining room. The air smelled like Windex and tomato soup and somewhere down the hall the lights flickered. He knew what he was about to ask and he knew what it would mean for his Good Kid image.

Honestly though? Mattie didn't care about his Good Kid image anymore. He wasn't sure being a Good Kid had anything to do with actually being good. Because the good thing to do—the right thing to do—was to save Carter, and saving Carter was going to involve a lot of bad things.

Stealing? Possibly.

Sneaking around? Most definitely.

Lying? Without a doubt.

But, right now, it was going to involve misleading poor Carter the Clone. Mattie faced him. "Where do *you* think teachers hide stuff?"

SOMETIMES A WRONG CAN MAKE A RIGHT

AT LONG LAST, I NOW WELCOME YOU TO MATTIE LARIMORE'S Great Beginning—only it isn't so great. It's a rather small decision that ended up having much bigger consequences. Great beginnings—and horrible beginnings—can be like that. They don't feel great or horrible at all. They feel natural, maybe even inevitable, and you only realize their importance after they've passed.

Or, in this case, you only realize their importance after *Mattie Larimore's Big Book of Bad* becomes an international movie phenomenon.

"Where would teachers hide stuff?" Carter the Clone repeated. He stopped at the dining hall's double doors and leaned one shoulder against the wall. "Like when Dad was talking about loopholes?"

"Yeah."

"Why?"

"Uh . . . um . . ." Mattie faltered under Carter's stare. The clone was studying him suspiciously, and Mattie realized he never should've opened his mouth. He shoved his hands in his pockets and pretended to be very interested in how the hallway light was flickering. "Oh, you know, why not?"

Carter nodded as if this made perfect sense, and Mattie slumped with relief. "I don't know," Carter told him.

"But you have to know!"

"Why?"

Mattie swallowed. Did something just flash in Carter's eyes? Did the clone know what Mattie was up to? "I just thought you might," he said at last.

"Oh." Carter shrugged. "I know lots of stuff, but not that. See ya." He opened the dining hall door and almost crashed into Marcus. Mattie cringed. The clone had been standing on the other side. Lately, it seemed like Marcus was always around and always *listening*.

Was he reporting back to Rooney?

"Hi, Mattie," Marcus said.

"Hi," Mattie squeaked and scurried past him. It didn't do any good, though, because every time Mattie looked up, he saw Marcus watching him, *studying* him.

"Why is Marcus staring at you like you have something he wants?" Caroline asked as she sat down next to Mattie.

"I think he knows I know," Mattie whispered to her.

Caroline jammed her fork into her salad. "That's not good."

"No," Mattie agreed. "I have to find Carter—the real Carter. He has to be somewhere we would never think to look. Do you have any idea where that might be?"

Caroline brightened, and then frowned. "I don't know where that would be. I mean, that's kind of the definition, isn't it? Somewhere we would never think to look."

Mattie nodded. Over at the eighth-grade table, Carter and Marcus scraped their chairs back. Carter took his tray to the trash, but Marcus kept his eyes on Mattie.

"Look away," Caroline whispered, furiously jabbing at her salad.

"I can't," Mattie whispered back. It was like Marcus had some sort of tractor beam in his eyeballs that kept pulling Mattie in.

Then Marcus walked around the eighth-grade table and Mattie sighed with relief. Marcus was leaving. He was going to class. He was—

Walking right toward them!

This was how it was going to end!

Marcus looked straight at Mattie and cracked his knuckles. He made his hands into fists and then . . . he kept walking.

Caroline winced as Marcus passed. Mattie felt like wincing too. Actually, Mattie felt like passing out. He wouldn't, of course. Marcus might come back and kick his unconscious body into next week.

"Do you think he heard?" Mattie whispered.

"I don't know," Caroline breathed as the dining hall doors slammed shut. "I don't know where Carter is, and I don't know how we're going to find him, but we better do it fast."

"But *how* are we going to find him?" Mattie wondered as he helped Eliot clean the windows during their afternoon applied mathematics class. "Carter could be anywhere."

Before Eliot could answer, Mr. Karloff walked past them in a gust of cologne and cleaning spray. "Remember, students! This is real-life math! Math you will need in the real world!" Mr. Karloff stopped at the whiteboard, his hands on his hips. "How many fingerprints do you see? Count them up and wipe them away!"

"I love this class," Eliot said as he scratched at a bit of grime caked in a corner. "I just tell him I saw thirty-six fingerprints and he takes my word for it."

Mattie considered the window. There were far more than thirty-six fingerprints on the glass. He turned to his friend. "I need you to focus," Mattie said. "What if it were Caroline? What if she were cloned?"

Eliot paused to consider this. "Would I get to program her?"

"Eliot!"

"*Fine*, I wouldn't like it either."

Mattie dipped his sponge in the bucket again. Unlike Mrs. Hitchcock's classroom, which was always hot, this classroom was always cold, like a cellar on a summer day, and Mattie's fingers were numb. "I don't even know how to find Carter. I mean, he could be anywhere, right? We didn't even know Munchem had a basement until last month. What if there's some other hidden room?"

Eliot nodded. "Yeah."

"So we have to think like kidnappers. If you stole someone, where would you keep him?"

Eliot thought about this. "You think there's more space in that basement?"

"No!" Mattie stopped scrubbing and looked at Eliot. "Well, I guess there could be. Wherever they have Carter would have to be really well hidden—or maybe it's close to the school. Maybe it's in some shed or something. Bad guys love sheds. They're always locking people up in them."

"It would have to be soundproof." Eliot was quiet for a moment. "Mattie, what if they're not keeping Carter hidden away?"

"Huh?" Mattie eyed Mr. Karloff as the teacher circled the other side of the classroom. His father's words about hiding something in plain sight suddenly looped through his head, but he wasn't any closer to figuring out what that could mean.

"How many fingerprints?" Mr. Karloff called out to the class. "What happens when you multiply the fingerprints by four more hands?"

Mattie had no idea. He did, however, know that many fingerprints on her windows would enrage his mother. Mattie glanced back at Eliot. "What do you mean?"

"Um, what if they're not keeping Carter? What if he's already gone?"

Mattie opened his mouth, closed it, opened it again, but nothing came out. Before, all he could think about was hiding places and now all he could think about was how his life might turn out if Carter was already gone.

If Carter were gone then Mattie wouldn't have anyone to argue with. He wouldn't have anyone to give him advice about the proper care and feeding of parents. He wouldn't have *Carter*.

And it would be Mattie's fault.

Mattie swallowed hard. "You think he's *dead*?" Mattie bellowed the last word. He bellowed it with all his might and with all his breath and, for a moment, he sounded exactly like Mr. Larimore. Mattie didn't mean to be so loud, but he was startled.

And scared.

"What's going on over there?" Mr. Karloff demanded. He crossed the room in quick, choppy strides. "What are you two doing?"

"L-lead!" Mattie stammered. "I think there's lead in the paint."

Mr. Karloff's face screwed up with confusion. "Of course there's lead in the paint."

"Wait." Eliot put down his rag and leaned away from the window. "Lead paint can give you cancer."

Mr. Karloff nodded. He put one hand on Eliot's shoulder. "The best things in life always do, son. Now back to work!" he shouted.

Mattie leaned in closer to Eliot. "My brother isn't dead. You don't know that. We saw Maxwell get up and walk around after they cloned him—and Hitchcock said they don't put them down or whatever. Rooney has to be keeping them somewhere."

Eliot studied Mattie's face for a moment and then nodded. "So what's your genius idea for finding him then?"

"I don't know."

"There's just one thing I don't understand," Eliot said.

"Just one? You're way ahead of me."

"Like, how does Carter the Clone know all the same stuff the real Carter knows?" Eliot looked at Mattie. "You said it was like he knew who you were before, right? Like he knew you two were supposed to be brothers?"

"Yeah, but I don't think he remembered how we were down in the basement. I mean, he knows about the machine, but only because Headmaster Rooney made him take out the wrenches.

I don't think Carter actually remembers we, you know, put them in there."

"That's weird."

Mattie nodded. "It's like he has some memories, but not all—or maybe he just remembers the really important stuff?"

They stared at each other. They had no idea. They didn't know how the clones had the same memories as the students they replaced. They didn't know where Rooney was keeping Carter. They didn't even know how many fingerprints they were supposed to be counting.

Mattie was beginning to think he didn't know anything.

"Okay," he muttered, trying to piece together what he could. "Where would you keep bad students? It would have to be somewhere soundproof and secret, but easy to get to because they have to eat, right? Right. And that leaves—"

Eliot sprayed the closest window with more cleaning solution and rubbed until the glass squeaked louder than Beezus. "Wait. Where's the one place students are never allowed?"

"The basement?" Mattie guessed.

"Yeah, but *besides* the basement?"

The headmaster's office . . . the janitor's closet . . . and suddenly Mattie knew. He dropped his rag. "The teachers' lounge."

ALWAYS HAVE A PLAN

YES, INDEED, THE TEACHERS' LOUNGE. THE SOLE PLACE SOUND-proofed well enough that teachers can laugh at their students' essays. The *one* place where teachers can hang upside down as they sleep.

Fine. Be that way. It may not be soundproofed and teachers might not sleep hanging upside down, but the teachers' lounge is still someplace that is only spoken about in hushed tones.

And students are never *ever* allowed to go in there.

"You really think this will work?" Mattie whispered to Eliot.

Eliot frowned. "You have a better idea?"

Mattie shook his head.

"That's what I thought," Eliot said.

Even though Mattie didn't have a better idea for sneaking into the teachers' lounge, it didn't mean he thought this plan would work. After Mattie realized they needed to search the teachers' lounge, he'd been at a loss to figure out how to do it.

It was Eliot who suggested sneaking in during a fire drill.

"But they'll do a head count once we get to our assigned posts," Mattie reminded him. "Karloff and his Santa belly will know we're gone."

"Yeah, and it'll still take them maybe twenty minutes before they realize it. Think about it: the teachers' lounge is on the back hall—no one will be around, and if they are, they'll be leaving for the front lawns. We could take ten, fifteen minutes, and run back. We'll tell them you were in the bathroom."

Mattie had opened his mouth and then shut it. Eliot had a great point. But now that they were hiding in an empty classroom doorway and sweating while they waited for the fire alarm to go off, Mattie's heart seemed determined to crawl up his throat.

Eliot watched the clock on the wall across from them. The spindly hands trembled as they ticked. "The fire alarm should go off in three . . . two . . . one."

Whoop whoop whoop!

Eliot took a step forward, but Mattie grabbed his arm—just as Mrs. Hitchcock rushed past. She was patting her pockets as if she'd lost something. It made the fuzz from her cardigan drift to the floor in fat puffs. They waited for a beat, and then a beat more.

"Okay," Mattie said. "Ten minutes. Let's do this."

While Eliot watched the deserted hallway, Mattie opened the faded and scratched teachers' lounge door. He leaned inside and took a look around. Empty.

"C'mon." Mattie motioned to Eliot. Mattie was prepared to see something amazing—shocking, even.

"This isn't what I expected," Mattie said. The room was small, crammed with furniture and sagging shelves. The walls were beige. The couch was beige. The floor was beige except in certain places where it was stained. The whole place smelled like old books and older coffee.

"Why would anyone want to lounge in here?" Mattie asked, turning in a small circle.

Eliot shrugged. Out in the hallway, the siren continued to whine.

"So." Mattie braced both hands on his hips. "Where would you hide students?"

"Maybe there's a secret passageway or something?" Eliot suggested, checking their time on a bookshelf clock. They had six more minutes. "See if you can find a door."

They looked and they looked, but there wasn't a door. In fact, there wasn't even any type *of* door—not a trapdoor, not a hidden door, not even a hole the boys could sneak through. There wasn't anything besides the few tables, the fewer chairs, and a microwave that was crusty on the inside.

Mattie's stomach squeezed tight as he studied the inside of the microwave. Unsurprisingly, he'd found nothing, and while it had seemed quite unlikely anything to do with Carter would be inside a microwave, Mattie felt it was equally unlikely to discover his teachers were cloning their students.

Who knew what else he might have missed because he hadn't looked?

Mattie closed the microwave's door. "We were wrong. There's nothing here."

"Maybe there's a trick to it?" Eliot peeked behind some bookshelves pushed against the wall. "Try moving some of the books."

"You really think if I move the right book, the bookshelf will move to reveal some sort of passageway?"

"You really think there's a cloning machine in the basement?"

"Good point." Mattie surveyed the closest drooping bookshelf and lifted a copy of *You Are Not Your Students*.

Nothing.

He moved two dog-eared versions of *How to Be Good Enough*.

Still nothing.

Mattie checked the tabletops and spotted a coffee-stained desk blotter. There were small notes about upcoming tests . . . someone's phone number . . . and . . .

"Yobbo," Mattie whispered. Why was "yobbo" written at the corner of the desk blotter?

"Wait a sec," Eliot muttered. His face was squished between the bookshelves and the wall so Mattie couldn't see Eliot's expression, but he knew that excited tone. Eliot had found something.

"What is it?" Mattie asked.

"I believe it's two students breaking the rules," Headmaster Rooney said. "Is that what this is? Is it?"

Mattie gulped, Eliot gulped, and Headmaster Rooney laughed.

"My office," he roared. "Now!"

———

Headmaster Rooney was quiet. He was quiet all the way down Munchem's longest hallway. He was quiet as they walked down the steps and past the portraits and up the sunny corridor that led to Miss Maple's desk. He was even quiet as he ushered Eliot and Mattie into his office and closed the door.

An unsuspecting student might assume Headmaster Rooney was quiet because he wasn't that angry. In fact, an unsuspecting student might assume he or she was just going to receive detention or maybe have to write lines on the white-board for a few hours.

Mattie, however, wasn't an unsuspecting student. Mattie had lived with Mr. Larimore for eleven years and he knew that quiet angry was way worse than shouting angry. But, right now, all Mattie could think was the following:

He was going to be cloned.

He was going to disappear.

And his parents would never know the difference.

Mattie stood in front of the headmaster's desk and took a breath so deep he hiccupped.

"What was that, Mr. Larimore?" Headmaster Rooney demanded.

"N-nothing, sir!" Mattie stammered. Eliot and Mattie stood before Rooney's desk. Mattie couldn't bring himself to meet the headmaster's eyes so he stared at the framed pictures instead. It wasn't helpful. In all of the pictures, the headmaster smiled like a shark—with all his teeth and yet something more.

"Admit it! I caught you returning to the scene of the crime!" the headmaster yelled. "Criminals always return to the scene of the crime!"

"What?" Mattie took a step back. "No! Wait—what crime?"

Headmaster Rooney was turning more purple by the second. "You're lying! You know what crime! Come clean this instant!"

"No!" Eliot yelled, his blue eyes enormous. "We didn't even know there was a crime!"

"Ah-*ha*!" The headmaster laughed and laughed. He laughed so hard that his head rolled back and Eliot and Mattie exchanged a look that said, *I think this man is insane.*

The headmaster suddenly stopped laughing. "So you *are* telling the truth! And people say bad kids can't! I must be getting through to you two delinquents—am I getting through to you?"

"Yes, sir!"

"Good," the headmaster said and leaned in so close to the two boys that Mattie could smell the tuna fish on his breath. "Now, tell me the truth: What were you doing in the teachers' lounge during our fire drill?"

"Nothing," Mattie said.

The Rooster's brows rose into angry orange points. "Nothing? It didn't look like 'nothing' to me."

"We were just curious," Mattie said slowly. "You know how kids are," he added and tried to shrug like his mother always did when she said that. Mrs. Larimore had used the expression "you know how kids are" plenty of times, and Mattie was confident it would work here too.

Rooney wiped white spittle from the corners of his mouth and glared at Mattie. "Stop lying. What were you doing in there?"

Mattie gulped. His brain kept spinning around answers he couldn't use. They were looking for Carter. They were looking for hidden doors. They were—

"Looking for Karloff's birthdate," Eliot said.

"*Mr.* Karloff," Headmaster Rooney snapped.

Eliot nodded. "*Mr.* Karloff's birthdate. We wanted to get him a present."

Headmaster Rooney leaned back in his chair, steepled his fingers, and studied Eliot for a long, long moment. "And why would you want to do that?"

"He's our favorite teacher," Mattie said. "He always looks so jolly. Like Santa."

"He's the best," Eliot agreed and grinned until the Rooster rubbed his forehead like it suddenly hurt.

"Mr. Larimore?" Headmaster Rooney said.

"Yes, sir?"

"I expected better from you. What do you think your father will say when I tell him you broke into the teachers' lounge when you were supposed to be participating in a fire drill?"

Mattie tried not to gulp. What *would* Mr. Larimore say? Probably a great many swearwords.

Headmaster Rooney scowled. "I was assured you were a good child."

Mattie slumped.

Headmaster Rooney braced both hands on his desk and leaned forward. "Considering this is your first offense and I am feeling generous, I'm going to let you two off with a warning. Do you feel grateful?"

Grateful? Mattie didn't feel grateful. He felt astonished. Why would the headmaster let them off with a warning?

"I said: Do you feel grateful?"

"Yes, sir!"

"Good, very good." The headmaster rubbed his hands

together and studied the boys through narrowed eyes. "But let me make myself very, very clear. If you break the rules again, there will be consequences, and I am *very* sure you will not like them."

WHEN CLEANING SOMETHING GROSS, USE SOMEONE ELSE'S TOOTHBRUSH

MISS MAPLE STOOD OUTSIDE THE HEADMASTER'S OFFICE WAITING for Eliot and Mattie. It was hotter than ever in this wing of the old house, but Miss Maple wasn't sweating a bit. She was smiling a smile that belonged in a toothpaste commercial and arranging stacks of blank papers on her desk.

"That went well, didn't it?" she asked them, her golden curls bouncing.

"Yes, Miss Maple," they said. The boys watched as she put some of the blank papers in a left-hand pile and some in a right-hand pile.

"Wasn't the headmaster kind to let you off with just a warning?" Miss Maple continued.

"Yes!" the boys said in unison, but they knew the Rooster wasn't kind.

"Wasn't it wise of him to know you'll be good boys from now on?" Miss Maple added.

"Yes!" the boys said in unison, but they knew he wasn't wise either.

He was weird, though, Mattie thought. Very weird. The Rooster wasn't nice, the Rooster wasn't wise, and the Rooster most certainly did not let bad kids off with just a warning.

Miss Maple considered Mattie and Eliot as she sat down at her desk and moved her huge purse to the floor. "I won't see you back here like this again, will I?" she asked. Her smile looked even whiter under the overhead lights.

"No, Miss Maple."

"Good. Now run along or you're going to miss lunch."

Eliot and Mattie didn't just run. They fled. They galloped down the long gallery, past the dusty pictures, and up the stairs into the rear hallway. They ran past the dining hall. They ran past the science wing. They didn't stop running until they reached the overgrown courtyard where, once again, Mattie had to catch his breath and stomp ants trying to crawl up his leg.

"I thought you had blacked out back there," Eliot panted. He collapsed onto the nearest bench. For something made out of stone, it wobbled an awful lot, but Eliot didn't seem to care. "You just stared into space like my grandpa does."

Mattie swatted at his ankles. "Sometimes I have to think."

"Yeah, well, think faster next time."

"There can't *be* a next time," Mattie reminded him. He rubbed both fists into his eyes, feeling very much like punching something. Or breaking something.

Or maybe just screaming really, really loudly.

They weren't any closer to finding Carter! All Mattie had found out was that the teachers liked burned coffee and watched the same British television shows as Caroline.

Yobbo whatever, Mattie thought as he glared up at the stone angel. Someone had drawn eyeglasses on her. She looked even angrier than Mattie, which was incredibly satisfying.

"C'mon." Mattie turned to leave. "Let's go before we miss lunch and Karloff yells at us."

Eliot scraped along beside his friend, but both boys were quiet as they climbed the stone steps to 14A. Mattie couldn't stop thinking about the Rooster's talk of consequences. He knew it meant cloning. He was sure of it.

Which meant Mattie *couldn't* get caught again.

Or maybe it meant he should just give up?

"I can't give up," Mattie whispered.

"What?" Eliot stopped and turned around. Sunlight was streaming through the upper windows, illuminating the dust in the air. It gave Eliot a dirty halo. "Are you talking to yourself now too?" he asked.

Mattie faced his friend. "I can't give up on Carter even if the Rooster does clone me."

"Dude, he'll only clone you if he catches you. Key word: *if*."

Mattie tried not to roll his eyes. Eliot sounded awfully confident for a kid who seemed really close to peeing himself when Headmaster Rooney threatened them. Eliot also sounded smug, which he often did when he had an—

"Wait." Mattie peered closely at his friend. Eliot's eyes were wide and glassy. "You have that look again."

"What look?"

"That look you get when you're thinking about something, when you have an idea. You always look like your brain hurts."

"That's not nearly as flattering as you think it is."

Mattie grabbed Eliot by the shoulders. "What's the idea, Eliot? What's the plan?"

"I think it's time I introduced you to Marilyn," Eliot said and turned around. He took the last steps two at a time, and Mattie had to scramble to catch up.

"Marilyn?" Mattie didn't remember meeting any student named Marilyn. He knew Caroline, obviously, and there was Eloise from their applied mathematics class, and that blond girl who never talked in biology, but he couldn't remember a Marilyn.

"Who's Marilyn?" Mattie asked.

"My computer."

"We're not allowed to have computers."

"I know."

"But you have one and you named it Marilyn?" Mattie gawked. "Is she a robot too? Like Doyle and Carter?"

"Don't be stupid. Of course she isn't. That would be insane. Now," Eliot said, pointing one finger to the ceiling above them. "Boost me up before Kent comes out and wants to know what we're doing."

Mattie stared at the foam ceiling tiles above their heads. They had made it back to the hallway leading to 14A—and not only had they made it back to 14A, the boys were standing in the very same spot where they had met on the first day of school.

"I don't understand," Mattie said slowly. "How is Marilyn going to help us find Carter?"

Eliot sighed as if Mattie was especially stupid and Eliot was especially long-suffering. "We can't go sneaking around anymore, right?"

"Right."

"But we have to save Carter, right?"

"Right."

"So," Eliot said slowly, "we need someone to sneak around for us. I hard-wired Marilyn into the school's phone lines so we can use the Internet. I'm going to use her to check Rooney's, Karloff's, and Hitchcock's email. People leave all sorts of stuff in their inboxes. Maybe it will be stuff we can use."

"That's a great idea!"

"I know. Now boost me!"

Eliot stepped on Mattie's interlaced fingers and the boys

teetered left and then teetered right as Eliot grabbed for the ceiling.

"Hurry up!" Mattie panted.

"Stop wobbling!" Eliot gasped and, after another two misses, he worked his fingers between the plastic foam ceiling panels, hoisted his forearm over the ledge, and kicked his way into the attic. Mattie stared up at the ceiling as bits of dust and dirt floated down.

A rope ladder dropped and smacked him in the face. "Ow!"

"Hurry up!"

Mattie hurried. The ladder swung a bit too much to make the whole thing fun, but he did get to the top without hurling. Or falling on his head.

On his hands and knees, Mattie slowly crawled inside while his eyes adjusted to the dark. It was colder up in the attic than it was down in the rooms. It was dirtier too—and that was really saying something considering this was Munchem. There were cobwebs in the corners, dust covered everything, and something gritty clung to Mattie's palms. He brushed his hands off on his pants and then saw the computer or, rather, he saw Marilyn.

She was covered in a plastic shower curtain, but Mattie could still see the red and green lights. They looked like eyes in the dark.

Eliot carefully removed the computer's plastic wrapping and Mattie sneezed.

"Do you mind?" Eliot asked.

"Sorry." Mattie sneezed again. "Is this what you were doing up here? On that first day, when you and Caroline fell out of the ceiling, were you setting this up?"

Eliot nodded. "My parents love it here because we're not allowed to have computers. Munchem is like a detox program for people who love computers, and I love computers."

"What's a detox program?" Mattie asked.

Eliot paused, screwing up his mouth as he thought. "I think it's like vacation. My mom goes on them, and when she comes back, she's happier like she's been on vacation."

Mattie nodded like that explanation made sense. It didn't. But Mrs. Larimore always said that if you didn't understand something you should smile and nod until you *did* understand it or the person just went away—so Mattie smiled some and nodded more.

Eliot looked at Mattie like he had sprouted another head. "The problem is," Eliot added, "I'm not relaxed when I don't have my computer and I'm definitely not happy."

And, true to his word, Eliot did indeed look very happy as he settled on his knees in front of Marilyn. He tapped a few keys on the keyboard and the monitor sprang to life. A few taps more and strings of small letters and numbers flew across the blue screen. It didn't make any sense to Mattie, but Eliot nodded along with the lines as if they made the most natural sense in the world.

"Here," Eliot said after long, long moments of clicking. He tilted the monitor in Mattie's direction. "Look."

Honestly, Mattie couldn't *stop* looking. The screen was filled with Karloff's inbox. There were emails about class schedules and grades and detentions.

"Wow." Mattie shook his head, unable to believe what he was seeing. "Marilyn's like magic."

Eliot snorted. "No way. She's much more expensive."

"That one." Mattie pointed to an email exchange between Mr. Karloff and Mrs. Hitchcock. It was at the very bottom. "What's in that one?"

Eliot clicked on the email, and Mattie leaned over Eliot's shoulder as he read out loud: "'Due to the delay on pod delivery, we will have to postpone the final project.'"

"Pods?" Eliot asked. "What are pods? Something for science class?"

"I don't know. Keep scrolling down." A few lines down, Mattie's hands went clammy.

The headmaster wants all the students done
as soon as the pods are delivered.

All the students? Mattie swallowed. All the students!

"Eliot, they're going to clone all of us!" Mattie stared at the floor and then at the ceiling and then at Eliot. He couldn't believe the teachers were doing this. He couldn't believe they were going to *get away* with doing this.

"No wonder the Rooster didn't bother punishing us. He knew he was going to clone us anyway," Eliot added.

"Do grown-ups even worry about what's right and what's wrong?" Mattie asked. "Or is that just something they expect us to do?"

"Um . . ."

"We have to fight back." Mattie jumped to his feet and slammed his head into a rafter. Then he crouched, which wasn't nearly as satisfying as standing up in a huff, so he jammed one finger into the air. "We have to find the others."

"Right." Eliot nodded.

"And then we have to call the police," Mattie continued, jamming his finger even higher. "And the police will have to believe us because we'll have witnesses."

"Right," Eliot said again, weakly.

"And we have three days before the dinner so that's what?" Mattie asked. "Seventy-two hours? We can do that."

"No pressure," Eliot said with a sigh.

It was a lot of pressure. Mattie stuffed both hands in his pockets and stared at the attic floor. They needed to do all of that, and they couldn't do any of it without finding the other students first.

"Eliot?" he asked. "Could you look at aerial maps on that thing?"

"On *Marilyn*, yes. Why?"

"Just trust me." The squeezing in Mattie's stomach had turned to fluttering. He had an idea. "Can you look up Munchem?"

Eliot pulled up a map site. He entered Munchem's address and the camera swung low, zooming down until it reached woods, then fields, then an enormous mansion sitting like a spiny, brick birthday cake in the middle of all those woods and fields.

"Welcome to Munchem," Eliot muttered. He scrolled up. He scrolled down. He zoomed in and out so they could see more Munchem details.

"Look," Mattie said, pointing at the screen. "You can even see the mushrooms by the garden wall."

You could also see the falling-down wrought iron fence by the falling-down cemetery and the foggy windows in the first-floor bathrooms. You could see the enormous circular drive-way and the gargoyles by the gates. You could see everything, but neither Mattie or Eliot could see anywhere that looked suitable for hiding at least five students.

Eliot sighed. "There's nothing here."

"Go back," Mattie said. "To the cemetery. What's that tomb thing?"

Eliot wrinkled his nose. "A mausoleum?"

Mattie nodded, his heart beginning to race. A mausoleum. It was a big stone box with massive double doors. It sat perched on a small rise at the back of the cemetery.

Mattie looked at Eliot. "We've been thinking about this all wrong. It isn't about where students aren't allowed to go. It's about where we would never go, and none of us would ever go to the cemetery."

KNOW THE VALUE OF A GOOD OPPORTUNITY

"WE CAN'T GET OUT THERE," ELIOT SAID FOR THE ELEVEN millionth time. He followed Mattie down the shallow stone steps that led to the lunchroom. "There's no way. We'll get spotted for sure."

Eliot was right. They would get spotted. The cemetery was past the meadow, almost to the forest. Anyone would see them running across the grass. Anyone would—

"That's why it won't matter if we do get spotted!" Mattie said.

"What?"

Mattie spun around, excited. "We're going to volunteer!"

"What!"

"We'll volunteer! We'll have permission to be out there!" Because while the Munchem cemetery was home to various members of the Munchem family, a particularly bad-tempered raccoon, and, possibly, one (or ten) students who didn't graduate, it was also home to some of the worst weeds and leaf piles on the entire campus.

"We have a free afternoon," Mattie explained. "We'll volunteer to help in the garden, and as we work our way toward the cemetery, we can get a better look."

Eliot paled. "You're insane. There's no way that will work."

"What will work?" Caroline bounced down the steps that led from the first-floor corridor to the second-floor classrooms. She skidded up next to them, her blazer flapping open.

"We think they might be hiding Carter in the cemetery," Mattie whispered. It was time for afternoon classes, and the hallway was getting crowded. Kent brushed past them and Mattie bumped into Caroline. "I want to use our free afternoon to volunteer to weed the cemetery."

"It won't work," Eliot repeated.

"It'll totally work," Caroline said. "I know Rupert's schedule. We can leave as he goes on break. Let's do it."

And, thanks to Caroline, Mattie felt like they would "do it." After lunch, they'd collected plastic bags and gloves from

Rupert, who'd been surprisingly accommodating about the project.

"He's going on break," Caroline informed them as they made their way toward the north wall gate. "He takes break from one until whenever he feels like coming back. Usually around dinnertime."

"So we have a couple hours before anyone will know where we are," Mattie whispered as they passed Mr. Karloff.

The teacher glared them. "Where are you three off to?"

Mattie held up his plastic bag. "We're volunteering!"

Mr. Karloff grunted something—Mattie wasn't sure what— but he didn't stop them and now Eliot, Mattie, and Caroline stood on the other side of the north wall, in the middle of the dead gardens. From here, it was easy to see the meadow below the school, the tree line beyond the meadow, and the very edge of the cemetery's spiny fence in the distance.

"You shouldn't come, Caroline," Eliot said, shaking his head.

"Of course I'm coming!" Caroline huffed. Her scarf kept riding higher and higher on her neck, overtaking her chin. "Last time, you two geniuses got caught."

Mattie and Eliot glared at her, mostly because they knew they couldn't say anything. Caroline was right.

"We are going to get caught," Eliot moaned. "And we're going to get cloned and no one will *ever know* what happened!"

Mattie patted Eliot's shoulder and tried to smile like Mr. Larimore did when one of his employees was sad. "We're not going to get caught. Well, I'm pretty sure we're not going to get caught."

Eliot rubbed his hands against his sweater. "You know they bury students who don't make it out in the cemetery, right? There's supposed to be one big hole and they just dump the bodies in there and—"

Mattie took off. He bolted for the gate at the bottom of the hill and, still arguing, the Spencers ran after him. It was cold. It was thrilling. It was a *long* run. Mattie was panting by the time he reached the tilted cemetery gate.

"I don't get it," Mattie said as they crept through the grave-yard. Eliot tripped on the cracked brick path and bits of stone scattered. "When my parents buried my grandma, we did it in another state, not our backyard."

"My mother says grief does funny things to people," Caroline said, patting the head of a stone angel perched on top of a tomb. It looked friendlier than the courtyard stone angel, but not by much.

Caroline braced both hands on her hips. "I like it here. It's nice to get out, you know?"

Mattie didn't know. The graveyard looked just like the rest of Munchem, which was to say it was shabby and had plenty of things Mattie could cut himself on. Long tufts of yellow grass grew between the headstones, and a tree branch had fallen on the fence, crushing the delicate iron scrollwork. They circled around and around looking for, well, anything really.

Mattie spent several minutes peering under fallen head-stones, but all he found were worms and one small, yellow flower. It had grown up through a crack in the stone path and, to Mattie at least, it looked a bit heroic. Maybe even brave.

Or maybe Eliot's rope ladder had smacked Mattie's head harder than he thought and now he was delusional. Stuff like that happened constantly on *Como Pasa El Tiempo*.

"Doesn't look like there's a tunnel," Eliot said after kicking the grass about for several minutes.

"And nothing's under the fallen headstones," Mattie added.

"So that means . . ." Mattie, Eliot, and Caroline all looked up at the two mausoleums. They were against the back fence. The right mausoleum leaned against the left one, like it had passed out. It reminded Mattie a bit of his uncle at holiday dinners.

"We need to check in there," Mattie said, sounding very brave for someone who had to drag his feet forward.

"I don't want to check in there," Eliot said.

"We have to," Mattie told him. "We can't give up!"

Caroline pushed ahead with an exasperated sigh. "No one thinks we should give up, Mattie!"

"I do," Eliot said. "I think we should give up."

Mattie and Caroline ignored him. They climbed the stone stairs and studied the ornate doors, the heavy stone arches, and the scowling gargoyles perched on top of those stone arches.

"This is how people die in horror movies," Mattie muttered.

In truth, Mattie had only ever seen parts of horror movies—and those were parts he'd had to sneak—but Mattie had seen enough to know broken-down carnivals, deserted old houses, and graveyards were to be avoided.

And yet here he was.

Or, rather, there his brother might be.

"Carter is so going to owe me." Mattie grabbed the door handles, giving them a little shake. To his shock, they turned easily, like they were used to being opened. Mattie looked at his friends. "This seems too easy."

"Maybe because nothing's in there," Caroline said with a worried wobble in her voice.

Mattie swallowed. "Ready?"

"Wait a second." Caroline stooped and tightened the laces on her tennis shoes.

"Your shoes are fine," Mattie said, watching her. "What are you doing?"

Caroline stood and brushed off her hands. "Making sure I can run faster than you two if zombies leap out of there."

Eliot rolled his eyes and, together, the three of them pulled open the doors. They were ready to be brave. They were ready to find Carter. But mostly they were ready to get this over with.

Too bad the mausoleum was empty.

"I guess that explains why they didn't lock the doors," Eliot said, sticking his head inside to look around the empty building.

Well, technically, it was *almost* empty. There was a lone

tomb at the very center, but there were no doors, no ladders, no stairs. There were, however, birds' nests in two corners of the mausoleum, bird poop on the floor, and something that smelled like . . .

Mattie sniffed.

"Another dead end," Caroline groaned.

"Don't say dead!" Mattie took another sniff. "It smells like burned hair."

The smell was an excellent reason to march right into the mausoleum. Burned hair might equal clones. It might equal clone-making machines. It might equal Carter.

But it would also mean going into that scary stone building.

With the shadows.

And the possible zombies, or vampires, or teachers. It was a toss-up really. Anything could be hiding in the dark.

"Well, boys." Caroline squared her shoulders and lifted her chin. "Adventures aren't always pony rides down rainbows. Let's go." Caroline stalked inside the mausoleum and began to check the far walls. She ran her hands up and down the stones, looking for . . . Mattie wasn't sure actually.

"Are you two coming?" Caroline asked.

Mattie took a deep breath—which smelled like rotting leaves and dust and burning hair—and marched inside.

Eliot hung back to prop open the doors, letting in as much afternoon sunlight as he could. "Guys? This is weird. I think the doors usually *are* locked. Look." A small loop of chains and a large padlock were tucked in a neat pile next to the wall.

"If it's usually chained, why is it unlocked now?" Eliot asked.

"Because someone's coming back," Mattie said, his heart trying to rush up into his throat. "We'd better hurry."

Caroline and Eliot traced their hands over the cold, rough walls, and Mattie searched for cracks in the stone floor.

Maybe there was a trapdoor? Maybe there was . . .

Mattie straightened. "The dust and bird poop are all smeared."

"Gross," Caroline said.

"What's your point?" Eliot asked.

Mattie wasn't sure. Yet. After all, Mattie was around dirt all the time. Thanks to his time at Munchem, Mattie had found dirt in his ears, in his socks, and even up his nose—and none of those discoveries had been particularly intriguing until now, because right now Mattie had noticed how the dust on the floor was lighter where he stood.

Mattie studied the floor some more. The dust was lighter all the way to the heavy double doors. Almost like something— or *someone*—had been dragged across the mausoleum's floor.

The hairs on the back of Mattie's neck prickled. He turned, following the dusty path.

"What are you doing?" Eliot asked. "Do you see something?"

"I don't know," Mattie muttered. The path didn't go very far. In fact, it stopped right in front of the tomb. Mattie stopped right in front of the tomb too.

"Oh, boy," Mattie said.

"What?" Caroline asked. "What did you find?"

"I think, maybe, this thing might move," Mattie said, running his hands over the cold, smooth edges of the tomb. He ran his fingers up to the corner and down the lid, across the sides, and found, what . . . a speaker?

Mattie peered closer. Yes, it was a plastic security speaker, like the kind people used to gain entry to the Larimore properties. You said a password into the speaker and the door would open.

Only there wasn't a door.

And Mattie didn't know the password.

"What is it?" Eliot asked, coming around to look.

Caroline followed him. "Oh," she said.

"Yeah." Mattie nodded. What could the password be? He leaned a little closer, pressed the small green button at the base, and said, "Munchem."

"Mattie!" Eliot grabbed him. "*Anyone* could be on the other side! What if they're looking at us *right now*!"

Mattie shook Eliot off. "What if Carter's right there?" He pressed the button again. "Munchem."

Nothing happened.

"Academy," Caroline guessed.

"Rooney," Mattie tried.

"Password," Eliot said at last. Caroline and Mattie looked at him and he shrugged. "What? You'd be surprised how frequently that works."

But it didn't work. Nothing worked. Mattie felt his chest getting tighter and tighter. They were so close, he just *knew* it. What was the password? What would the teachers use? What would the clones—

"Yobbo," Mattie blurted, pressing the green button as hard as he could.

The tomb began to creak. The tomb began to rumble. The tomb began to *move*. It slid sideways, revealing a long set of stairs that descended into a long, dark tunnel. Mattie, Caroline, and Eliot peered over the side.

"Not it," the Spencers said together.

Mattie blinked. "You can't be serious."

"You know the rules of Not It," Caroline said, crossing her arms.

Mattie knew the rules of Not It. The Spencers stood to the side as Mattie took one step down and then another. Unlike the stairs in Headmaster Rooney's coat closet, these were the kind of stairs you would push someone down to make their death look like an accident. They were steep and dim and Mattie shuffled along, keeping one hand on the wall. He tried not to think about the dark.

And what might live in the dark.

And what might be waiting for him in the dark.

Mattie squeaked.

"Mattie?" Eliot called. "Are you okay? Can you see anything?"

Mattie squinted. The shadows might have a shape after all. "I think? Maybe? It's almost like—" Mattie took another step and tripped and fell straight into the dark.

NEVER GET TRAPPED IN A DEAD END

BAM! BAM! BAM! MATTIE BOUNCED DOWN THOSE STAIRS. *Whump! Whump! Whump!* His head thumped against the steps and then the wall and then the steps. *Clump!* Mattie landed on his butt.

Clump! Clump! Eliot and Caroline landed beside him.

"Ow," Mattie muttered and rolled on his side so he could see his friends. Above them, the tomb slid shut. "What happened?"

"We ran after you," Caroline said. "It seemed like a good idea at the time."

"And now?" Mattie asked as they stared up the dark staircase and at the tomb's smooth stone bottom.

"I'm not so sure," Caroline answered. She craned her head.

Above them, an orange light flickered to life. "How many secrets can this stupid school have?"

The three friends got to their feet and straightened their clothes. They were in a large circular room with a low ceiling and lots of boxes covered in sheets. To Eliot's right was a metal desk and computer with multiple monitors.

Security, Mattie thought. He recognized the grainy images of the cemetery above them. "Well, at least we'll be able to see who's coming," Mattie said, jutting his chin toward the monitors.

"Oh, goody," Caroline said, dusting off her shirt. She paused. "Wait. Tell me those aren't new coffins!" She jammed one finger in the direction of the boxes. "Tell me right now!"

Mattie couldn't. They looked exactly like new coffins. Long and thin, the closest had a white sheet draped across the top. Mattie lifted one corner. There was a glass top underneath the sheet. He leaned closer to the surface until he could see something fuzzy underneath the glass. Something fuzzy and round and—it was a head!

It was a human head! Mattie jumped backward. "Ah!" he yelped.

"What?"

Mattie's sneakers squeaked as he kicked himself away from the box. "It's a *head*!"

Eliot and Caroline crept to Mattie's side. The head wasn't just any human head. It was *Doyle's* head.

Actually, Mattie tugged the sheet farther back and breathed a sigh of relief when he realized it wasn't just a head, it was Doyle. All of him. Doyle's hands were folded neatly on his stomach and his eyes were closed. He looked like he was sleeping.

"Is he dead?" Caroline breathed. She sounded scared and the dim orange light made her eyes shiny as plastic.

"I don't think so?" Mattie smushed his nose against the glass. Doyle's face never moved, but his chest lifted and fell ever so gently. "I think he's asleep."

"It's like he's in a glass coffin," Caroline whispered.

Doyle was lying on a white satin cushion inside the glass box. White, flexible tubes pumped air across Doyle's face, making his caterpillar eyebrows flutter. Mattie listened closely and could hear faint music being played inside the box. It was almost . . . nice.

"Maybe it's more like a toy box," Mattie suggested because it sounded less scary and Caroline looked awfully close to tears. "You know, like they put action figures in—wait, do you think these are the pods the teachers were talking about?"

"Probably," Eliot said as he examined the control panel attached to Doyle's pod. "I think they're frozen."

Mattie pulled back. "What?"

"Cryogenic freezing." Eliot peered into Doyle's pod. "It slows everything down. The teachers wouldn't need to feed the kids or anything."

"It can also help with wrinkles," Caroline added. "Our parents are testing it in their laboratories."

"Seriously?" Mattie wondered.

The Spencers shrugged and Mattie jumped down. "Help me find Carter?"

Caroline hugged both arms around herself and nodded. They trailed from pod to pod. There was Marcus. There was Jay. There was Maxwell.

And there was Carter.

Mattie was so relieved that his knees shook. He'd found his brother! And his brother was okay!

Now we just have to get out of here, Mattie thought and rapped on the glass top with his knuckles, hoping Carter would wake up. He didn't. Mattie knocked harder.

"Would you stop that?" Caroline whispered fiercely. "We're making enough noise as it is!"

Mattie stopped and Carter still didn't move. Mattie wiped away a bit of the dust and then realized he was leaving fingerprints everywhere. He started to clean away the fingerprints and realized it was too late. If anyone came into the room after them, it would be obvious someone had been wiping the dust from the tops of the pods to look at the students inside.

Mattie's thumb ran across an indentation in the metal on the side of Carter's pod. He recognized the symbol. It was the Larimore Corporation logo.

In fact, the more Mattie looked around, the more he

realized that almost everything here was made by the Larimore Corporation. Mattie felt bad—like he had personally done this, and he knew that was dumb. He hadn't forced Headmaster Rooney to buy this stuff. It wasn't his fault his dad's company made this kind of equipment. You didn't blame the pencil for misspelling words. So why did Mattie feel so anxious?

"Look at all the empty pods," Caroline said, clutching Beezus. Mattie swallowed. He knew Rooney meant to clone all the students, but seeing the pods in person and knowing what they were meant for, well, it was scary all over again.

"Hey, look at this!" Eliot knelt close to the far wall, peering at some thick metal pipes. The pipes went from Doyle's pod to the wall above. If they were very quiet, they could hear the soft, soft whir of air being pumped through them.

"What if they're keeping him asleep?" Eliot asked. "What if it helps the clones somehow?"

"How would it help the clones?" Caroline wanted to know.

"How should I know?" Eliot stood and started to follow a line of electrical cables. They were fat and heavy and lay like snakes on a summer day. "It's almost like . . ."

Caroline and Mattie climbed down as Eliot squeezed between Doyle's pod and the wall. They followed him and found Eliot on the other side, peering into a metal cabinet filled with electronic boards and wires.

"What's that?" Mattie asked.

"A gigantic computer tower," Eliot said, sticking two

fingers into the computer's insides. He tugged at one wire and then another. "It's simply fascinating."

Caroline rolled her eyes. *"What's* fascinating?"

Eliot dug around a bit more. "These are network cables." He leaned back, studying how the electrical lines left the cabinet and followed the wall. "And the network cables are hooked up to the machines, and the machines—" Eliot jumped to his feet and traced the cables as they snaked across the floor. He scrambled on top of Doyle's pod again and stared down at Doyle. "The machines are hooked up to the students!"

"Well, that explains everything," Mattie said.

"Totally," Caroline agreed with another eye roll. "I feel so much smarter."

Eliot blinked at both of them. His mouth hung open a little as if he couldn't believe they were being so stupid. "Think of Doyle's brain like a hard drive," Eliot finally explained. "That's where a computer stores all its data, and if Doyle's brain is the hard drive then Doyle's clone can pull all his memories from him."

Mattie gasped. "That's why they know so much! They're just pulling their memories from the real students!"

"Exactly." Eliot dusted off his hands and stared down at Doyle. "They pull just enough information so they can pass as Doyle or Carter or Marcus and override the bad stuff with the Rooster's files."

"Kind of like saving over the old files?" Caroline asked.

"More like only accessing what he wants and"—Eliot snapped his fingers—"*that's* why they won't let us have electronics!"

"What?" Mattie stared at him.

"Electronics could interfere with the computers and that would screw up the clones!" Eliot explained. "Pretty smart— and with all those pods? Think of how many students they could clone! They really could do all of us!"

Mattie thought Eliot sounded a little too excited by the prospect. "Eliot."

Eliot was oblivious. "I want to take some stuff," he said, his eyes glassy like he'd been eating candy for days. "Think anyone would notice?"

"YES!" Caroline and Mattie said.

"Fine. Whatever." Eliot scowled and slid off Doyle's pod. He put both hands on his hips and stared at the students, the boxes, and all the wires and cables dangling around them. "It's just all so beautiful," Eliot whispered and dabbed his eyes.

Caroline gave Mattie an anxious look. "Do something," she hissed.

Mattie stared at her. What was he supposed to do?

Caroline planted one hand between his shoulder blades and shoved him forward. "We have to get out of here! Someone could come back any minute!"

Well, Mattie could definitely agree with Caroline on that.

"So, Eliot," Mattie said, glancing around the room. "If we

unplug Doyle and Carter, will the clones forget who they're supposed to be?"

"Maybe? I don't know. I've never seen anything like this."

Mattie looked at the Larimore Corporation logo stamped on the closest metal panel and shook his head. "Yeah, me neither."

"I mean, we could try. It might not hurt anything. Of course, it might also be like unplugging a thumb drive while you're still using it."

"What do you mean?"

"Well, if you did that in real life to a thumb drive, you could hang up your computer and lose whatever you were working on."

"Oh." Mattie looked at his brother and tried to decide what parts of Carter he might lose if they just yanked out the plug.

"Maybe we should try!" Eliot ran to the nearest box—Doyle's—and started to tug on the biggest networking cable. "Let's see what happens!"

"No!" Caroline cried. "You can't just start yanking on stuff!"

"Why not?"

"Because those are *people*!"

Eliot stared at her. "No, they're not. This one's . . ." Eliot looked down. "This one's Doyle."

"You can't do it!"

Eliot gave the big networking cable a jerk. "Actually, I can."

"You can't do it because I said so!" Caroline's hair stood up even higher and her eyes bugged even more and Mattie took a step back. And then another.

"Fine," Eliot grumbled and dropped the cable. "But we need a plan. We need to do something."

"We *need* to get out of here," Caroline added. "We can figure out a plan later, but if we stay here, we're going to get caught and then we'll end up just like them!"

And, as if they were starring in their very own scary movie, the computer began to beep.

"Oh, no." Caroline swallowed. "What does *that* mean?"

Mattie dashed to the closest monitor and his heart double-thumped. "Karloff. He's heading for the cemetery."

"We have to run!" Eliot grabbed his sister's arm and hauled both of them toward the stairs. "Open the tomb!"

"Wait!"

The Spencers stopped, turned, and stared at Mattie. "Don't run. Let's hide."

"But Mattie, we can still get away," Caroline panted.

Mattie shook his head. "If we leave now, we won't get to see what they're up to."

BE CAREFUL WHERE YOU HIDE

"HIDE!" MATTIE WHISPERED. ELIOT AND CAROLINE SCATTERED, and Mattie dashed after them. They ran right. They ran left. They ran ever so briefly around in a circle and then Caroline jumped into an empty pod and the boys dove underneath it.

Caroline closed the pod's top with a *click* as Mattie wedged himself next to Eliot and all three of them held their breath as the tomb scraped open.

A pair of shoes came into view.

"C'mon," Mr. Karloff snapped. They were *his* shoes and Mattie realized it as soon as the teacher spoke—although he probably should've realized it when he saw the super-shiny loafers. Mr. Karloff did love polishing his shoes. Mattie could see the overhead lights reflected on the toes. "Hurry up, Marcus!"

Marcus's shoes appeared. Or, at least, Mattie assumed they were Marcus's shoes. They were standard black Munchem-approved loafers, so technically they could have belonged to almost any student. Then the loafers jerked. They danced to the right and started doing some sort of tap dance to the left.

Tap dance? Mattie stared. Yep, the clone was definitely tap-dancing—and he was good at it.

"Oh, for heavens' sake!" Mr. Karloff fumed and stomped closer to Marcus. Marcus kept dancing.

Beep! Beep! Bloop!

Marcus stopped dancing.

"Finally," Mr. Karloff said. "Now c'mon, Marcus. I don't have all day to reset you."

Mattie and Eliot watched the teacher's feet shuffle past.

"Stand over here, Marcus," Mr. Karloff instructed. Mattie couldn't see the teacher's feet anymore, but he could still see Marcus's. The clone stood next to the real Marcus's pod. There was the sound of fingers tapping on a keyboard and then something went *whoosh, whoosh.*

Eliot nudged Mattie's elbow and pointed at Marcus's pod. Mattie didn't understand. What did Eliot want? What—oh.

Oh, no, Mattie thought.

A cable had been knocked loose from the pod. It lay on the floor, the end pointed accusingly in their direction. If Mr. Karloff noticed, he would plug the cable in again. If he plugged the cable in again, he would have to lean down. If he leaned down . . .

249

Mattie gulped. If Mr. Karloff leaned down, they would be spotted for sure.

"Ah!" Mr. Karloff's shiny shoes rushed into view. "This is what your problem is!"

Mr. Karloff knelt to grab the disconnected cable and spent several moments trying to jam the connector back into the socket.

Jam! Mattie watched and started to sweat.

Jam! Jam! Eliot watched and his hands started to shake.

"There!" Mr. Karloff cried as the connector finally connected and Marcus the Clone started dancing again. He pirouetted toward Mr. Karloff, and Mr. Karloff jumped to his feet, swearing.

"No!" Mr. Karloff yelled. "Stop it!"

He wrestled with the clone again and pushed more buttons. Finally, Marcus the Clone stopped dancing. Mr. Karloff slumped against the pod, trying to catch his breath. "Stupid clones," he muttered. "Stupid computers. Stupid pods. Stupid . . ." Mr. Karloff's voice trailed off. Mattie assumed he didn't know the proper name for the cable he was cursing.

"This will be so much easier when we get better equipment, Marcus." Mr. Karloff got to his feet and tapped away on the keyboard once more. He sounded like he was trying to beat it to death. "No more having to fix you every time a rat knocks something loose. No more traipsing across campus every time you have to be reset. No more getting your system overloaded all the time."

What was Karloff talking about? Mattie looked at Eliot, hoping Eliot understood, but Eliot was staring into space, his lips mashed into a thin line like he was thinking.

"There!" Mr. Karloff said again. He sounded satisfied and banged on the keyboard a bit more. "Now you should be fixed and I can get back to my tea."

"Thank you, Mr. Karloff," Marcus the Clone said. He sounded extra chipper. "I feel much better!"

"Well, good," Mr. Karloff returned. "Now let's get back. You can clean my bathroom before you go to dinner."

"That sounds great!" Marcus said, following Mr. Karloff across the room, up the stairs, and out of the tomb.

———————

Mattie and Eliot waited in the dark until they were sure Mr. Karloff and Marcus the Clone were long gone. The waiting was even harder than the hiding. Mattie counted and counted, trying to keep track of the seconds so he could add them into minutes, but after the three-minute mark, he lost track and just lay on his belly, feeling his heartbeat slow back down to normal.

It took a while.

"No wonder the whole place is looking cleaner," Eliot whispered.

"*That's* what you can't believe about this?" Mattie asked. Under the pod, it smelled like new plastic and cold concrete. Mattie's nose prickled like he wanted to sneeze. He rubbed it with one hand.

"Well, *yeah*," Eliot whispered back. "Furthermore, if they have the clones, they shouldn't need *me* to clean those crusty toilets. It's gross." He craned his head, trying to get a better look at the stairs. "Do you think they're gone?"

"I hope so." Mattie dragged himself forward on his elbows and peeked around the pod's edge. In the dark, the stairs were just a solid blob and the tomb door was completely invisible. Both boys listened and listened, but they didn't hear the *scuff scuff* of shoes or the whisper of incoming voices. "I think we're okay," Mattie whispered.

"Then why are you still whispering?"

Mattie cleared his throat. "Better?"

"No. Your foot is in my face."

"Oh." Mattie scooted to one side. "Now?"

"Now it's in my ear."

Mattie dragged himself out from under the pod and the overhead lights flickered on, making the room look eerie and greenish. "Caroline?"

Caroline said nothing. Eliot popped up next to Mattie and brushed himself off.

"Caroline?" Eliot tapped on the pod's glass.

There was still no response.

"Ugh," Eliot muttered, glaring up at the lights. "It's like the Rooster wants to make the whole thing creepy."

"It's already creepy," Mattie said.

"Fine. Creepier. Happy?"

"No." Mattie wasn't happy at all. He'd found his brother, but had no idea how to wake him up. He was stuck underneath a tomb, and now Caroline was ignoring them. Mattie knocked harder on the tinted glass, and that's when he noticed the lights.

There were three of them. They were green. They were blinking. And they most certainly had not been green or blinking before Mr. Karloff arrived.

"Is this thing *on*?" Mattie asked. His voice skidded so high he sounded like a Martha or a Matilda or a Mary. But Eliot didn't notice. Eliot was banging on the glass now too.

"Caroline? Caroline!"

Caroline lay on her side, one hand curled by her hip, the other curled in a fist. She looked like she was fast asleep, and she wasn't waking up.

"We have to get her out of there," Mattie said, checking the glass door's handles. They were locked tight. "Can you get it to open?"

"I don't know!" Eliot fumbled with the buttons on the side. He pushed the green ones.

Nothing.

He pushed the yellow ones.

Still nothing.

"What do I do?" Eliot began to push all the buttons and yet nothing continued to happen.

"Try the green buttons again," Mattie cried. "I'll lift up the door."

But nothing worked.

Panting, the boys peered down at Caroline. There was a leaf stuck to her sweater. No, Mattie realized. That wasn't a leaf. That was a Beezus.

"What do I do? What do I do?" Eliot moaned, studying the keypad. The green lights kept blinking and he slapped his palm against them. "We can't leave her here!"

"We won't!" Mattie reassured him. "We'll figure it out. You're really good at computers, right? You can fix this!"

"I can't," Eliot moaned. "I don't know the first thing about *these* computers. What if I hit the wrong button? *Anything* could happen."

Or nothing could continue to happen, which was almost worse. Caroline was stuck. She was going to get caught and because the boys wouldn't leave her, they were going to get caught too.

Mattie forced himself to think clearly. He walked around the pod and stopped. "What about the red button?" Mattie asked, pointing to the pod's broad, shiny side.

Eliot joined him and the boys stared at the red button. It sat alone, close to the pod's top.

"What if it's an alarm?" Eliot asked, his voice climbing. "It could bring the teachers."

Mattie nodded slowly. The button could indeed be an alarm and it could indeed bring the teachers. "But what if it's the lid's release?"

Eliot looked at Mattie. Mattie looked at Eliot. Eliot leaned forward and jammed his thumb against the red button.

NEVER LEAVE SOMEONE BEHIND

THERE WAS A *CLICK CLICK.* THE RED LIGHT BY THE RED BUTTON illuminated. The pod's top swooshed up with a chilly breeze and Caroline's eyes slowly opened. She blinked at the ceiling and then at Mattie and Eliot and then, finally, she sat up.

Eliot threw his arms around her. "You're so stupid!"

"You're stupid!" Caroline thumped her brother, but he didn't let go. She looked around the room. "What's going on? Where am I?"

Eliot pulled back. "You don't remember? Did you hit your head?"

"No!" Caroline snapped, but she pressed both hands against her head to be sure. "I don't think so. What's going on?"

"Oh, my God," Eliot moaned. "She came back an idiot. My parents are going to kill me."

Mattie shoved Eliot to the side. "You're under the cemetery," Mattie said. "We went into the mausoleum and found that tomb, remember?"

Caroline's stony expression indicated she clearly did not.

"Uh, we figured out how to move the tomb," Mattie continued and pointed to the stairs behind them. "We came down and found the other students. They're sleeping in these pod things."

"I don't remember any of that," Caroline said. Her dark eyes were wide.

"What do you remember?" Mattie asked.

"I remember . . ." Caroline twisted to see the room and the stairs and the door tucked into the ceiling. "I remember standing at the stone wall—the one by the garden—and Mattie ran off and we followed—"

"That was almost an hour ago," Mattie interrupted.

"The pod made you forget," Eliot said. "I wonder if . . ." Eliot spun around to study the control panel again. "I wonder if the longer you're in the pod, the more you forget?"

Mattie stared at his brother's pod. How much would Carter remember? Would he know what happened? Would he remember who Mattie was?

"Do you think Carter will forget he's a jerk?" Mattie wondered.

"It's science, Mattie, not magic." Eliot helped his sister down from the pod. Caroline was a little wobbly on her feet, and Beezus clung to her shoulder like a pirate on a pitching ship.

"I can't leave him," Mattie said. "We have to get him out. We'll take him to the police and we'll tell them—"

"What?" Eliot asked, supporting Caroline with one arm. "He won't remember anything. He's been in there for over a week, Mattie. What if we hurt him?"

What if they did? Mattie stared at his friends and then stared at Carter's pod. He just couldn't bring himself to leave.

Caroline disentangled herself from Eliot. She was standing on her own now, much less wobbly and much more like herself. "Mattie, we'll come back for him and, next time, we'll be ready. We'll get caught if we try to drag him back to school. Do you *want* that?"

"No!"

"Then let's go!" Caroline said and all three of them darted for the stairs—but not before Mattie took one last look at his brother's pod. Carter had been in there for days. How much of his memory would be lost? How much of what made Carter, well, Carter would still be there?

"C'mon, Mattie!" Caroline grabbed Mattie's hand and hauled him up the steps.

They paused at the very top, listening for voices before Eliot pressed the exit button to release the tomb. It slid open and they emerged into the mausoleum, shut the tomb behind them, and ran into the cemetery. Mattie never thought he'd be so happy to see that ugly, broken-down angel.

Or the prickly grass.

Or the sky.

Or . . . well, everything.

"What a disaster," Caroline said after Eliot explained everything she had missed. She tried to untangle Beezus from her hair. It didn't work very well. The poor rat had wads of her hair clutched in his paws and teeth and his eyes were bugged out of his head.

"We're in worse shape than when we started," Caroline said and gave Beezus a yank. He ripped free from her head with a chunk of her hair.

Mattie frowned. He kind of sort of might possibly agree with Caroline on this one. "At least we know where they are," he said at last.

"But how are we going to get them out?" Caroline wanted to know.

Mattie had no idea how they would do that. He turned to Eliot. "What do you think?"

"I think we're in pretty bad shape," Eliot said with a nod.

Mattie's heart squeezed. Eliot didn't have to sound nearly so pleased about it. Then again, it wasn't like it was Eliot's brother who was trapped down there.

"But," Eliot continued, holding up one finger and smiling. "We do know one more thing than we did before."

"What's that?" Mattie asked.

Eliot's smile spread into a grin. It was the same grin Mattie would eventually recognize every time Eliot's magnificent mind thought of something magnificent. "Now we know the clones can be overloaded—"

"And," Caroline interrupted as a grin eerily similar to her brother's spread across her face. "When the clones are overloaded, they malfunction."

"What are you . . . *oh!*" Mattie straightened. They were talking about what Karloff said, about the clones—how they were always getting overloaded and when they overloaded they went wrong. Now Mattie was starting to get it.

"Exactly," Eliot said. He rubbed his palms together. "Think of the mayhem."

Mattie nodded. "The Rooster won't know what hit him."

REMEMBER YOUR GOAL

THE SPENCERS THOUGHT ABOUT THE ROOSTER AND MAYHEM and clones. They laughed and laughed. Mattie didn't laugh, though. He couldn't stop thinking about how his brother was stuck deep beneath the mausoleum.

"We have to wake them up," Mattie said. "We have to get Carter and everyone out of there. If we tell the whole school what happened, Rooney and the teachers will have to stop."

Caroline's expression turned worried again. "Mattie, if all the adults are in on it, who's going to make them stop? Who's going to help us?"

Eliot nodded. "She's right. If we free the others, the Rooster and the teachers will just put them back."

Mattie studied his friends. They had a very good point and

it was definitely a problem. But surely there was a way around the very good point and the definite problem?

Maybe?

Mattie chewed his thumbnail. It didn't help him come up with any ideas, but it was something to do. His mind kept coming back to calling the police, but every time he thought of it he was reminded of one of his father's favorite topics: the burden of truth. For Mattie, it had always sounded like when you stood up for what was right. But Mr. Larimore said it was so much simpler than that. It was just having to prove something did or did not happen. Just like now. Mattie had to prove Rooney was cloning students.

But how? How could he convince the police to come to the school? How could he convince anyone of what was going on in the basement and cemetery? Take a piece of pipe? A chunk of wires?

Mattie looked around the cemetery and then at the school in the faraway distance. He looked at the overgrown grass and the overgrown ivy. He looked at Munchem's imposing iron fence. The gate was so far down the driveway, Mattie almost couldn't see it, but he knew it was locked. It was always locked except for when—

"The parents!" Mattie cried.

Eliot and Caroline stared at him. "What about them?" Caroline asked.

"They're the only people coming to Munchem who aren't

in league with the teachers!" Mattie ran to the entrance of the cemetery, looking from the gate to the school and back again. "We have to overload the clones during the end-of-term parent dinner. They'll be so horrified, they'll call the police and the Rooster will get arrested!"

The Spencers looked at each other, and Mattie crossed his arms. "It's the only way."

Caroline nudged her brother. "He's right. We need help."

Eliot shook his head. "Nope, what we *need* is a way to overload the clones while we're stuck at that dinner. How's that going to work?"

Eliot was right. If they were sitting at the dinner, they couldn't mess with any of the clones' wiring. Nervousness began to creep through Mattie again. "What are we going to do?" he asked.

"I have an idea."

But like any good idea, Eliot needed time (plus a few items from Marilyn).

"This better be worth it," Eliot muttered to Mattie as he carried a small pile of computer parts into their room. It was evening two days later, and Room 14A was empty since the boys were preparing for the parent dinner.

Preparing might be a bit of a stretch. Doyle was somewhere—probably delivering more baked goods. Bell and Kent were in study hall again—or were still, Mattie wasn't quite clear on that. Eliot was muttering to himself and gluing black plastic to a small metal frame. And Mattie? Well, Mattie was staring at his essay.

What kind of person had he become at Munchem?

What kind of person indeed. Since arriving at Munchem Academy, Mattie had thrown a dirty sponge into Doyle's face. He had sneaked into the headmaster's office. He had found a cloning machine. He had tried to save his brother—only to get his brother caught and cloned. And now—Mattie sighed—now he had to fix it.

Eliot burst into laughter and held the small metal frame closer to the lamp. Mattie watched him and noted that Eliot had a laugh that was bigger than he was and maybe a little bit like an evil scientist's laugh before he melted down a hero.

"What are you doing?" Mattie asked.

Eliot shook his head and hunched over his desk. "I'll show you in a minute."

Mattie squirmed and looked at his essay again. By now, he could recite it backward and forward and while standing on his head—which he couldn't actually do, but thought would be far more useful than reading paragraphs on what he'd learned at Munchem.

"The point isn't what you think is important," Mrs. Hitchcock had reminded him for the eleventh—or eleven millionth—time earlier that afternoon. "The point is what your *parents* find important, what the world will find important."

All term, Mattie had been looking forward to this. He was going to see his parents. He was going to get his chance to make it up to them and to go home. But if he did well, he'd go home and leave Carter.

And if he didn't do well, he'd have to stay here and risk getting cloned.

"Prepare to be amazed," Eliot announced. He held a black plastic remote control above his head. It was pieced together with silver tape and had a crooked antenna. "Ta-da!"

Mattie cocked his head. "You're going to play a movie for them?"

"No." Eliot scowled. "Remember when I said lots of electronics could interrupt the clones and make them mess up? Well, I'm going to do that. I'll overload the clones' systems and force a malfunction."

"How?"

"Spark gap generator." Eliot held out the remote for Mattie's inspection. "The energy creates an electromagnetic pulse—kind of like when speakers crackle right before your cell phone rings. The only problem is it's really small so I'll have to be close to the clones."

"Where did you learn to do this stuff?" Mattie asked.

Eliot shrugged. "Other kids read comics, I read computer manuals."

Mattie studied the silver tape and the crooked antenna. The plastic remote was small enough that Eliot could probably tuck it inside his Munchem red sweater. If he kept it under the table at dinner, no one would ever know it was there.

"Does it work?" Mattie asked. Eliot narrowed his eyes. "I mean, *how* does it—"

The door to 14A swung open and Doyle bounced through. "Dinnertime!" Doyle smiled at them and, slowly, Eliot began to grin back.

"How's it going, Doyle?" he asked, easing the remote into one hand. Mattie's heart tripped when he saw Eliot's thumb began to move over the keypad. There was the faintest crackling.

"It's going great, Eliot!" Doyle's eyes went bright as he set down his schoolbooks on the study table.

"How great?" Eliot asked.

Doyle didn't answer. He couldn't. Doyle's head snapped back, his shoulders straightened and stared at something only Doyle the Clone could see. One arm raised above his head, finger pointed to the ceiling.

"Eliot?" Mattie said, his eyes cutting from Eliot to Doyle and back again. "I think—"

"I think it works," Eliot said as Doyle began to pirouette around the room. One part of Mattie was horrified. Another part of him was impressed with Doyle's ballet. All he needed was some tights and a ballerina bun.

Doyle spun past them as Eliot tucked the remote in his pocket. "Prepare to be amazed at parents' night," he said.

"Prepare to save the others on parents' night," Mattie reminded him.

"Same difference."

RECOGNIZE YOUR TEAM IS YOUR BEST ASSET

MUNCHEM HAD NEVER LOOKED SO CLEAN. MATTIE KNEW
Mrs. Hitchcock had asked the upperclassmen to decorate the
dining hall for the end-of-term dinner, but he hadn't expected
it to look nice—well, as nice as one could make a dining hall
look, which was to say there were decorative streamers and
embroidered place mats. But it still smelled like old fish.

Headmaster Rooney paced the length of the room, eyeing
each of the students. His dark suit was pressed and his red
hair was slicked down. It made him shorter than usual and
maybe that was why he looked so angry.

"Now listen up!" Rooney shouted. The force of his voice
rocked him onto his toes. "Your parents will be joining
us shortly. You are to greet them. You are to eat with your

roommates and, after dinner, you will read your essays when you are called upon. Do you understand?"

Everyone muttered and looked at their shoes.

"DO YOU UNDERSTAND?" the headmaster shouted.

Everyone nodded and still looked at their shoes. No one wanted to meet the headmaster's eyes. Well, no one but Mattie, who couldn't look away. Again.

"What are you doing?" Eliot muttered. "Look away."

"I can't!" Mattie whispered. This is what mice must feel like sitting in front of a snake, he thought as the headmaster glared at him.

"Go on then," Headmaster Rooney said, eyeing Mattie. "I expect your best behavior tonight or *else*."

Mattie's heart jerked into his throat. He forced himself to walk calmly to his place in line, next to Eliot and the other boys from 14A, as their parents arrived.

"Dude," Eliot muttered, turning his head toward Mattie as the room began to fill. "Doesn't Doyle's mom look just like him?"

Doyle's mom did indeed, and Mattie was so transfixed by how she embraced her clone son—and how the clone embraced her—that he entirely missed the woman waving at him.

"Mattie?" she cried. People stopped, people stared, and Mrs. Larimore smiled.

"Yes, it is me," she said, placing one hand against her chest. "I know. I'm excited for you too."

Eliot's eyes bugged. "Is that your mom?"

Mrs. Larimore shoved past two other mothers and teetered toward Mattie. Her high heels made *clackety clackety clack* noises against the hardwood floors that made Mattie's chest feel tight. He knew he missed his mother, but he didn't know he missed her noises too.

"Mom!"

Mrs. Larimore threw her arms around him. She smelled like roses and laundry detergent and *home*. Mattie buried his face in her neck.

"Where's Dad?" Mattie asked when he finally pushed himself away.

"Just saying hello to your brother." Mrs. Larimore nodded her head to their right and, sure enough, there was Carter the Clone shaking hands with Mr. Larimore and the headmaster. Mattie had never seen his father look so happy. Mr. Larimore's jowls quivered as he pumped Headmaster Rooney's hand up and down. Headmaster Rooney looked just as delighted. It made Mattie wonder if the Rooster would want a picture with his dad too. Then the headmaster's eyes met Mattie's, catching him staring.

"Do you have your poem ready?" Mrs. Larimore asked, touching her fingers to her dark, upswept hair.

"Essay, Mom."

"Are you ready to read your essay?"

Not at all, but Mattie nodded and Mrs. Larimore smiled

like that made her happy. He was good at making her happy, Mattie realized.

"Mrs. Larimore," Headmaster Rooney called. "Could I have a word with you?"

Mattie tensed as his mother began to pull away. "I'm really glad you're here," he whispered. "I think I'm going to need your help."

"Of course, sweetheart." Mrs. Larimore squeezed his hand in both of hers. "I've missed you so much. I've almost convinced your father to let you come home. Just be good tonight, okay? That shouldn't be so hard for you, right?"

Mattie clenched his jaw. "Right."

And really it wasn't hard for him. Mattie sat with the other boys from 14A. He ate his vegetables. He used his napkin. He watched his parents from across the room and felt worse and worse.

"It's going to be fine," Eliot told him and took an enormous mouthful of ham.

"Did your parents come?" Mattie asked, using his fork to push mashed potatoes around on his plate.

"Nah, they're too busy coming up with a new lipstick line. I bet Caroline's monkey's completely pink by now. Are you going to eat that?"

Mattie wasn't, and he let Eliot eat all of his ham and most of his mashed potatoes. In fact, Mattie didn't know how Eliot could eat at a time like this. It wasn't just that Mattie's parents were here and he might get to go home. It was the clones and the remote control and rescuing the students. It was *everything*, and Eliot was eating like it was nothing.

Maybe Eliot really did have superpowers.

At the head of the tables, Mrs. Hitchcock stood up and faced the crowd. "And now, ladies and gentlemen," she began. "We have a brief interruption to honor our wonderful headmaster."

"What?" Caroline squeezed in next to Eliot in a blur of red Munchem uniform and dark hair.

"Go sit back down!" Her brother whispered, wiggling closer to Mattie. "You're going to get us caught!"

Caroline pushed hair from her face. "I can't see what you're doing from over there!"

"You're supposed to eat with your roommates—"

"Hush!" Mattie breathed. Marcus the Clone had just joined Mrs. Hitchcock. He held a small brass plaque in his hands.

"Headmaster," Mrs. Hitchcock continued. "Could you join us?"

Headmaster Rooney wiped his mouth and stood. He looked surprised, but somehow Mattie was pretty sure he had known what was coming.

"I would like to take a few moments to tell you all how Headmaster Rooney changed my life," Marcus began.

"I don't remember anyone mentioning this," Caroline whispered, drumming her fingers against the tabletop. "At this rate, we'll never get to the essays."

Caroline was right. As usual, Mattie was beginning to realize. Then again . . . "Eliot," Mattie whispered. "This is our chance! Use the remote!"

Eliot hesitated.

Why was he waiting? Mattie nudged him. "Do it now!"

Eliot sighed and dragged the remote out from under his jacket. He muttered something about the tragedy of ruining perfectly good robots and Caroline kicked him.

"Ow!"

She kicked him harder.

Eliot shot his sister a murderous look. "I'm on it, okay? Okay?"

He propped the remote between his knees, grumbling. Mattie cut his eyes back to Marcus and saw Carter had now joined them too.

And here came Doyle. And Jay. And Maxwell. All of the clones were joining Rooney and Mrs. Hitchcock at the front of the dining hall.

"Thanks to Munchem," Carter announced, "I have a new perspective on life."

"I'll say," Caroline muttered.

Carter continued talking about the challenges at Munchem and how they'd made him a better person. Or a new person entirely, Mattie thought. Next to him, Eliot's fingers were flying over the remote. He typed. He tapped.

Nothing happened.

"They're too far away," Eliot whispered.

Still up at the front of the dining hall, Headmaster Rooney dabbed his eyes and shook all the clones' hands. "At Munchem Academy," he said to the audience, "we believe making good students is a science!"

Everyone clapped. Marcus and Carter stood behind the headmaster and smiled like they were running for class president. Then, quite suddenly, Marcus—who was on the very end of the stage—stepped to the side.

Mattie straightened. He craned his head to get a better look and, sure enough, Marcus the Clone made another side step . . . and another.

"You're doing it!" Mattie whispered. "You're really doing it!"

"What part of 'genius inventor' did you not understand?" Eliot whispered back, his eyes still pinned to the clone. "Of course I'm doing it!"

Mrs. Hitchcock had noticed Marcus's twitching and was edging closer to him. She was almost close enough to grab him. If she pulled Marcus away—

"Hurry!" Mattie gasped.

"I'm trying!" Eliot retorted

Marcus the Clone broke into dance. His arms flailed. His head bobbed. His legs, well, his legs did their own thing. Their own separate things, actually. Marcus the Clone looked like he wanted to do the splits or needed to go to the bathroom. Mattie couldn't decide.

Caroline and Eliot and Mattie watched as Mrs. Hitchcock grabbed Marcus. She righted him with a jerk and everything continued.

Like nothing had happened.

Headmaster Rooney grinned at the crowd. "Because at Munchem Academy," he said and winked, "the best you is a new you!"

The parents clapped, the teachers smiled, and Mattie stifled the impulse to yell. He wanted to stand on top of the tables and shake his fist in the air. Both of which would have been supremely satisfying, but neither would have actually accomplished anything.

Except . . . Mattie did stand up. In the dim lights of the dining hall, it wasn't that noticeable. Or maybe it was because all of the teachers were watching the clones.

Or maybe it was because Mattie was so short.

It was hard to tell, but Mattie didn't care. The teachers weren't watching him, his parents weren't watching him—they were too enchanted with the clones—and the double doors were still open. Mattie had his window of opportunity and he was going to take it.

"What are you doing?" Eliot tugged on his friend's sleeve. "Sit down! I'll try again when the clones do their speeches in the auditorium."

Mattie shook his head. "I'm going to get Carter—the *real* Carter," he said, edging away from the table. "It's the only way."

ALWAYS HAVE A BACKUP PLAN

HEADMASTER ROONEY WAS WINNING. HE WAS WINNING, AND if Mattie didn't do something fast, the whole thing would be over. Unfortunately for Mattie, he wasn't particularly fast. His legs were short and his lungs were burning before he even reached the hallway that led to the back gardens.

Mattie spun around the corner and slipped. He righted himself and kept going. He ran past Mrs. Hitchcock's classroom and the dingy lockers on the first floor. He ran past the stairs to the science wing and ran out the rear doors that led to the garden.

He ran so fast he was wheezing by the time he reached the garden gate. Mattie grabbed the handle with both hands and yanked. The gate sprang open and Caroline dashed past him.

"Hurry up, Mattie!"

Eliot ran after his sister. "C'mon, Mattie!"

Caroline was almost invisible in the dark, but Eliot's blond hair looked white in the moonlight. It bobbed down the hill and across the field toward the cemetery. Mattie trailed them, but not by much.

Clouds drifted past the fat white moon. Mattie could see the cemetery coming into view. There were the spikes and a headless gargoyle sitting on the spiny iron fence.

Mattie ran faster. He dashed between the tilted tombstones and shoved through the mausoleum doors. Inside was just as cold and dark as he remembered. Mattie fumbled about looking for the green button at the bottom of the plastic speaker.

"Yobbo!" Mattie finally whispered. The tomb slid sideways and, this time, Mattie and the Spencers clattered down the stairs together.

The overhead lights clicked on, humming like bees. Mattie hopped down the last step and dashed over to Carter's pod. "Are you sure this isn't going to hurt him?" he asked Eliot, hand hovering above the pod's handle.

"Let's find out," Eliot said.

Mattie swung around. "Eliot! We can't hurt him!"

"I'm almost entirely sure he'll be fine," Eliot admitted. "Like ninety-nine percent. Look at Caroline. She's fine."

Mattie looked at Caroline. She rolled her eyes. "Mattie,"

Caroline warned, pointing to the stairs and then the tomb above. "We don't have time for this!"

It was true. They didn't. Mattie took a deep breath and faced the pod. He hit the red button. He wrenched open the top and nothing happened. Carter kept sleeping.

"Carter," Mattie said, shaking his brother's arm. "Carter, wake up."

Carter did not wake up. He remained stiff and lifeless, like the time he pretended to be dead to scare Mattie.

"Try punching him," Caroline suggested.

"Don't do that," Eliot said and started tapping away at the pod's keypad. "We'll try this." He hit the green keys and then the blue keys and then the green keys some more.

Mattie's eyes went wide. "What are you doing?"

"No idea, but—"

Carter sat up in a *whoosh* of cold air. He scrubbed one hand across his face and blinked at the overhead lights.

"Carter!" Mattie jumped up and threw his arms around his brother. Carter felt solid and familiar and his Munchem shirt was a tiny bit crispy from the cold. "I'm so glad you're okay! Wait—" Mattie stopped squeezing Carter and studied him *"Are you okay?"*

"What?" Carter stared at Mattie and then he stared at Mattie's arms, which were still slung around his waist. "Where am I?"

"Um." Mattie took a step back and looked at his friends.

Eliot's eyes were huge, and Caroline waved one hand like *Go ahead and tell him. I mean, really, what else are you going to do?*

Or maybe Mattie thought that because he knew Caroline a little too well by that point.

Mattie took a breath and faced his brother. "Headmaster Rooney cloned you and while your clone has been running around pretending to *be* you, you've been stored down here."

"Whaaaaaat?"

"Headmaster Rooney cloned you and while your clone—"

"Shut it," Carter snapped. "I don't want to hear about the stupid clones!"

"Then what's all this?" Mattie yelled. He grabbed his brother's arm and shook it. "Look around you! What's all this?"

Carter eyes grew wider and wider. "Are you *insane*?"

"No. I saved you. Look around!"

Carter looked at Mattie instead. He looked at Mattie's face and then at Mattie's hand and then at how Mattie's hand gripped his arm like he would never let go. Carter looked at Mattie like he was seeing him for the first time, which Mattie knew couldn't be right because Carter had always known him.

"You look different," Carter said at last.

"I *am* different," Mattie said. "And I'd really love for you to explain how you got down here if I'm making all this up."

Carter's gaze took in the whole room. He studied the other pods and the stairs and the Spencers. He was quiet for so long that Caroline started to make little growling noises because she knew—just like Mattie and Eliot knew—that they didn't have time for this.

Finally, Carter faced his brother. "Okay," he said and swallowed. "Tell me everything, Mattie."

Mattie recounted it all, even the part about Doyle's baked muffins.

"Muffins?" Carter repeated. "Doyle *bakes*?"

"Yes," Mattie said with a nod. "*And* he irons socks instead of kicking seventh graders."

"That's some machine."

"Yeah."

"And I was cloned too?"

"Yeah." Mattie hesitated. "We were all down in the basement when Rooney came in, and you knew what was going to happen, but you sacrificed yourself anyway. It was my fault and I'm sorry. I've been trying to bring you back ever since."

"Huh," Carter said, blinking and staring at his brother. "Huh," he said again.

"Do you remember now?" Mattie asked. Sometimes hope felt like a bird in his chest. It flew higher and higher.

"No," Carter said at last. "I wish I did though."

Mattie sagged. He wished his brother remembered too.

"Guys?" Caroline huffed. "Maybe you might want to hurry this along?"

Mattie took a deep breath, but this time it didn't loosen

the knot in his throat. "We don't have much time, Carter. Will you help us?"

Carter looked at Mattie then he looked at the Spencers then he nodded his head. "Yeah, okay, Mattie, but here's what we're going to do—"

"Why does he get to decide?" Caroline demanded. She crossed her arms and glared at Carter. "He just woke up. How do we know he's not brain-scrambled? Maybe Eliot should check him."

"No," Mattie said, stepping between his friends and his brother. "I know what we're going to do. I have a plan."

"Since when do you have plans?" Carter asked. He looked at Caroline, who rolled her eyes. "Is he always this bossy now?"

"No," she said. "Sometimes he's asleep."

"Hey!" Mattie said. "Knock it off. Both of you." Mattie stood a little straighter. "Okay, this is what we're going to do. Caroline?"

"Yes?"

"I need you to distract Carter's clone and hold him until we can show both Carters *together* on the school stage."

Caroline cocked her head. "Like cage the clone up or something?"

"Yeah, exactly." Mattie nodded hard. "You usually let stuff loose, so just reverse it. Do you think you can?"

"I can do anything with duct tape." Caroline tossed her hair. "It's a talent."

AND THEN HAVE A BACKUP PLAN
FOR YOUR BACKUP PLAN

"I'M NOT PRETENDING TO BE A CLONE," CARTER REPEATED AS he followed Mattie back through the garden. Caroline had long since disappeared into the shadows, muttering about duct tape and clone lures. Mattie kind of wanted to know what could possibly be a clone lure, but, at the same time, he was afraid to ask.

"I'm just going to confront the Rooster and get it all out in the open," Carter added.

"But it won't get out in the open because he'll stop you!" Mattie tugged on the garden gate. It wouldn't budge. He tugged and tugged and—*wham!* It swung open, nearly smacking him in the face. "You have to have witnesses! If you stand up to read your essay, you'll have everyone's attention—"

"I don't have an essay," Carter complained as he followed Mattie into the garden. "I never bothered to do it."

"That's why you're going to read mine." Mattie took his folded essay from his pocket and passed it to Carter as they hurried past the dead flower beds. "Everyone will be watching and when Caroline and Eliot free the other kids, you'll have even more backup. Your clone will be there and the other clones will be there and everyone will believe us."

Right? It was a small voice in Mattie's head, but it turned his hands and feet to ice.

"They'll have no choice," Mattie whispered as they edged closer to the school.

"Are you still doing that thing where you talk to yourself?" Carter asked.

Mattie ignored him. He had Eliot's remote tucked into the waistband of his pants and, with every step, the plastic dug into his spine. The boys hovered close to the doorway, listening for any other footsteps.

Nothing, Mattie thought with relief. He took a deep breath and motioned for Carter to follow him. He kept one hand on the wall, steadying himself as they went inside. His legs seemed kind of shaky when he climbed out of the pod, but he was getting better.

"Tuck in your shirt," Mattie said. The school was warmer, but not by much, and his breath rose in fat, round puffs. "You're not dressed like the other Carter and I can't fix that and—"

"What are you two doing?" Miss Maple rounded the corner and stopped. She had both hands on her hips and her head was high. The light from behind turned her into a tower of shadows.

Mattie's heart swung high. Miss Maple! They could tell her what was happening! She would help them!

"What are they doing?" Mr. Karloff appeared next to Miss Maple. He stomped toward the boys, his shoes slapping the tile. "What's the meaning of this? Mattie? Carter! How did you get out here? You're supposed to go on *now*!"

Carter stared at Mr. Karloff. He opened his mouth, shut it, and opened it again.

"He must need rebooting," Miss Maple said. Mattie's stomach sank. She knew. Miss Maple was in on it too.

"Clearly," Mr. Karloff muttered and grabbed both boys by their arms and hauled them toward the auditorium. Miss Maple tripped along behind them, her heavy purse rustling like she had something alive inside it.

Mattie was afraid to look, but he also couldn't. He was too busy scrambling to keep up with Mr. Karloff. They hustled down the hallway and past the dining room and up the stairs. Mattie could hear a muffled loudspeaker and soft clapping.

Please let Caroline have found the other Carter, Mattie thought. Please please please.

"Wait," Mattie puffed. "Where are our parents? I need to see them!"

"You can't see them," Miss Maple said. She had a smile in her voice, which meant Miss Maple sounded just like she always did—bright and sunny. But there was something about the bright and sunny that left Mattie cold. In fact, Miss Maple seemed a little *too* happy when she added, "They had to go."

"Go?" Mattie dug both feet into the tile. It didn't slow him down. Mr. Karloff just dragged him along. "How could they *go*?"

They *can't* go! They had to be here for Carter's big reveal! Mattie needed Mrs. Larimore to hug Carter the way she hugged Mattie. He needed Mr. Larimore to yell and make a fuss. It was his father's greatest skill, and Mattie had never needed it more.

"Yes," Miss Maple continued, and she sounded more and more pleased. "They had to go and they didn't say good-bye because they didn't have time."

"Glad to know some things never change," Carter muttered.

Mattie slipped and Mr. Karloff pulled him upright. His parents couldn't go. They were supposed to save Carter and Mattie. They were supposed to help save all the kids.

And they were supposed to take Mattie with them. It was that small voice in his head again. It was so small Mattie almost couldn't hear it, but he could *feel* it, and it made him feel small in a way that was worse than just being short.

The auditorium doors were shut tight. Mr. Karloff hauled the Larimore boys around the side, shoving them through a side door to the backstage. It smelled like old velvet and old papers. Miss Maple sneezed.

"You," Mr. Karloff said to Mattie, pushing Mattie into a plastic chair. "You better not move. I have plans for you. And *you*"—Mr. Karloff looked at Carter and pointed toward the stage where Headmaster Rooney was waiting and smiling at the crowd—"you get out there."

Carter looked at Mattie, then he looked at Mr. Karloff, then he looked at Headmaster Rooney. Headmaster Rooney looked back like he was counting all the ways he was going to torture the Larimores if Carter didn't get out there.

"Whatever," Carter said and marched past the moldy curtains and onto the stage. He had Mattie's essay clenched in his fist and there was faint applause as he walked to the headmaster's side.

"And this is Carter Larimore," Headmaster Rooney began, wrapping one arm around Carter's shoulders. "He'll be reading from his essay, 'How Munchem Academy Made Me a Better Person.' Carter? Take it away."

Mattie looked over his shoulder and listened for any sounds coming from the hallway beyond the door. Nothing. Still no Eliot. How much longer would it take to free the others? And where was Caroline? Had she been able to catch Carter the Clone?

Miss Maple dug her fingers into Mattie's shoulder and shook him. He turned back around and clasped his shaky hands between his knees.

Come on, guys, Mattie thought. We need you.

On stage, Carter cleared his throat. He unfolded Mattie's essay and looked at the parents and teachers and students. He cleared his throat again. "'How Munchem Academy Made Me a Better Person' . . . by Ma—Carter Larimore."

The microphone screeched and the headmaster scowled. Mattie started to sweat. Did the Rooster know? He was studying Carter awfully hard. His brother wasn't dressed like the other clones. The others were wearing Munchem blazers and shirts. Carter was wearing a Munchem shirt, but it looked slept-in.

Mostly because it *had* been slept in.

"At Munchem," Carter began to read. "I've learned about the merits of a clean dorm and a clean classroom. I've learned to live up to my potential. I've learned—"

Carter stopped reading. He stared at the audience. Mattie knew they were in trouble. Carter could only play good for so long—or he had just spotted his clone on the other side of the stage, hidden in the wings.

"Oh, boy," Mattie breathed as Carter the Clone waved. Ribbons of silver duct tape hung off his arm.

"What the devil?" Miss Maple whispered and dug her fingers even deeper into Mattie's shoulder. Mattie barely noticed, though. Carter the Clone waved again and the real Carter gaped. He patted the back of his head like he couldn't believe his hair really stuck up like that.

"Carter?" Headmaster Rooney leaned a little closer. His attention was pinned to the audience ahead of him. He still hadn't seen the clone to his right. He had *no idea*.

But Miss Maple did. She glared at Rooney and gave Mattie a shake. It snapped his back teeth together.

"Is everything all right?" Headmaster Rooney asked Carter.

"Of course it's not all right." Miss Maple dragged Mattie to his feet as Caroline suddenly came into view. She was breathing hard and looked furious with the clone. "It's not all right at all, you fool!"

Headmaster Rooney couldn't hear Miss Maple's furious whispers. He was too busy studying Carter, and Carter was too busy smiling at Rooney. He was smiling the same evil smile he had on his face when he dunked Mattie in the pool or peed on Mrs. Kirby-Clegg.

"It's just nerves, sir." Carter's eyes were wide and his voice trembled. "We can be nervous, can't we? You don't expect us to be *robots*, do you?"

Headmaster Rooney blinked. He blinked again. He looked at the audience and then he looked at Carter and then he saw Carter the Clone standing in the wings.

"We are so dead," Mattie whispered.

And indeed they would be. Mattie needed the clone to come out. He needed proof. He needed the other students. But, right now, he needed to make sure Headmaster Rooney didn't clobber the real Carter.

Mattie wrenched himself from Miss Maple's grasp. He would have to defend Carter. Or punch Rooney. Or *something*.

Miss Maple swore. It was long and impressive and contained variations that even Mr. Larimore didn't know. She grabbed for Mattie. When that didn't work, she grabbed for the closest rope.

Miss Maple yanked, Mattie ducked, and the moldy velvet curtains began to sway.

"Uh-oh," Mattie said as the curtain swung shut. Now they couldn't see the audience. Now the audience couldn't see *them*, and the audience definitely couldn't see Carter the Clone sit down hard like someone had just deactivated him.

Which maybe someone had, Mattie thought as he held the now broken remote in his hands. He'd fallen on it and now the plastic box was in pieces. Lots of pieces. If he survived this, Eliot was going to kill him.

Mattie jumped to his feet, and Headmaster Rooney crashed into him. Then Miss Maple took a swing at both of them with her purse. It swooshed past Mattie's head.

"C'mon, you fool!" Miss Maple grabbed Rooney by his arm. Beyond the curtains, parents' voices began to rise.

"What's going on back there?" someone's father yelled.

"Is everything okay?" someone's mother called.

Mattie opened his mouth to yell that it was not okay *at all* just as Miss Maple pulled the fire alarm with all her might.

Whoop whoop whoop!

"Stop!" Mattie cried. Miss Maple gave him a kick. Mattie kicked back, but he missed. Rooney and Miss Maple ran through the side door, disappearing into the hallway.

"Carter! Caroline!" Mattie cried. "They're running away!"

But were they? Headmaster Rooney and Miss Maple weren't running for the garage with its school buses and vans. They weren't running for the road. They weren't even running for the woods. No, they weren't running away at all. They were running straight for the cemetery.

They were running straight for Eliot.

NEVER LET THE BAD GUYS GET AWAY—
UNLESS YOU'RE THE BAD GUY, IN WHICH CASE: RUN FOR IT!

MR. KARLOFF AND THE CLONES DASHED PAST MATTIE.

Whoop whoop whoop!

"Argh!" Mattie cried as he lunged for Marcus the Clone's ankle. Marcus easily shook him off, but Mattie was up and running. Too bad for Mattie that everyone else was running too.

Parents were going right and left. Students were following parents. Mattie tried to follow the teachers and the clones as best he could, while being pushed sideways and backward.

Carter, Caroline, Rooney, and Miss Maple were heading toward the cemetery. Mattie quickly realized that the teachers and the clones were heading in the opposite direction, for the parking lot. They galloped past panicked parents and plunged through the great double doors. They ran down the steps and across the gravel drive.

Cars were everywhere. The teachers and clones went straight for a white van waiting by the grass. Mr. Karloff got there first. He opened the sliding door, and everyone dove in.

Well, everyone except for Mattie, who was too far behind to stop them.

He stared at the bright red taillights as Mr. Karloff floored the van down the driveway and toward the road. Mattie sagged as parents and students milled around him. No one knew what had just happened. The proof was getting away! *Mattie's* proof was getting away!

A potbellied man shoved past Mattie. He pivoted, searching the crowd. "Where'd the teachers go? Where's that Rooney?"

Mattie opened his mouth and heard a shout, but it wasn't just any shout. It was Carter's voice.

"You better run for it!" Carter yelled.

Mattie plunged back into the crowd. He charged through the school and out the back doors toward the fields. He was fast, but he wasn't fast enough. Carter and Miss Maple and Headmaster Rooney were well ahead of him, running across the meadow toward the cemetery as if their hair were on fire.

Mattie's chest tightened. Headmaster Rooney is going to catch them, he thought, tearing across the grass. *Have to catch up!*

Mattie ran with all his might, but the others' legs were longer—way longer—and he fell behind. He was just passing the tumbledown headstones when he heard another shout. Something was happening down in the mausoleum.

The tomb was still pushed to the side, so Mattie pounded down the stairs. He stopped at the last step, gaped, and almost went back up. Eliot had definitely freed the others.

But they weren't going anywhere.

Doyle and Marcus were staggering around the room. Maxwell was barfing in one corner, and Eliot and Caroline were running from Miss Maple. She had her handbag and was swinging it with all her might.

"Run, Mattie!" Caroline yelped as Miss Maple clocked her in the shoulder. "Run while you still can!"

Mattie couldn't run. His feet felt pasted to the floor. He stared at Rooney, who was standing in the middle of the room, tears streaming down his face. It was so odd, so unexpected, so very un-Rooster-like. He was crying like he was on *Como Pasa El Tiempo*, like his heart was broken, like everything he'd ever wanted had been destroyed.

But what Headmaster Rooney had wanted was *wrong*!

Mattie knew it was wrong, and yet now he could almost see things from the headmaster's point of view: the Rooster had wanted to have a great school. He had wanted to create something bigger than himself.

Even villains thought they were heroes.

"You!" Headmaster Rooney cried, stabbing one finger in Mattie's direction. Everyone turned around.

"Get him!" Miss Maple shrieked and dove for Mattie. Carter grabbed Miss Maple around the waist and she rammed her elbow into his temple.

"Run, Mattie!" Carter yelled.

Mattie was already running.

"Not that way!" Carter yelled, but it was too late. In his panic, Mattie went left when he should have turned back and now he was just running in circles. With Miss Maple and Headmaster Rooney puffing right behind him.

"I've got you now!" Rooney snarled.

Mattie skittered under the closest pod, crawled along on his hands and knees, and popped up on the other side. Miss Maple swore. Headmaster Rooney grunted. Mattie ran faster, feeling like he was leading a horrible parade.

"Mattie!"

Mattie glanced over his shoulder. Carter was waving frantically. Why? Mattie yelped as Miss Maple's fingers dug into his collar.

"Come here, you little brat!" she screamed.

Mattie ducked again. Why was Carter waving? Now was not the time for waving—wait.

Mattie darted another glance and realized Carter wasn't waving. His brother was *pointing* at the now-open pods.

"Aargh!" Miss Maple cried as Caroline tackled her behind her knees. They both hit the concrete floor in a puff of screams and kicks.

Which left just Headmaster Rooney running after Mattie, and Eliot running after both of them, and the pods were now open—

Mattie knew what Carter meant. He knew what he was going to do. Mattie slowed, looking over his shoulder to Eliot.

"Push him, Eliot!" Mattie cried.

"What?" Eliot spluttered.

"Push! Him!"

And as Mattie jumped onto the nearest pod, as he ran across the cushion and jumped down the other side, Eliot did indeed push Headmaster Rooney. He shoved him with all his strength. The Rooster stumbled and fell facedown into the pod. Carter snapped it shut.

"Moof, moof, mwah, mwah!" Rooney cried. Mattie couldn't understand the headmaster through the thick glass, but he was pretty certain Rooney was saying, "Let me out this instant!"

Or possibly, "I'm going to clone all four of you when I get out of here!"

"Mattie!" Caroline cried as Miss Maple gave her a kick. "Help!"

Miss Maple kicked her again, and Caroline's grip loosened. She fell to her side as Miss Maple ran for the stairs.

"I'll get you for this!" Miss Maple shrieked. "You just wait!"

"Get her!" Mattie yelled, but it was too late. Miss Maple took the stairs three at a time and disappeared into the dark.

"Let her go! She doesn't matter!" Carter tugged Mattie

back to the pod containing Headmaster Rooney. The head-master slammed his palm against the glass and yelped.

"Dude," Eliot whispered. "You don't see that every day."

"Nope," Mattie wheezed, still trying to catch his breath. In the movies, you could always tell who the bad guys were. In real life, bad guys looked like regular people. Mattie thought that was even scarier.

"What are we going to do?" Caroline moaned.

"We could clone him," Carter suggested, flicking the glass to tease the headmaster. "See how much he likes it."

"Why would you want *another* Rooster?" Eliot demanded.

"Cloning Rooney would make us as bad as he is," Caroline said, crossing her arms. "Stop antagonizing him!"

Carter flicked the glass harder.

"We should call the police," Mattie said. "We'll go back to the house and get some of the parents. When we show them this"—Mattie waved at the pods and the room and the comput-ers and, well, everything—"they'll have to believe us."

Caroline nodded. Carter nodded. And Eliot? Well, Eliot leaned over and turned on the pod.

BE CAREFUL YOU DON'T OVERDO IT

"WHAT ARE YOU DOING?" CAROLINE'S EYES WERE WIDE AND her hair was huge. She grabbed for the pod's control panel. "Turn it off!"

"No," Eliot said as he blocked her. Behind him, the headmaster stopped pounding on the glass. He began to giggle. Then he started to laugh. Then he passed out.

"Eliot!" Caroline smacked her brother's arms and chest. "He's going to forget everything!"

"Yes." Eliot nodded and then nodded some more. "I think that's for the best actually."

The best? Mattie lunged for the control panel too and Eliot waved both of them off.

"I don't understand," Mattie told him. "We have to tell the police."

Eliot gave Mattie a big shove. His expression was worried, and it stopped Mattie dead. "But what happens after we tell the police?"

Carter nodded. "I was thinking the same thing."

What? Mattie looked at Carter and then at Eliot. "They'll arrest Rooney and the rest of them."

"We'll be heroes," Caroline added.

"And Munchem will close," Eliot said quietly.

Carter nodded again. "Exactly."

Everyone paused to think about this. Carter stared into space. Mattie scrunched up his nose. Eliot scratched his cheek and Caroline smoothed down her hair.

"We won't go to school together anymore," Eliot continued. "You know what Mama said. 'Caroline, if you can't make Munchem work, you'll have to go to that girls' school.'"

"And I'll have to go to military school," Carter said.

"And I'll get sent to another boarding school without Marilyn," Eliot said. "I'd hate that."

Mattie stared at his friends and his brother. He wasn't sure where his parents would send him if Munchem closed, but he knew wherever it was, it wouldn't have the Spencers or Carter around and the realization made Mattie's knees go a bit weak.

He had friends now and they were important to him.

When did that happen anyway? How could something that felt so strong have snuck up on him? Did it happen when Eliot showed him Marilyn, the supercomputer? When Caroline introduced him to Beezus? Or was it just now, when they fought the Rooster and won?

Mattie had no idea how he had changed, but he did know he was different now. Maybe those were the best changes, the ones that crept up on you, the ones that stowed themselves away inside you so you could discover them later.

"I don't want to go to another school," Caroline said. "I can't be myself there. I belong here."

"Yeah," Carter said. "Me too."

"Me three," Mattie said and everyone looked at him in surprise.

"Mattie," Carter said hesitantly. "All you've wanted to do since you arrived is go home. Are you sure?"

Mattie nodded. "I think I fit in better here."

"I think you're more *you* here," Carter said.

"I think so too," he said.

"But what about the machines?" Caroline asked.

"And what about the clones?" Eliot added.

Carter nodded. "What about the other teachers? You said they were all in on it."

"Maybe it won't be a problem," Mattie said slowly, watching the real students. Doyle and Marcus weren't staggering anymore and Maxwell wasn't barfing in a corner any longer, but they still looked baffled. "Mrs. Hitchcock and Mr. Karloff were getting into the Munchem van. I saw them as I ran down here. They had the clones with them. I think they knew they were in trouble. I'll bet they're halfway across the state by now."

Carter rubbed his chin. "Which means . . ."

Everyone turned to study the now unconscious headmaster. He was drooling on his satin pillow and his hair stood up in spikes. Mattie thought it made him look like he had horns.

"What if we left him in the pod?" Eliot suggested.

Mattie peered down at Headmaster Rooney. "He would forget about the machine and the clones and we could pretend like nothing happened."

"But something *did* happen," Carter said, and he said it a bit testily. But can you really blame him? After all, Carter did get cloned. He studied the real Doyle, Maxwell, Jay, and Marcus with a frown.

Mattie looked at his brother. "It will have to be our secret."

Carter sighed and scuffed his shoe against the concrete floor. "I can't believe no one is ever going to know how we saved them from being cloned *and* saved Munchem from being closed."

"But we know," Mattie said, and he turned the pod's dial as far as it could go. The friends stood back and watched Headmaster Rooney snore. "You think you could speed this thing up?" he asked Eliot.

Eliot's eyes went bright. "Give me twenty minutes."

Mattie shook his head. "We have ten *maybe* before we have to get back."

Because Eliot was even more amazing than Eliot thought, they only needed six. Eliot upped the pod's power and adjusted several connections. He typed out something long and involved on the keypad that made the motor under the pod whirr and whine.

And when the Rooster opened his eyes again, he grinned at Mattie as if Mattie were his favorite thing in the whole wide world. They pushed back the pod's cover and the headmaster sat up.

"What's going on?" the headmaster asked.

"You tell us," Eliot said. "You always answer your own questions. That's kind of your thing."

"Thing?"

Eliot frowned and looked down at some of the wires he had reconfigured. The blue was now connected to the black and the red wires were dangling uselessly. "I might have overdone this a bit."

"What do you remember?" Mattie asked the headmaster.

"That you're very short."

"Wow," Carter said, nodding. "Good job, Eliot. You turned him stupid . . . stupid*er*."

Mattie wasn't so sure. He studied the headmaster. He studied his watery blue eyes and the spittle at the corners of his mouth, and finally asked, "What if he's faking?"

Eliot shrugged. "What if he is?"

"Yeah," Caroline agreed. "It'll be way worse for the Rooster if he does remember. Think of all the trouble he'll get into if he confesses."

Caroline's right, Mattie thought. She's usually right, he also thought, but he put that second thought away because something else just occurred to him. "Carter? All this stuff is Larimore equipment. Do you think Dad would get in trouble?"

Carter hesitated. "I don't know—if we stick to the plan though, who'll find out?"

Exactly. They just needed to stick to the plan. Mattie turned back to Rooney. "Hey, Headmaster?"

"Yes?"

"We need to get back to school, okay?" Mattie helped Rooney down from the pod. The Rooster swayed a little when he stood up. "You're going to need to get some new teachers—"

"And someone else to clean," Carter said.

"And a better heater," Eliot added.

"And no more frogs in biology!" Caroline huffed.

The real students cheered, but Mattie didn't think they knew what they were cheering about, and the Rooster nodded, but Mattie didn't think he understood what they were saying to him. Maybe he really wasn't faking it?

Rooney grinned at him. "Frogs for everyone but biology!"

Mattie patted the headmaster's sleeve. "Not quite, but nice try. Let's get you back to school."

And together they locked up the mausoleum and led the real students through the cemetery (which was still too dark) and up to Munchem (which still had people running around and around).

Mattie thought, This didn't turn out too bad.

Ahead of him, Carter took the headmaster's arm and grinned. His teeth were extra white in the moonlight. "Don't worry about a thing, Headmaster. I'll tell you everything you need to know."

MATTIE LARIMORE'S BIG BOOK OF BAD

ALWAYS LIVE HAPPILY EVER AFTER . . .

OR HAPPILY UNTIL THE NEXT JOB

AND *THAT* WAS HOW MATTIE LARIMORE MET THE SPENCERS and freed his brother and saved the other students and kept Munchem safe and yet nobody knew.

It wasn't the most glorious of beginnings for a master thief.

Truth be told, it might not have been the most glorious of endings either because when Eliot and Mattie led a dazed and confused Headmaster Rooney back to the school, they realized what a mess they'd left behind. The students were still milling around, the parents were still with them, and the few teachers that were left looked as confused as Headmaster Rooney.

"We are in so much trouble," Caroline muttered.

Mattie thought he might very well agree with her and then

Doyle's fat-headed parents stepped away from the crooked pillars that held up the crooked arched doorway, and Mattie could see who was still there, still waiting.

"Mom! Dad!" Mattie raced to his mother's side and flung his arms around her waist. He pressed his face into the soft silk of her blouse. Miss Maple had lied. His parents *hadn't* left. "They told us you left!"

"Leave?" Mr. Larimore demanded. "How in blazes could we leave? Someone's blocked our car."

And, indeed, someone had. The big black SUV couldn't move forward or backward because other big blue SUVs were parked on either side. Mattie scuffed his feet against the gravel and wondered who would do that, but he didn't have time to wonder for very long because Mr. Larimore was stomping toward them, shaking his cell phone to emphasize every word.

"I went outside to make a call and your mother came with me," Mr. Larimore said.

"He might've needed something," Mrs. Larimore explained.

"Then people started running around." Mr. Larimore pinned both hands to his hips and glared at everyone. "And no one knew what was going on and a bunch of people ran right past us and took off in a van—like *hippies*!"

"Oh, no, dearest," Mrs. Larimore said, patting her husband's arm. "Hippies smell *much* worse."

Mr. Larimore ignored her. He pointed his cell phone at the

headmaster. "What kind of school are you running anyway, Rooney?"

Headmaster Rooney blinked. "A brick one?"

Everyone fell silent and stared at him. Rooney turned around and around, trying to figure out what they were looking at. Mattie forced himself to laugh. "Oh. Ha ha, Headmaster Rooney. You're so funny."

"Am I?" The headmaster blinked again. He patted the top of his head, trying to smooth down his spiky red hair. It seemed like the pod was as bad for Rooney's hair as it was for his memories.

"Ridiculous," Mr. Larimore grunted. "Why, if I ran this school, it would be in tip-top shape! Tip-top, do you hear me?"

"Yes," Headmaster Rooney said.

"Good!" Mr. Larimore paused and looked at his cell phone. It was blinking, but he shoved it in his jacket pocket. "Do you know what else I would do?"

"No?" Headmaster Rooney guessed.

Mr. Larimore nodded until his jowls quivered. "I'll tell you what else I would do." He directed the headmaster to the granite steps.

Eliot's eyes bugged out. Mattie knew the look. Panic. Eliot didn't think Headmaster Rooney was in any shape to have a conversation with Mr. Larimore. But Mattie knew that Headmaster Rooney was in the *perfect* shape to have a conversation with Mr. Larimore because he would just keep asking

Mr. Larimore questions about what Mr. Larimore thought.

And Mr. Larimore loved that.

"Mattie," Mrs. Larimore said, grabbing him in an enormous hug. "I want you to come home. We miss you terribly."

Mattie hesitated. It was everything he had worked for, everything he was supposed to want and yet: "I can't, Mom. I'm sorry."

"But why?"

Mattie thought about it. "Because I might fall into my bad habits again?"

"But you were always so good!"

Except for when I stole a train, Mattie thought.

"Mom, do you know how brave Carter is?" Mattie blurted and then regretted it. He didn't regret asking his mother if she knew her son was brave—he was worried about how he was going to *explain it* if she asked for an example.

Thankfully, Mrs. Larimore wasn't big on explanations. "You two are so cute when you're not trying to squish each other." She beamed at her boys and placed one hand against her heart. "You're almost always exactly what I want you to be!"

Mattie didn't know what to say. It was true. He had always tried to be exactly what they wanted him to be, but maybe that wasn't what he wanted anymore. Not exactly, at least. At Munchem, he had learned that doing the right thing wasn't always the same as following the rules. He'd also learned he could do almost anything if Eliot and Caroline were there to help. He might even have learned how to get his brother to stop calling him girls' names, but, of course, he couldn't tell his parents any of that.

"He can't leave now," Mr. Larimore announced. Mattie and Carter's father had deserted the headmaster and the small group of teachers—and the much larger group of parents—and was rushing toward them with bright eyes. "This is going to be great, Mattie. Your headmaster has a good head on his shoulders. He took all my advice. In fact, he's going to have me help him find more teachers—better teachers. It'll be good for people to see me give back. There have been *issues* at the company again. Wait. Is that another reporter?"

There did indeed seem to be someone running across the meadow, toward the trees. There was the faintest flash of red too. Was it a camera? Or a clone?

The teachers and clones had gotten away. Mattie wasn't sure where they'd run to, or why the teachers would've taken the clones, but a sickening feeling told him he was going to find out eventually.

And we'll be ready, Mattie thought. In the meantime, though—

"Just smile, Dad. Even if it is a reporter, we're a happy family. Let them take a picture."

"You might have a point," Mr. Larimore said, rubbing his palms together. "Let them see my warm, personal side. It's going to be an amazing new term at Munchem Academy. You and Carter are going to do great."

Carter looked at Mattie. "You ready, Lassie?"

"It's *Mattie*."

MATTIE LARIMORE'S BIG BOOK OF BAD

ALWAYS LISTEN TO THAT VOICE
INSIDE YOUR HEAD

AND *THIS* IS WHERE ALL THOSE LESSER BOOKS STOP. THEY claim the beginning is over and Mattie's life of crime is set on its one true course—and, in a way, those books are right because all beginnings are made up of endings. You can't begin anything without ending something else, which is why this superior—and highly accurate—book ends here before Mattie's story begins to get worse.

Much worse.

Or much, much better. It rather depends on your perspective and how you feel about Mattie's eventual destiny, a truckload of glitter, and a few unfortunate explosions—and also clowns.

Everyone hates clowns, though, so perhaps that will be something to bring us together.

But, of course, Mattie doesn't know anything about glitter or explosions or clowns yet. At this moment, he's on top of the world. He has friends and Munchem and nothing but possibilities ahead of him.

Only we know how those possibilities are going to turn out—and I know better than anyone—but that's a new beginning and this is our latest ending.

For now.

ACKNOWLEDGMENTS

The Commander would like to send enormous thank-yous to the team at Disney Hyperion, especially his editor, Tracey Keevan. He feels so lucky Mattie and friends found a home with her. It's been a total privilege.

Another big round of thank-yous to Jared Stamm, copy editor extraordinaire, who makes the Commander look far more polished than he might actually be.

In addition, the Commander wouldn't be anywhere without Wonder Agent Sarah Davies, who wasn't fazed at all when the Commander wanted to do comedy. And the idea to do comedy wouldn't have even occurred without Phoebe Yeh's encouragement. Sometimes book ideas come on their own. Other times they happen when people believe in the Commander more than the Commander believes in himself. Thank you, ladies. He's a better writer because of you.

As always, there aren't enough thank-yous in the world

for Natalie Richards, who reads everything the Commander writes and helps him make it so much better than he could ever make it on his own. Equally enormous thank-yous to the Commander's long-suffering sidekick, Boy Genius, and his parents.

Many medals for service above and beyond the call of duty for Megan Miranda and Stephanie Winkelhake, who also worked on *The Boy Who Knew Too Much* and made it so much stronger. The Commander truly wouldn't be here without y'all. He's so lucky to have you in his life.

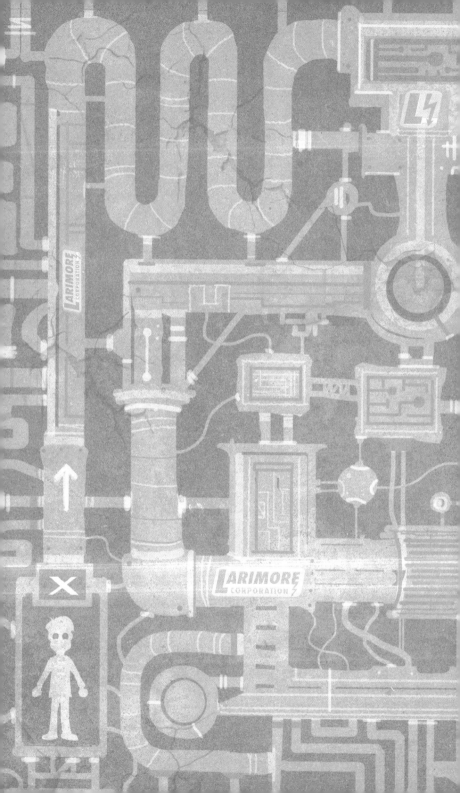